Land of the Living

Books by John Hearne:

LAND OF THE LIVING
AUTUMN EQUINOX
EYE OF THE STORM

LAND OF THE LIVING

BY JOHN HEARNE

HARPER & ROW, PUBLISHERS
NEW YORK AND EVANSTON

H4363L

for

EDNA MANLEY, *of Jamaica*

and

FRANK COLLYMORE, *of Barbados*

and

ARTHUR SEYMOUR, *of British Guiana*

*an affectionate tribute to their spirited and
lifelong concern for the imagination
of one territory*

Contents

───────────── ★ ─────────────

Epigraph

───────────── ★ ─────────────

*"The earth is green where our fathers died—
but no greener than where our fathers did
not die."*

AMERINDIAN PROVERB

Part One
EXILE

I

———————————— ★ ————————————

I

The last touches to a design of insane plunder were the deaths of my mother, sister and father in Auschwitz or Belsen or Dachau—I was never able to discover which of these synonymous machines had consumed them. For a long time after that, I mean, it was difficult to believe that a real I had survived and not merely a solid ghost remaindered from the body of six million living Jews. Even in England, with its dispassionate, pervasive reverence for law, I waited for another crisis in which we would be the axiomatic sacrifice chosen to appease another unpredictable rage of history.

But now in Cayuna, I feel that some sort of obscure, powerful resurrection of myself has begun to stir. The island has claimed me.

Perhaps, though, I have been paradoxically fortunate in this: that the mindless convulsions of terror with which Europe so nearly destroyed itself had already started before I could really become a European. And what remains from before that time are accidental fragments: unrelated clarities from a world shattered beyond any hope of reconstruction.

They emerge gratuitously, like old coins discovered by a child in a patch of waste: the mosaics of pale stone laid carefully beneath the vines to reflect the Rhineland sun; falling asleep in the *Residenztheater* and waking, my sister's irritable

13

pinch throbbing in my arm, to hear the golden jingle of Pappageno's entrance, so that even now that first, astonishing moment of submission to aesthetic delight is inextricably bound up with the sharp pain from her powerful fingers, the reproachful knit of her thick smooth eyebrows and the heavy scent of Chanel on the deep breast against which my head had fallen; the sudden visits, during the summer, of my mother's friends as they passed south from a dozen cities to Italy and the Riviera, leaving behind them a general, exciting impression of vivid faces, strange gaudy clothes, little magazines with bright, distorted designs on the covers, rapid gossip in three or four languages and frequent, incomprehensible laughter; sitting with my father, at dusk in a café facing a little pink Mediterranean square, and eating ice-cream while he blew the smoke from his cigarette under the table to drive the mosquitoes away from my bare legs.

We make these small descents into memory, from one face to another, to the touch of a hand or a small pleasure, to a half-forgotten sadness, to a word, to a moment of loaded silence, to ourselves. It is from this sort of frail stuff that we pretend to build an enduring structure in time. What a pretence. For the past is, really, inaccessible and our most patient, most honest reconstructions are all fulfilments of a present need. Whatever we call the truth has in it a taint, an inevitable, tarnishing shadow of expediency. Cynically or in pure faith we reassemble a series of ephemeral attitudes, but always for our own consolation. And to establish the evidence of our identity, we all have to loot the uncomplaining dead.

II

"I didn't realize," Oliver Hyde said this afternoon, "that Marcus Heneky was going to be such a deceptive old man. I thought I had him taped. Then I saw what I'd done, in print, and knew I'd missed by a mile."

14

He reached over and took the red-covered *Newsletter* from where I had dropped it beside me. Opening it, he glanced at the leader he had written on the Reverend Marcus Heneky and the Pure Church of Africa Triumphant.

"No," he said, "not good enough," and gave a small, comic growl of disgust as he tossed the magazine back to the striped canvas of the veranda swing on which I was stretched out. "What's wrong with it, Stefan? What beat me?"

"There's nothing wrong with it," I told him. "It's a fine piece of writing."

We had all spent the morning at the sea, coming back here for lunch, and now, lying flat on my back, my head resting on my hands, I was drowsy with the animal contentment of my salt-scoured, sunbaked, comfortably fed body. The white ceiling above me was flecked with patches of light wherever the sun found a small gap in the packed leaves of the creeper that grew up a wire trellis all along the veranda. As I watched, a lizard crawled from under the eaves and began to stalk the moth that clung to the ceiling just above my head. The lizard was a croaker, the only ugly member of its kind in Cayuna: grey, leprous and flabby, utterly unlike the long, delicate fingers of pulsating flesh, brilliant as polished stone or subtly glowing as pastel, that scuttle about every garden in the island.

"Look at that," I said and pointed to the ceiling. Oliver's eyes followed the line of my finger.

"Do you think he'll make it?" he asked.

"Yes, but if you'd like to put half a crown on the moth, I'll cover it."

"Done."

"Don't make a noise now," I warned him. "I know you, Oliver. You never play fair if you can avoid it."

It was all over on the ceiling as I spoke. The croaker's obscene, upside down waddle dissolved into a noiseless blur, potent, terrifying and concentrated, and the little jaws were fast on the speckled brown tissue of the moth's wing. The

15

insect fluttered desperately and tumbled to the tiles beside Oliver's chair. On the ceiling, the croaker began to ooze back to its nest under the eaves, a segment of wing held like a wafer in the nearly invisible slit of its mouth.

"The bastard," Oliver said, stilling the untidy flutter by his chair with the toe of his sandal. "They're the ugliest, greediest brutes in creation."

"They pay their way," I told him. "If it wasn't for them, this island would belong to the insects. I'm going to do a monograph on them one day. A hundred thousand words. It'll make me famous."

"A hundred thousand!" There was a lilt of genuine, astonished interest in his voice. "You mean that you could really find a hundred thousand words to write about a croaker?"

"Half a million words if I wanted to," I told him. "Their sex life alone would be good for six chapters. And that's just a beginning. You don't know us scientists once we get involved with a line nobody has followed before."

I turned my head and smiled at him, inviting him to share my half-serious, half-fanciful ambition, and he chuckled and tossed his chin with indulgent mockery.

"You'll never do it, Mahler," he said derisively. "You're too lazy. All you want is that soft billet you've got now teaching undergraduates how to open up frogs."

"That's a wicked lie," I said dreamily. "I'm preparing myself for a big leap. You wait and see. Maybe I'll discover a new sub-species and really cause a stir. Mahler's Lizard. *Lacertus cayunae mahleri.*"

Lying there, I felt drugged with the assurance of profound happiness that had come into my life with people like Oliver and the others whose murmured voices came to us from the far end of the house on the back verandas. The details of these years when I had been alone or alien were remote and faint, like the fossilized imprints of plants or skeletons that no longer belonged to an evolving world.

16

Suddenly, Oliver leaned forward from the big shabby straw chair and tapped me imperiously on the chest. I gave him a cautious attention. Like most small men, he can be very intense, and now, with his thin brown hair tousled into a spiky crown and his slight body hunched above me, he had the absorbed, business-like concentration of a terrier before a hole.

"That was very slick, Stefan," he said. "Very neat. I hardly noticed when you changed the subject. But let's get back to my problem, eh?"

"What problem?" I protested. "You did a fine piece on Heneky. I told you that."

"No. It had all the facts, in correct order. But there's something missing. You know that. I haven't placed him."

"Why d'you think I should be able to tell you?" I asked him. "I'm not even a Cayunan. I couldn't begin to see him in a context the way you can."

"Balls," Oliver said amiably. "You're a Cayunan now if you're anything at all, you damn Jew. And you've got a nose for these things. Besides, you knew him."

I sat up quickly.

"Only because of the daughter . . . Bernice," I said. "And I didn't really know him. Nobody did. Not even poor Bernice, and she tried, God knows. Let him lie, Oliver. You've said as much about him as there is to say."

Oliver gave an impatient sniff and for a moment his heavily lashed, dark eyes studied me reflectively. He smiled.

"Lord, but you're a lazy swine," he said fondly. "You're afraid to try anything outside those neat little classifications you foist on your poor students."

"You really think that?"

He shook his head and winked.

"No. I was only teasing. But why are you trying to dodge Heneky?"

"I'm not," I told him. "—But he's beyond me, Oliver." For a moment, the face of Marcus Heneky formed itself before me,

17

raw, declamatory, as starkly obsessed as a face in a cathedral window. And with it, I saw the calm, indomitable face of Bernice. I shook my head quickly. "No," I continued. "He's too complicated for me, Oliver. I wouldn't do him justice."

"That's it," he said. "That's it, Stefan. Did any of us do him justice? God, but he's got himself stuck in my conscience as a writer. Think of all the words we've used on him. Every goddam journalist in this island has had a crack. And he's still a paper doll. A silhouette."

"Your version isn't." I told him. "Seriously, boy. It isn't unctuous or patronizing or shocked like the others. I think you've got what there was to get for now. Marcus—Heneky— was the sort of man you wait for time to erode down to his essential shape." I put out my hand and patted his knee and smiled my sympathy. "Maybe you're right, you know. I don't seem to have your sort of audacity when it comes to people. I prefer to worry about the things I can define easily. Like the croaker up there—or *Carcinus sycoraxae*, for instance."

"*Carcinus sycoraxae!* What the hell is that, Stefan?"

"Land crabs. The ones we had for lunch. Their behaviour patterns are very interesting. You know those annual migrations they make to the sea? I think it's because Cayuna was once all submerged except for the big peaks."

"You mean they haven't caught on yet that the situation has changed? That they think the peaks are still only a few yards from the sea?"

"I wouldn't be at all surprised," I said. "I brood about them all the time."

He grinned suddenly and got to his feet with one of his abrupt, emphatic movements that always look as if he's forcing his body to keep pace with the quick, restless scanning of his mind.

"All right," he said. "You can relax. I'm closing the case on old Heneky. For now, at least. I'm going in for a drink. Coming?"

"Tell Joan to bring one out for me," I said. "I've reached a pitch of absolute comfort. Like a cat on a fat lap. It won't last, but I want to hold on to the moment."

" 'And live in eternity's sunrise,' " he quoted. "Who said that?"

"William Blake. You can't catch me out, Oliver. Now go and annoy the others and tell Joan to bring me a drink. Scotch, if Fabricus hasn't finished it."

He turned and went through the opened french windows into the drawing-room. I listened to his brisk, lightly placed footfalls across the boards and then to his voice suddenly raised as it romped with playful aggressiveness among the undulating murmurs on the back veranda. Andrew Fabricus said, "Oh, go away, you horrid little man," and Andrew's wife, Margaret, added something I couldn't distinguish and all the others laughed softly. Then the amiable clash became immersed in the familiar harmonies of an established intimacy and the flat, syrupy Caribbean drawl seemed to be suspended across the cool, shuttered house as consequential yet unobtrusive support to the casual, golden happiness that had descended on me like a benediction.

When Joan came to the door with my drink I was propped on all the cushions against the arm-rest of the swing. I looked at her from an immense, loving distance.

"Hullo," she said and sat on the edge of the swing before me. "I thought you wanted a drink."

"I do, but it's too much work to hold a glass. Raise it to my lips."

She giggled and put the edge of the frosty glass to my mouth. I drank and the burning coldness of the ice, the sharp assertion of the liquor, the bland liveliness of soda-water all seemed new and remarkable. As I drank I put my hand inside her partly unbuttoned blouse.

"Don't," she said, pulling away so quickly that some of the drink spilt with a luxurious chill on my warm body. She

19

pointed with her chin, over her shoulder, down the steps to the garden where two children, one, the boy, the colour of old bronze, the other, a girl of three, with fair, wiry curls and a skin like finest olive oil, were trotting round and round a susumba bush with the serious exaltation of fanatics pursuing a vision. "Suppose the children saw you." She took a handkerchief from her belt and dabbed me dry.

"All right," I said loudly, taking the glass and kissing the cold film of moisture from the palm of her hand. "But I'll make up for it later. I'll do that and much worse. I'll ravish you like a beast."

"Stefan!" she protested. "Not so *loud*! They'll hear you inside."

"You're my wife, aren't you? I have a right to ravish you if I want."

"No, you don't. They can put you in prison for that."

"In Cayuna? In the last outpost of masculine privilege? They wouldn't. They'd raise a public subscription for me."

"You fool," she said softly and leaned on me, her cheek against mine and her lips cropping gently at my ear. "I thought you were going to work when we got home."

"It's only a dissection. I'll be able to tumble you between cuts."

She locked her fingers behind my neck and leaned back at full arms' stretch. Her face was bright with ingenuous anticipation and promise.

"Maybe," she said. "Maybe I'll take pity on you." She unclasped one hand and passed the tips of her fingers over my lips and jaw. "I don't think I'd like you without your beard now. It makes you look like an Old Testament prophet."

"As old as that?"

"No, no. A young one. John the Baptist, or Moses when he fled from Egypt and rescued that girl at the well. What was her name again?"

"Zipporah," I told her. "Jethro's daughter."

"Yes. That's the one. . . . I wish you weren't losing your accent so fast, though. You had such a lovely accent when I first met you. Now you're beginning to sound just like Oliver or Andrew."

"Joan," I said suddenly, "I'm so happy. It's almost frightening. I feel as if my blood had turned into honey."

"Why?" she asked, with a gently smiling, maternal attention as beautiful, in its way, as her luminous desire of a moment before. "What's made you so happy, Stefan?"

"Everything!" I finished my drink in one gulp and waved my free hand as if I were carving a shape of happiness from the impalpable ingredients caught in the air of this Sunday afternoon. "It's a sort of arithmetical progression. . . . All of us down at the sea this morning. . . . Oliver wanting my opinion and advice. . . . Hearing your voice back there, among all the other voices, as if I had never heard it before, but recognizing it as if I had always known how it would sound. . . . An essay one of the students gave me earlier this week that shows we've made the sort of contact one can only hope for. . . . Everything. . . . A man of my age is in no condition for this sort of happiness. I've blundered accidentally into the world those two inhabit." I pointed to the two children who were now forging across the lawn with an air of large, inexorable purpose. "But while I'm in it I want to enjoy it. Before I get thrown out."

I put my arms around her waist and drew her close against me. She was laughing softly with the contagion of my pleasure.

"You're a strange one sometimes," she said. "I can never guess what you're going to say next. Maybe that's why I married you."

"No," I said. "That's not why. I'll tell you why."

I drew her closer and with my lips against her ear began to whisper a rush of calculated obscenities. She struggled and hid her face against my neck, her cheeks growing warm as I sur-

21

rendered to a tumult of wild, internal laughter and contrived increasingly ornate fantasies of pure smut.

At last she put her hands on my shoulders and pushed desperately, struggling free when I was too weak from that silent, lunatic laughter to hold her to me. Her eyes were jumping in an agony of embarrassment and her face glowed as she jumped to her feet.

"Stefan! You mustn't! You—You——"

Suddenly she clapped her hand over her mouth, looked at me from under her lashes and gasped as a little explosive laugh escaped her.

"That wasn't funny," she said, and shook helplessly. "You wouldn't say things like that to a—a whore." Once again she trembled as an irresistible chuckle seemed to leap from the pit of her stomach like a clown from a drum. "Well, would you?" She looked at me with a sudden, touching naivety of interest.

"No," I said. "There'd be no fun in saying things like that to a whore. Besides, they're very prudish. It's only a wife who can really appreciate artistic filth."

I flung myself back against the back of the swing as the laughter rose in me like fumes of alcohol.

"I'm going inside," she said primly. "I'm not staying out here to be insulted."

She turned and walked to the doorway, and paused, with one foot resting on the low step up into the drawing-room. When she spoke she kept her head bent, with a terrible, shy dignity, like a girl's, that utterly transfigured the thickened, forty-year-old body: even the now ineradicable lines of her past hard drinking seemed somehow honourable and arresting, like the scars on a soldier.

"You know," she said quietly, "if I didn't have you to love, I think I'd die. I don't mean kill myself. I just wouldn't take the trouble to go on living. Do you love me, Stefan?"

The appalling, bathetic sincerity of her quiet submission bit suddenly into my unreflecting contentment with a hurt like uncomforted tears.

"Yes," I told her after a moment. "I love you very much. But sometimes I simply don't have the words to tell you."

"I know," she said. "I know you do really. It's only that I wish I could have been still beautiful when you met me. It doesn't seem fair to you that I'd begun to look like this. I used to be a lot of woman before I tried to drink Cayuna dry. Ask Oliver."

"You are beautiful," I said. "I love what you are now. What I married. Not that other woman, whoever she was. Understand?"

"Yes." She had put her hand against the jamb, leaning her weight against her stiffened arm and looking at me over her shoulder. "But you're—you're so distinguished. You're one of those men who get better looking the older they grow. When you're my age somebody is going to try to take you from me. Somebody young who hasn't spoilt herself with all the things I did. And you're going to want her."

"For God's sake, Joan!" I said. She had already resigned herself to betrayal, as a refugee in the most tolerant haven learns to anticipate neglect, abuse or the boredom of his hosts; and like the refugee, she was using her condition compulsively, in a sort of mute blackmail. I looked at her with the exasperation and guilty resentment we keep for those who fling themselves too nakedly on our strength, freedom and sense of honour. "What's wrong with you?" I asked her sharply. "What else d'you want me to say? All right, if it'll make you any happier—I'm sorry for the infidelity I haven't committed yet. I'm ashamed. It was a moment's madness and lust. . . . You've invented a new form of repentance, haven't you? Maybe everyone ought to adopt it. It would make life so straightforward. We could all repent of our future sins at about fifteen and then go ahead with a clear conscience. It would be like carrying traveller's cheques or a banker's draft."

Her eyes began to glisten and she lowered her head.

23

"I'm sorry," she muttered. "I didn't mean to go on like that. It just came and I couldn't stop it. It has nothing to do with us really—it's Oliver and Sybil. He's going to leave her. So she says."

"What!" I jerked upright on the edge of the swing. "You don't mean that. When did she tell you this?"

"This morning down at the beach. When you and Oliver and Andrew were out by the reef."

"I thought she was looking pretty wretched this morning. I put it down to the time of the month or something. But why, Joan? What's happened?"

"Somebody else has happened. . . . That Scottish girl Government brought down to do the survey."

"Mary Seton? The sociologist? I didn't think she'd met Oliver more than a few times. At the paper. In the way of business. . . . The little bastard! The cunning little bastard. How did he keep it so quiet?"

"They've been using that cottage Isaac Azoud has up in the hills. You know Azoud has a thing about Oliver. He'd do anything for him. Anyway, Oliver and that sly, red-haired bitch have been making love up there for months, and now Oliver has told Sybil he's going."

"Just like that?"

"Just like that. Sybil's promised to do anything if he won't leave her. She'll even accept the other woman. The fool. I wouldn't humiliate myself like that for any man. Not even for you." She sighed. "I'm a liar. I suppose I would." She pushed her hand through the heavy, fine mat of her grey-streaked brown hair. When we were first married, she used to dye it, dreading any additional emphasis on the difference between our ages. Until I had begged her to leave it, finally convincing her that the wide bands of grey among the fading but still glossy brown gave it a curious vitality.

"Hell," I said heavily, "what a sad business. D'you think anything can be salvaged?"

24

She shook her head.

"No. Sybil wouldn't have told Margaret and me except that she had reached the end of something. She says Oliver has been as cruel as the devil these last few weeks. Not physically, of course, but the things he's said."

"Oliver! Cruel!"

"He has it in him, you know?"

"Yes," I agreed reluctantly. "I suppose he does. Like all of us. That sounds like the end, Joan. Once the man starts being cruel. . . ." I shrugged. "And he's such a tough honest little brute. He hates pretending. That would make him nastier."

"Sybil has done too good a job with him," she told me. "You don't know what Oliver was like in the old days, before you came to Cayuna. The man you see now is all Sybil's work. He wouldn't have been able to leave anybody a few years ago."

She was looking straight at me, with the fearful, selfish appraisal of a woman who sees in her friend's failure to hold a man, her own future inadequacy. Like a hypochondriac in a city where plague has been rumoured, furtively and minutely examining a healthy skin for the first symptoms, seeing in every temporary blemish the certain portents of infection. I rose quickly and went to her and put my arm around her waist and kissed her on the cheek.

"Don't take it so hard," I whispered. "There's nothing we have any right to do. And don't worry about you and me. That's all right. It always will be. I'm not likely to need another in the way I need you."

The whispered avowals were as much for my own re-assurance as hers. It is only in the sham battles and training manœuvres of our affairs that love survives without the exercise of these banal declarations. With marriage, we realize that all the explosive charges, the booby traps, the whining, in-visible bullets have suddenly become real and that we're not going to escape the most savage hurt unless we exchange these constant small solicitudes and stubborn, irrational hopes. This, really, lies behind the intangible shock of sympathy that sometimes warms two couples who know each other closely: the sudden recognition that each is committed to an advance against a future of entrenched opportunities for boredom, disloyalty and the irrevocable cruelty of a moment's carelessness.

Joan gave a small, lopsided smile. One of those smiles with which women confess their triumph at having forced a protestation of love and shame for having exposed their need so urgently. She nuzzled her face against my shoulder.

"I am a nuisance," she said. "I don't know why you put up with me."

"Oh, you'll do," I said. "It'd be too much trouble to trade you in now. . . ." I gestured to the back of the house. "Sybil's putting a good face on it. I'd never have suspected."

"That's the sort of girl she is."

"Who's supposed to know?"

"Nobody, officially. Margaret will tell Andrew later, but he's probably heard it already from Oliver. Those two have always told each other everything. Ever since they were children."

"Hell," I said again. "What a stupid, dismal business. For all of us. We'd made something so solid between us. You know, it was close without being incestuous. This is going to spoil it."

"I know one person who's going to be happy when she hears," Joan said wryly. "Edna Hyde. She's never quite believed that she has a black daughter-in-law."

"The old fool."

"She won't be the only one. A lot of people feel like that about the sort of marriage Oliver made. That it isn't real. It's something horrid from the way we were brought up to think. People like Oliver and Andrew and me were always 'us', and people like Sybil were 'them'."

26

"That depended on the point of view." I smiled at her. "Remember you were 'them' to 'them' too. . . ."

"Stefan!" the boy shouted from the garden. "Deborah says you must come here."

"That means he wants something," I told Joan as I looked back at the two children. "I'll join you in a minute."

I patted her rump and watched her stride across the drawing-room to the back of the house. From behind, her walk had a proprietorial generosity and lightness and I was sure that, whatever her concern for Sybil, she was happy again. I turned and went down the steps to the garden.

The children came trotting across the dry, faded grass from the shade of the aurelia hedge where they had been grubbing in the earth. In the flawless glare of mid-afternoon their skins had the hard, glazed patina of sculpture in fine wood.

"What is it, Peter?" I asked as he took my hand. "I thought you were supposed to have a sleep after lunch. You ought to show Deborah what a good boy you are. Don't you go to sleep every afternoon, Deborah?"

She squatted by my feet and began to play with the buckle of my sandal.

"I'm hot," Peter Fabricus said. "Wet us with the hose, Stefan."

"All right," I told him. "Take off your clothes. This is just for a minute, though. Then you must go to bed with Deb."

I went and fetched the garden hose coiled by the steps and brought it back to the standpipe sunk into the middle of the lawn. Peter had already stripped and was capering in an exhibitionist, purposeless fashion around Deborah as she struggled gravely with the buttons and straps of her little sun suit.

"Come along, Deb," I said and finished screwing the hose to the tap. "Let's give you a hand." I knelt on one knee as she came over to me. Her body, as I held it against me and unbuttoned the gay scrap of cloth she wore, had the unbelievable

27

delicacy and warmth of life you can feel throbbing beneath the plumage of a little bird. "There you are," I said as she stepped out of her sun suit, "now you're a nice naked girl."

When I turned the tap and the first silver arc of water glittered against the sky, Deborah Hyde suddenly found her voice. She gave a throaty, ecstatic squeal, leapt with tumbling abandon and fell soggily under the stream. Peter joined her with a forced, competitive yell and for a minute they squirmed delightedly on the patch of grass that was rapidly turning to mud. Then I adjusted the nozzle of the hose and made a broad misty spray and chased them with it, playing it on them until they were clean again.

"Look at the rainbow, Deborah," I said, pointing to the bright spectrum held in the droplets of the spray. "Go on. See if you can catch it."

She began to plunge her hands repeatedly into the fan of water, squeezing her fists into chubby balls as she tried to drag the shifting rainbow from the spray.

"I've got it!" Peter yelled. "I've got it! I've got it, Stefan."

He pushed Deborah aside and hugged his arms tightly to his chest, leaping exaggeratedly and raising his voice until the pitch broke. Deborah sat with a neat bump and remained on the grass, looking up at him with placid, adoring contemplation.

"That's enough now," I said, helping Deborah to her feet and hosing the fresh dirt from her bottom. "In you go, Peter, and remember to help Deborah up the steps."

They ran off without a word and began to climb the wide, shallow steps from the garden to the veranda, the boy taking them easily enough, the girl, with devout concentration, leading from the same foot at each ascent.

I unscrewed the hose, coiled it and carried it back to the shade of the ferns by the steps. Tiny, damp footprints darkened the whitestone, those on the lowest step already fading as the dry wind lapped the smears of water. Playing with the children had made me thirsty, but I did not want to join the others yet. I needed a moment alone to put Joan's news about Sybil and Oliver into a perspective of new acceptance. Now there would be fresh and necessary dissimulations, delicate adjustments with which we would all try to rescue the achieved affinities of our circle.

I went to the middle of the lawn and gathered the warm, milky smelling fragments of the clothes the children had forgotten and came back to the steps and sat on the highest, in the shade, and lit a cigarette.

I would never, I realized suddenly, be completely free again. Somewhere and somehow in the past five years, the small, potent felicities, the strict yet nourishing exactions of this afternoon had been made possible and I had ceased to be the permanent tourist forever insulated from the subtle fulfilments of the real inhabitants.

But at what point had this occurred? By what unconsidered assaults of experience had I been brought to these degrees of love and need?

As the child Deborah had grasped at the rainbow in the spray, I tried to pull from the accumulations of the past five years some significant order of events. Perhaps, too, I tried with something of her innocent belief that what I reached for was a tangible truth and not a mere deception of light staining a fine mist of elusive particles. . . .

2

---------- ★ ----------

I

The water in the narrow channel, that day three years ago as we came up through the Caymanas Marshes from the sea, was black and still. The surface was blotched with oily smears quite different from the twinkling dance of silver flakes across the blue skin of the bay where we had spent the morning. On either side of the channel there were plaited walls of mangrove, with dull, tough foliage tangling above the labyrinths of grey, gnarled roots. When the wash of our little boat lapped sluggishly at the banks and the water heaved and subsided, you could see a greasy plaster of dark mud and tiny crabs scuttling across the knots of wood. Little tributary creeks led into the main channel and at the mouth of each creek a file of alligators waited for the schools of small fish to come out: each brute sunk deep into the water, with only the four glistening knobs of its eyes and nostrils to show where it lay. Down by the sea, the heat had been dry and a salty breeze had blown across the baked smell of the white sand, but here we seemed to burrow deeper and deeper into the folds of a dirty, steam-soaked blanket. When you tried to draw an easy deep breath, a brackish, too sweet stench caught in the back of your throat. As the boat pushed through the water ahead of the raucous little outboard, the birds in the dark tunnels on either side began to rouse. We ran a gauntlet of irregular, screeching protest, and once, from perhaps a mile away, the stupendous boom of a bull alligator crashed among us. Long after the last echoes had died, I could feel a twitch of aboriginal terror along my nerves: as if that wild, jurassic declaration had spoken not merely of sexual need but of an unused, slowly teeming world too old and ferocious for us to share; a world in which we warm-blooded creatures of mind and milk were not so much intruders as unborn.

Then the dense, tepid air began to freshen as the channel widened. Ahead of us, a kingfisher flickered from iridescence to dullness as it hurtled erratically into clear light and back into the greenish murk; the bows dipped as the boat slid from the flat, stagnant water and on to the brown corrugations of the wide lagoon; and as we passed from the shadow of the mangroves and the full glare of the sun came down on my head like a great paw-stroke, I winced and squeezed my eyes with my hand. A small, quite involuntary gasp of anguish escaped me and I squirmed on the narrow seat in the stern as the first gush of cold sweat itched on my skin and as my stomach turned implacably with nausea. I tried to concentrate on the boxes and jars of specimens stowed along the floor of the boat, but they swam lazily, like objects seen under water, and the suddenly concerned faces of my students had the unreal, minute clarity of objects focused through the wrong end of a telescope. I turned my head and smiled a bleak, embarrassed apology at Ruddy, the fisherman from Caymanas Village whose boat we had hired that morning and beside whom I sat.

"Teacher! You all right?"

Ruddy's face seemed to approach with the unrelated immediacy of a face in a dream.

"Yes. Yes," I muttered. "Little sick.... Pass in a minute...."

"Doctor Mahler! You're ill!"

Ruddy's face vanished. Inexplicably, against a slowly turning background of clamorous glare and vast, aching water, another face took the place of his. Miss Gay's. She was kneeling

31

among the specimen jars and boxes, looking up at me as I swayed helplessly in the sternsheets. The other students were trying to get nearer also, but in the confines of the little boat free movement was nearly impossible.

"No. . . . No!" I protested. By now I was so muffled in a wadding of sick pain that I was indifferent even to humiliation. All I could summon was a spasm of impatience, a petulant withdrawal from contact. "Only a headache," I told them, with the desperate, wavering urgency of a drunk. "Little too much sun. . . . Pass. . . . In a minute."

The band of my hat felt like a tourniquet and I knew that long before we reached the straggling cluster of huts on the grey shore across the lagoon, I was going to be very sick. It always happened like this. First the growing heaviness in my head; then the gradual accumulation of nausea and splitting pain; next the increasing tenderness of skin until even the pressure of my clothes became unbearable; finally the hapless surrender of the stomach. And it had nothing to do with the sun or the movement of a boat or anything else, directly. I doubted that it even had a name. It was a legacy from a period of terror and uncomprehended abuse: the price one paid, intermittently, for having escaped. Most of those I knew who, like myself, had escaped, paid one sort of toll or another: from their minds or their bodies. Mine was a modest tribute, except that it was often demanded at unexpected or awkward moments. I had felt it beginning as we came up the channel and had hoped to reach the privacy of the stand of sea grapes behind the village in time. It had been the sudden blow of unshielded sun on the lagoon that defeated me.

"Excuse me," I muttered thickly, turned my back, leaned over the stern, my face inches from the surface, and vomited into the brown water. The wake from the propeller caught the egg-yolk gush and spun it into trailing filaments. Then all the body's rejected stuff vanished into the cleansing depths and I was left wheezing and spitting at a pallid reflection which fol-

32

lowed swiftly just beneath the bright surface. My throat
burned mildly, my stomach fluttered and there was a congested throbbing in my head; but already I was feeling better.
I sat up and grimaced deprecatingly at the dubious, apprehensive faces before me.

"I'm sorry about that," I said. "It just couldn't be helped."

I did not apologize for my display but because it had caused
so much inconvenient concern, disturbing the well-earned
somnolence into which they had all been lulled by the boat's
steady glide and by the heat.

"Doctor Mahler! Don't blame yourself. How could you help
it? Are you feeling better now?"

As Miss Gay's deeply set, bloodshot eyes blinked at me with
a fierce devotion of tender reproof, I could see Miss Donaldson
and Mr. Henry exchange indulgent, knowing smirks that added
to the trivial mortification of the moment.

"Thank you, Miss Gay," I said, smiling as gratefully as I
could through a slowly thinning mist of vertigo. "I feel much
better. If you happen to have such a thing as an aspirin in your
bag. . . ?"

"Oh, yes, Doctor Mahler. Yes. Yes. I have some right here."

But long before Miss Gay's zealous fumbling in her handbag
had produced the aspirins, Miss Donaldson had languidly
handed a little wax-paper packet to Mr. Henry. He passed it
to me with the cup from the thermos flask.

"There you are, Stefan," Miss Donaldson said. "You'd
better take four. It's kill or cure."

I nodded my thanks and swallowed the small, bitter discs
with the iced water Mr. Henry had poured for me from the
thermos flask. Miss Gay crouched awkwardly on the floor of
the boat before the confused nest of her handbag, offering
mutely a large, economy size bottle of aspirins.

"Thank *you*, Miss Gay," I said, "Miss Donaldson seems to
have had hers nearer the surface. But I'll take a few of yours,
if you don't mind. Just in case I need 'em later."

33

When I held my hand out for her contribution, she shook too many from the bottle. Several spilled over the edge of my palm and fell to the floor of the boat. Mr. Henry sighed audibly and knelt beside her to help as she began to pick them up. I sighed too, silently, watching her, and wondering, as I often did, what possible compensation we could ever make to that heavy, sullen body, nearly horizontal upper row of teeth and that eager, incurably awkward heart. Knowing that there was none. She was the most brilliant student I had ever taught (sometimes, indeed, I was aware that my role was simply the humble preparation of a genius) and she had an infallible capacity for creating occasions of dilemma and unease. Like some innocent, deadly typhoid carrier she infected us all with her inexorable clumsiness. In her presence all the buried seeds of our ancient cruelty quickened into bright and odious flower. She was doomed to miscalculation and disappointment in all encounters of the spirit, and compared with Betty Donaldson's elegant, deliberate sexuality her shambling attempts to connect aroused something closer to protest than pity. Even our conscientious effort to view her with proud appreciation was corrupted by patronage, almost, one might say, by a sense of ownership.

Now as she settled back on her seat in the thwarts, with the untidily bulging handbag clutched to her stomach, I leaned forward to her.

"By the way," I said. "I nearly forgot. I got that report on the ecological congress. It came last night. If you come to the flat when we get back, I'll let you have it."

"Thank you, Doctor Mahler." For a moment her face was nearly handsome with alerted anticipation and eagerness, until she added heavily, "Oh, but I couldn't. You won't have finished it yet."

"I've read all I want to for the moment," I said. "Really. Besides, it's in French, of course, and I have to take it slowly. You'll be able to get what you want in half the time."

34

"I'll wait for a week or two, Doctor Mahler." Her voice rose on a note of nervous determination. "I couldn't deprive you of it."

"You're welcome to it, Miss Gay," I said. It had suddenly become imperative that she have the wretched thing. "I'm not using it. I was going to put it into the library tomorrow."

"Thank you, Doctor Mahler. Thank you. I'll come to your flat." She relaxed for a second into that still, unfathomable ecstasy with which the real scholars contemplate an acquisition of fresh knowledge, and then, as suddenly, stiffened and added with desperate emphasis, "I mean, I'll come to your flat for the report."

"Yes, Miss Gay," I said. Miss Donaldson had buried her face on Mr. Henry's shoulder. Wisps of laughter floated from her concealment like feathers from a torn eiderdown.

We were more than half-way across the lagoon now, and Ruddy pushed the tiller slightly to bring the bows straight on the village. Holding the course with casual steadiness, he leaned forward and put an immense, calloused hand, the size and colour of a stove-lid, on my shoulder.

"How you stay now, Teacher?" he asked with tender, protective respect (in Cayuna, the teacher holds oracular rank, something above the doctor, nearly superior to the priest).

"Fine, Ruddy," I told him. "I'm all right now. Really."

"You hol' on, Teach," he said. "When we land I will give you a little white rum fe' rub 'pon you head. . . . To draw de fever," he explained confidently.

"Thank you, Ruddy," I said, "but it isn't really a fever, you know. Just a bit too much sun."

"De sun in Braganza parish is de hottest sun in Cayuna," he said, "an' de hottest sun in Braganza stay here, above Caymanas Marsh. Dis is a sun can turn you to dust. I remember one time a white man—from foreign like you'self, Teach—come down fe' shoot alligator. An officer fellow from de regiment. Him come down, an' shoot him shoot like a machine-

35

gun. Him walk up an' down de swamp all day. Won't stop. 'Rest little, boss,' I tell him. Him wouldn't listen. Is like him an' de alligator have quarrel, personal. When evenin' come an' we go back to de village an' was tekkin' up a rum togedder, him suddenly drop dead. Burn up wid fever." Ruddy paused. "Stone dead," he added, with lugubrious pride. "Didn't even have time fe' say, 'Jesus Christ, tek my soul.' "

"That won't happen to me, Ruddy," I promised. "I'll be careful. Maybe your friend had a heart attack. Too much exercise all at once in the heat. Was he a fat man?"

Ruddy's whole face puckered thoughtfully, and he tilted his head in the judicious fashion of a fowl sipping.

"Him backside was fat," he said after a moment. "All white man have a fat backside. Dem favour like women in dat."

He cut the engine as he spoke and swung it down on its hinges into the stem. The boat lost way, settled deeper, drifted against a slapping of water and nudged its bow on to the coarse grey sand before the village. Ruddy jumped into the shallows as two men ran across the beach from under the palms where other narrow black boats were drawn up. The two men gripped the gunwhales at the bow and Ruddy crouched under the stern.

"Ah-h-h-HO!" Ruddy shouted and lunged up and forward with a grunt. And then, as if his shout had suddenly altered the usual continuities of living movement into the abrupt transitions of a frieze, the two men at the bows seemed to flicker before my eyes. At one moment they were flung back rigidly against the weight of the boat; in the next they were half-way along the sides, bent forward in a still explosion of gleaming and unanimous power, with only the wildly jumping cords of muscle and the crunch of sand beneath their slowly thrusting feet to mark the flow of terrific action that had dragged us past the water's edge. And with the end of their concerted action, the men were subtly diminished. For one second they had been ageless and magnificent exemplars, unconfined by time,

36

liberating the mind from its patient, clerical registration of decay. Now, as they straightened and grinned into the boat, they assumed their proper forms, like characters in a fairy tale from whom a spell fades at the clock-stroke. They chided each other anxiously, in sweet, thick voices, as they began to lift the specimen jars and boxes from the boat. For them, these commonplace creatures that they saw every day—starfish, seahorses, anemones, molluscs and the like—had become invested with a strange significance and were destined for rites not of mere analysis but of benevolent, incomprehensible magic.

I climbed from the boat quickly. My five students were gathering handbags, cameras, towels, swimming costumes, luncheon baskets and water bottles and climbing out too. Betty Donaldson was assisted to the beach by tenderly officious hands; the three male students attending her graceful descent to earth with the cooing solicitude, the smiling, ruthless competition for notice of courtiers about a queen. I gave my hand to Miss Gay and she jumped heavily to the warm sand beside me.

"Well, Miss Gay," I said as we reached into the boat together and lifted out the big, sealed tank of parrot fish, "I think we may congratulate ourselves on a profitable morning."

In Miss Gay's company, for some reason, one found all the shallow, consoling streams of small talk dried at the source; communication at this level was reduced to a muddy trickle of priggish banality.

"Yes," I repeated, with a determined, quietly hysterical heartiness. "Most profitable. What we got this morning ought to keep us busy for weeks."

Holding the tank carefully between us, we walked up the beach towards the great susumba tree under which we had parked the station wagon early in the morning. Ahead of us, Betty Donaldson's hips in their rudimentary shorts drawled an eloquent affirmation as her long, bare, brown legs carried her up the slope. The smallest of the specimen jars, the one into

37

which we had put the sea slug dived for by Mr. Henry out by the reef, swung casually from her crooked forefinger. Shreds of seductive banter from the three laden male students around her floated back to us, like the gay, worthless scraps of confetti thrown into the air at a carnival.

"Are you going to vote for her, Doctor Mahler?" Miss Gay asked me.

"Vote? For whom? What for?"

"For Betty? For Rag Week Queen? Haven't you heard about it?"

"Oh, that. Yes, I suppose so. She seems to be the people's choice, all right, judging by the posters. Is she going to win?"

"Of course," Miss Gay said with the happy pride of an elderly aunt as she gazed at Betty Donaldson's polished shoulders. "Nobody else has a chance. Roy Galbraith from Fine Arts has designed her dress already. It's beautiful."

The unsullied candour of her appreciation seemed to make the day suddenly brighter and to quicken the luxurious sense of convalescence I was feeling. I smiled at her as we negotiated the last stretch of rough ground before the station wagon.

"I shouldn't be telling you this yet," I said, "but you're a certainty too."

"Me? How?"

She looked at me with startled appeal, with unpretending astonishment.

"Yes," I told her. "For the Departmental Fellowship. Don't look so surprised, girl. Who else d'you think could have got it? All we're waiting for is the formality of finals and your results."

"But . . . but." Her voice had become frayed and I could feel a tremor in the tank we carried. "Suppose I fail, Doctor Mahler? I mean, what if my results aren't as good as you—you expect."

"Now look here," I said roughly, keeping my voice low so that the others couldn't hear us as we approached the station waggon. "You're not to talk like that, you understand. You're not even to think it. You're about the best thing to come out of Cayuna University since it started and there's absolutely no question of your failing. Your only worry is what you're going to make your special field. I mean that, Lois."

A small, cold panic seized me as I saw the possibility of my indiscreet encouragement flushing those timid creatures of insecurity and self-doubt that inhabited the fringes of her magnificent mind. With Lois Gay, nothing could be taken for granted except her instant, effortless apprehension of new fact: the extension of any spontaneous gesture could always become suddenly menacing or destructive.

At the station wagon, Ruddy, his two friends and the men were stowing the jars and boxes on the floor behind the rear seat. About twenty children, some as fair as Arabs or Sicilians, stood in a half circle around the car and watched with wordless absorption. Many of them had that subtle yet exhausted beauty of the small, isolated community where cousin has married cousin for too long. In another generation, imbecility and rare, half-forgotten diseases would begin to appear. As Miss Gay and I eased the tank to the floor of the luggage compartment and wedged it gently into place, more children came up from the little stream where they had been wallowing while their mothers pounded clothes on the flat, scorching rocks. They didn't crowd or scamper but took their places in the half circle ceremoniously, only the rapt, shining flicker of the dark eyes assured you that they were children like any other.

"Caymanas," Mr. Henry breathed to Betty Donaldson. "Look at 'em, eh. All they know down here are the two F's. Fish and——"

"Patrick!" she said sharply, smiling.

"All right. All right. I wasn't going to say it. . . . Hi. Ruddy! How many of these are yours, eh?"

"Dat one, sah," Ruddy said. "An' dis. Dat one, too. A nex'

one stay down at de house, but him is a bebby. Dis one might be fe' me also," he put his hand on a damp, bushy head beside him, "but I don't sure of it. She live wid me, dough."

Indulgent half-smiles passed between the students as I closed the back doors of the station wagon. Ruddy stepped forward.

"You all set now, Teach?"

"Yes, thank you, Ruddy. You've been a big help as always."

"An' how de stomach stay? You feelin' better?"

"Much better. It was nothing."

"Good." He cleared his throat slightly, stepped back a pace. "It would oblige an' honour me an' my friends, Teach, if you an' de oder ladies an' gentlemen partake of some refreshment in my house before you leave."

"Thank you very much, Ruddy," I said. "That's a good idea. I could really do with a little something."

In the two years that I had been coming to Caymanas Marshes, once or twice a year with the finals biology class, I has always hired Ruddy to take us out to the sea, and always, on our return, he invited me to his house in the same terms.

"Hey, bwoy," he said to his son, "run tell you mamma say dat guest comin'. Come, Teach. . . . Dis way. . . . Ladies. . . . Gentlemen."

At Ruddy's house we were placed neatly along two walls of the tiny dark living-room. I sat on the old horse-hair sofa between Betty Donaldson and Mr. Henry. Henry who was very short had to sit stiffly almost on the edge, for the leather covering had been worn glassy smooth and the front legs were distinctly splayed, tilting us forward. Ruddy, the two men who had helped him beach the boat and two more who had joined us at the house were ranged before the other walls. In the exact centre of the doorway leading to the kitchen, an enormous old gentleman, whose left leg had once been broken and set crookedly, sat and examined us all ceaselessly, with a mild, possessive pleasure, without uttering a word. Nobody had ever

40

told me who he was, or his relationship to Ruddy, but he was always there when I came to the house: a vast, benign presence who nodded to our greetings and to our farewells, kept an unbroken comforting silence, and around whom the restless, younger life of the house seemed to divide and flow like a river past a rock. There was a cool, pleasant stuffiness in the little, crowded room. Dark polish and closely shuttered houses are the only safeguards against the sun's exaction on an island like Cayuna. Admit light and moving air, as modern hygiene demands, onto gay, pale colours and the sun enters with them like a saboteur, lodges beneath every surface and furtively destroys reflection, withdrawal and sustained dialogue. ("The open veranda, the *stoep*," Oliver Hyde once told me with wry despair, "is the greatest threat to human evolution since the Ice Age. It's a colonial invention, needless to say.")

Ruddy's wife came from the kitchen as we settled ourselves. She was one of those strange, disturbing mixtures—not black, not brown, not any conventional formula of stirred colours— that you see only in Cayuna. You felt that here was an experiment of biology that had already justified its risk because of the new, troubling beauty and vigour it had. The quick, warm smile she gave us had the uncommitted curiosity of a wild creature's first contact with unclassified intruders. More than the men, who made periodic commercial excursions into the wider latitudes of the island, more than the children, on whom any influence might work equally, she reflected the essence of this village contained by its great swamp and prolific sea, insulated by a drab ten miles of barren, salty soil from the fat cane-lands of the interior, unimpressed, even, by the fierce, parochial loyalties that made up the true fabric of Cayuna.

She put a tray on the little table of glazed bamboo which stood in the centre of the room and was ordinarily covered with family photographs in brass or tortoise-shell frames. Now the photographs had been removed to the top of the har-

41

monium in the far corner, under the lithograph of a huge, jaundiced blue eye and a sampler on which was embroidered, The EYE of GOD watches YOU.

Ruddy rose as his wife edged neatly into the kitchen past the old man's chair and spreading bulk. The tray was crowded with all the evidence of a modest but undisturbed prosperity: a bottle of rum, a dozen assorted tumblers and mugs, a tall cut-glass pitcher containing coconut water, a plate of dry boiled shrimps on crackers with slivers of Scotch Bonnet pepper, a dish of small, salty oysters, a bowl of escovitched kingfish slices. When he had mixed the rum and coconut water, Ruddy lifted the tray and brought it round. He paused before each guest with a deliberate and exclusive gesture of attention that made mere politeness seem superficial. The dominant ridges and long hollows of his face were softened by a reverent delight, as if this act of hospitality was a ritual thanksgiving we all offered equally and which he led only by accident of his position.

I was given the large, thick, Diamond Jubilee mug on which a likeness of the old queen was floridly stamped: a heavy lidded old woman, pink and arrogant with the powerful tides of Hanoverian health, who gazed at this obscure, gentle corner of her empire with what seemed to be a great deal of satisfaction.

"Health, Ruddy," I said, raising the mug.

"An' good healt' to you, Teach," he replied, lifting his glass, first to me and then, in turn, to each of the others round the room. From the distant reaches of his benevolent self-communion the old man raised his mug in a gesture that did not so much toast as bless us all impartially. "When you comin' down again, Teach?" Ruddy asked.

"Oh, look for me when you see me," I told him. "Not for a few months. I'll write you."

"You gwine put all de t'ings you find down here in a book, Teach?" asked one of the men who had joined us at the house.

"I hope so. Eventually. This lady'll probably do it before me, though." I pointed to Lois Gay.

"True!"

Miss Gay smiled easily as they looked at her with respect and pride. They didn't belong to her category of real or imagined embarrassment. In this island just emerging from the hapless coma of illiteracy, the learned do not have to assume privilege, it is thrust upon them.

"Dem is from de university!" another man shouted into the ear of the old monument in the kitchen doorway. "De *university*! Where dem have all de books!"

The old man smiled gently and nodded a detached, tender approval. He held his mug out for more drink as if it were not really connected to his hand.

II

We spent an hour in Ruddy's house. A slow, comfortable hour that was curiously irrelevant to the pressures of our everyday lives. It was always a surprise to enter the rigidity of this world where factual exchange rather than opinion was the pattern of talk, and in which silence was not used for the preparation of new analysis but merely for the accumulation of fresh items of fact to be uttered, passed from mouth to mouth and stored. Compared with the harsh and articulate political allegiances of even the most remote settlements inland, Caymanas Village and its people inhabited a climate of almost medieval smugness: all judgements and attitudes were organic provisions, like the coconut trees along the beach. Because of the sea, and the generous swamp when the sea was too rough to fish, they had never gone hungry—what they sold inland was to adorn their lives. They knew tragedy, when someone drowned, but the brusque, contrived turbulence of the outside world was never quite real to them. Ruddy, for instance, besides his spanking new outboard motor (bought with ready cash, many of the notes, counted slowly on to Isaac Azoud's counter, from a series withdrawn from circulation) had recently acquired a large handsome radio. It was set in the corner beside the harmonium, immaculate and quite useless without the electricity that would not, in all probability, be brought here for another ten years.

I got to my feet and went through the pretence of consulting my watch. Betty Donaldson, Mr. Henry, Lois Gay and the others began to rise too.

"Man!" Mr. Henry said, patting his stomach. "That was a feast you give us, eh, Ruddy. I don't know what I'm going to the university for. I going to come live down here and get some good food to eat. No wonder you can't stop breeding pickneys."

Ruddy and the others laughed with unpretending pleasure. Formal appreciation of our encounter was what they had hoped for, and Patrick Henry knew exactly the rude subtleties of expected form. I hadn't learnt to use them yet; not, at least, as one member of a diverse, uneven yet intimate family to another. I would have stumbled through sincerities of gratitude and they would have found it all quite insipid beside Henry's facetious bawdy and warm patronage.

Betty Donaldson went to the inadequate opening the old man had left into the kitchen. She leaned in.

"We gawn now, Mrs. Swift," she called to Ruddy's wife. "Thank you for everything, eh." The tensionless Creole twang—so unsuited to the dry, marathon chase after abstractions, so matchless an instrument for describing the enigmas and treasons of mood—had coarsened unaffectedly, become rustic. Ruddy's wife came to the doorway.

"You was welcome, ma'am. You sure you have enough?"

"Lord, yes, me love. Thank you. I going have to sleep the whole way back to Queenshaven."

"Come again, ma'am. Drive good, eh."

After the limpid coolness of the little dark room, the air

44

outside seemed opaque with glare; the heat didn't burn cleanly but clung, as we pushed through it, like a thin paste. My stomach had settled itself efficiently after that humiliating reminder out on the lagoon, and there was a pleasant, glowing aftermath of spice and pepper all the way down from my palate; but my head still felt clogged and heavy, with a furtive nagging ache up the back of my neck and skull. The distant evening and the black velvet, gold studded night began to tease my anticipation like oases on the horizon of a thirsty traveller. As the brittle crust of sand on the little street powdered beneath my sandals and sharp fragments of shell lodged between my toes, I had one of those surges of panic bad temper which no European between the tropics altogether avoids: the blood's uneasy recognition of eventual defeat. With gloom and foreboding and a sour, tired admission of my absurdity, I watched Patrick Henry's resolute little body bounce beside Betty Donaldson. Suddenly, as they cleared the last house at the end of the street, Henry stopped, cocked his head inquisitively, and pointed towards the stream and the susumba tree under which we had left the wagon.

"Hey!" he yelled, his voice burred with startled exasperation. "Leave those, man! What you doing, eh?"

He leapt out of sight as if someone had jerked him on a string, and we hurried up to Betty Donaldson, who was staring after him and frowning.

"What's up?" I asked and stared, too, at Patrick Henry bounding like a golf ball across the fifty yards of grey, tussocky sand between us and the station wagon. The two doors at the back of the wagon were flung open, flat against the sides, and I could see a pair of long, black legs, thin buttocks in khaki shorts and the long, lean back of a man bent over and rummaging among the jars and boxes of specimens. The tank of parrot fish Miss Gay and I had stowed so meticulously had been taken out and set on the ground by his feet. The women and the children stood on the bank, looking at him, and even

45

at this distance, I could sense a caution and uncertainty in their stillness.

Patrick Henry skidded to a halt beside the stranger with an angry flourish of his short, thick arms; his head plunged into the opening above the bent back, and his deep, flat voice worried the still afternoon with protest.

"Hi, man! I speaking to you. What do you think you doing?"

I began to trot forward on his words. The station wagon and our equipment was university property, and until we got back I was responsible. I was as puzzled and irritated as Henry sounded; nothing like this had ever occurred before at Caymanas. A strenuous honesty, like their simplicity, was a part of the half-envious, half-patronizing legend the rest of Cayuna had created about them. But as I jogged through the loose, clutching sand, the man straightened and looked down on Patrick Henry; and I saw that what we would have to deal with was something quite different from the case of trivial delinquency I had expected.

He stood there and watched me as I came up: a tall, still figure, not simply thin but lean as a strayed domestic animal becomes gaunt and harsh on its own foraging. A tremendous, tensed hardness seemed to radiate from that narrow body and I had the sensation that he was encased by cured, unyielding wood instead of a warm envelope of vulnerable flesh.

"Well now," he said with an impersonal, waggish derision more corrosive than hate. "What a t'ing I see today. It not only de brown man run to de black, de white man run too." From far back in the rough forest of shaggy beard, matted hair and heavy writhing brows, his eyes glared with a bleak, unwinking ferocity in which we were not even reflected, as if we were the brute, anonymous means by which he contemplated ideals of hostility beyond our scope. "You t'ink say I was gwine fe' steal your big car?" he asked, thrusting his head at me with the flickering sinuosity of a snapping turtle. His face was pinched and lurid with joyless mischief, and he flung the

46

accusation at me like a man suddenly shouting from some dark, tormented dream. Then, as I stared back at him with careful indifference, his lips stretched in a meaningless, rigid grin and he lowered his head. Standing there, his hands resting on the handle of the great *coco-macca* stick before him, his head bowed in that sombre, inward contemplation, almost graven in his stillness, he was like a grotesque, impervious effigy brooding forever on all the hopes and agonies of some vanished martial faith.

By now the others had hurried across to us. The students had all affected the same air of casual involvement, but there was an apprehensive question in their quick glances from the man to Patrick Henry and myself. Only Miss Gay showed her alarm and disapproval clearly. She was from courteous, over-crowded Barbados where polite, almost parliamentary notice of every conflict is respectively served, and the stranger was clean outside the rules of the game to which she was accustomed. I could see her look with a prim interest and distaste at his wild head topped by the black-cockaded forage cap of his sect in Cayuna. Insulated as she was by the academic ghetto of the university compound, she had probably never seen one of the Sons of Sheba, except as a photograph in the newspaper when one of them was arrested for passing ganja, or when a group of them was beaten and shaved in a police station for disturbing the peace.

Ruddy and his two friends had dropped back. They came up slowly and reluctantly, their faces set in masks of elaborate neutrality and caution. When I tried to catch Ruddy's eye, he looked away sulkily, like a child of whom one asks too much.

"Just give me a hand with this, Pat," I said to Henry, and bent to one corner of the tank that the man had taken from the wagon. Henry glanced at him once with irritable resignation, shrugged and came over to help me. We had lifted it a few inches from the sand when the man started like a wakened sleep-walker, stepped forward, and planted his foot with

47

savage and deliberate force on the edge of the tank. The corner I was holding slipped from my fingers and the end thudded on the ground; the water heaved and slopped over the edge, and there was a turmoil of brilliant colour inside as the terrified fish raced from wall to wall. I straightened slowly. Beside me, Patrick Henry did the same, as Macpherson and Bent, the other two men in our party, closed up on us. Ian Macpherson, a slight, balding boy from British Guiana, took his place at my left shoulder and I thought how pathetic and incongruous his old-fashioned, gold-framed spectacles appeared. Louis Bent, the dapper, slickly handsome ex-teacher from Jamaica, wore that expression of complacently censorious outrage which is apparently handed to every teacher with his diploma.

Quite suddenly all the patient, generous accumulations of our day trembled on the edge of a squalid violence. And yet, looking at the impenetrable, fatuously exultant face before us, I was forced to acknowledge something pure, austere and dedicated: as if he were the solitary, indomitable witness to a persecuted but enduring truth. A wild and enigmatic dignity glared from his eyes and searched in my heart like a boathook. Behind the brimming challenge of that gaunt, crouched body in the patched, immaculate khaki shorts and open shirt, I could sense a sad, dumb need: the old, unappeasable hunger for a lost grace that inspires our most profound hope, our pity and our awe. For a moment, he was reflected in the light of selfless anguish. Then his lips parted vividly behind his beard and his private, desolate breath of laughter reduced him once more to a figure of compulsive mischief.

"What's wrong?" I said, very gently. "We didn't trouble you. You shouldn't do this to us."

He breathed deeply, as if he were burdened by too many perplexities for one man; the long ropes of sinew in his leg quivered as he thrust his foot more firmly against the edge of the tank; with a large, groping gesture, he indicated the speci-

48

mens, the car, the people facing him and the still, apprehensive watchers by the stream.

"Dese t'ings," he said heavily, with a sort of panting fierceness, and again he made that stiff, comprehensive gesture, like a man trying to convey the meaning of some really indescribable perception. "Dese t'ings. . . . Why you come here fe' steal black man's living?"

I shook my head and forced a soft, careless laugh.

"No, man," I told him. "You haven't got it right. We paid good money to get all those fish and things. Isn't that true, Ruddy?" I looked around for Ruddy. He and his friends had edged far off to one side. Now they stood nearer the women and children, wearing the same carefully non-committal, anxious expressions. "Tell him, Ruddy," I urged. "Tell him how much I gave you for the boat and for helping us."

"You give me enough, Doctah," he muttered dejectedly, and dropped his eyes when the man stiffly turned his head and frowned at him.

"You hear that," I said. "Now. . . ."

"I hear," he interrupted, with the brusque indignation of one dismissing a stupid lie. "An' I know say how de white man want to eat up de children of Africa an' hold dem in bondage. . . ." He began to shake, and his shining, angry gaze grew dull and blind; his voice took on a throbbing, exalted note. "Dis land an' de whole eart' belong to de white man, an' de black is his slave. You come here fe' mek more plot against we black. But our day come. Our God will come. . . . Black an' shinin' an' terrible. . . . Africa's children will turn and rule. . . ." He was swaying, now, in a series of abrupt convulsions, his voice hoarse. Beside me, Patrick Henry whistled in his teeth and said, "Ganja!" and I nodded without taking my eyes from the sombre, possessed figure before us. He seemed to claw dazedly for words in the air. ". . . Africa will rule an' de children of Africa will be as princes over all on dat day. . . . Blood will flow for de blood of we, an' de white man will be

49

broken. . . . It is written in de book dat each colour will have its day of glory an' dat de black shall be de last an' for evermore. . . . All nation shall bow down to Africa an' to de Emperor of Ethiopia an' to his people. . . ." He paused and sucked in a ragged breath like a single, harsh sob. Little, reddish points of light glinted on the opaque sheen of his pupils as, in a dragging, painful silence, he crouched implacably above the tank, his face creased brightly with that rigid, mirthless smirk.

In that heavy, expectant stillness, I could feel a tingle crawl damply across my skin; a miasmic projection denser than simple hate or even madness seemed to chill and darken the burning afternoon. Behind the inanely exultant face before us, I saw the haggard countenance of an antique, irremediable terror: something of itself, desolate and inaccessible, rising from the chaos that lurks at the centre of our small, decent achievements and from which we turn avidly into the factitious warmth of illusion, betrayal and sordid, desperate alliances of cruelty. Numbed by a sudden inadequacy I watched his heavy brows contract spasmodically and darken the drugged glitter of his unwinking eyes with a sort of quizzical sadness.

Then Patrick Henry moved forward, placing his feet with a peculiar, stiff-legged daintiness, as if he were stepping on a path of upturned faces. "Pat!" I said sharply, as behind us Betty Donaldson moaned, "Don't, Pat." He stopped and looked back, his face held in planes of an absurd but touching gravity. "Take it easy," I said lightly, smiling at him, and stepped forward two paces so that I was between him and the man. I put my hand on his shoulder and felt the nervousness thrumming in his taut little body like water rushing through a hose. "Take it easy, Pat," I said again.

He looked at me truculently, but with the unadmitted relief, I think, of a small boy prevented from completing an act to which his male pride has driven him.

"All right," he said irritably, and then, with a disgusted rasp in his voice, speaking round my body. "Here, man! What sort of damn foolishness is this, eh? All this white man, black man nonsense?" He waved his hand inclusively: from Miss Gay's dense blue-black, through Betty Donaldson's milk chocolate on peach and Ian Macpherson's raw copper, to his own freckled saffron. "You see what I mean? We all doing the same work, you hear? Which is something you and the rest of Sheba's Sons could consider. . . . A little work. . . . Instead of walking about looking to make trouble."

The man's hand twitched briefly, discarding Patrick Henry's words as one would toss aside the grey, crumpled, no longer relevant notes and reminders which accumulate in a jacket pocket. Under the restless, tufted brows his eyes became glazed and hot and suddenly assured.

"You," he said flatly, "an' all like you is traitor."

"I'm *what*?" I could hear Pat's voice thicken with frustration.

"All de rest of you is traitor too," the bitterly serene, utterly confident voice continued. "Except him," and his finger stabbed at me. "Him side is not we side, but all of you have join wid him. When de day of wrath come an' de righteous Jehovah overt'rows de enemies of peace den your blood will flow wid his. Him can't save you on dat day. For on dat day de white man will be broken, and all dose who have betray de children of Africa."

And saying this, not halting the level almost unemphatic flow of his words, his eyes fixed unblinkingly on our faces, he swung the *coco-macca* wide above his head, so fast that it blurred against the bright, hard sky, and brought the tip down against the tank, the stick descending like a neutral extension of his arm and the whole mindless, brutal action completed while we still registered only the abrupt tintinnabulation of bursting glass and the silvery leap of water into the air. It was over, really, before our incredulous judgement had accepted the

51

meaning of what he did: as we would have experienced, with the same time lag of disbelief, the effortless concentration of speed and ferocity in the hook of a cat's paw or the appalling sweep of an alligator's tail. Among the shards of glass on the damp sand the little fish arched and flopped, the shimmering mosaic of their scales already beginning to fade, as he whirled, in a tangle of stamping feet and flailing arms, to crouch again five yards away, the great *coco-macca* now held ready like a sabre, his face suddenly radiant with a dreamy, savage relish.

From a curious, unreal distance, I heard Lois Gay's astonished squeal, and I was vaguely aware of her darting past us, her mouth still open on that cry of protest as she ran to the station wagon, rummaged in the back and came running back, heavy, lumbering and earnest, her face blank and intent. She dropped to her knees in the act of running, careless of the splintered remnants of the tank, and with a tender, shaking haste began to drop the fish into the conical nylon net she had brought from the wagon. But I could feel only a detached interest in what she was doing, as I was only half-conscious of Ian Macpherson's grey, frightened face and the vacant, shocked collapse of Louis Bent's smug, schoolmasterish inflation. I was straining to keep my fingers locked on Patrick Henry's shoulder.

"Let me go," he gasped. "Let me go, Stefan. I'll fix him for that." He was nearly crying as he plunged madly in my grip.

"No," I said. "It's not worth it, Pat."

A dimly noted shaped that was Lois Gay galloped clumsily to the water's edge with the net of fish held before her, like one of those indistinct and irrelevant figures who sometimes operate on the blurred fringes of a dream.

"For God's sake," I panted over my shoulder to the apparently mesmerized Macpherson and Bent, "help me to hold him."

They started and Macpherson shook his head, and then they jumped forward quickly to my side. Between us we managed to hold the passionately writhing body until its furious lunges subsided into a confused shivering.

"Den what happen, white man?" The harsh, infatuated voice sneered as I tried to soothe the frantic boy. "Why de little brown bwoy carry on so bad? Him want mek trouble?"

"Nothing's going to happen, man," I said wearily. "You go about your business now and leave us. You've done what you wanted and nothing's going to happen."

"How you mean fe' tell me 'go on', you white bastard you? Why you don't come an' move me?"

"No." I shook my head. As I faced that sad, insensate hatred I seemed to see the figure of some pious and terrific longing, like a corpse shrivelling in the caustic air of a desert. "I can't make you move if you don't want to, man," I said. "You know that."

"You damn white shit," he said again, almost wistfully, and I turned to Macpherson.

"Take Pat to the car," I said. "Don't let him get out again. You'd better go with him, Betty. And keep him quiet, eh?" They all moved slowly towards the wagon, glancing sidelong at the man; Pat was still trembling like a newly broken horse. I waited for Lois Gay to come back from the lagoon's edge. Ruddy and his friends, the women and children by the stream looked on, motionless with that oblique and passive absorption. "Did you get 'em to the water in time?" I asked Lois as she came up.

"Yes, Doctor Mahler," she said crisply. "I don't know if they'll live though. Salinity in the lagoon might be too high." She went to the back of the wagon and slammed the doors shut decisively, turning the key we had left in the lock. She withdrew the key, turned and looked at the man. "Well!" she said severely and sniffed. Then she went to the driving side and heaved herself in behind the wheel. With a mild sense of surprise, I was aware of my shirt sticking damply to my back and drops of sweat tickling my ribs.

I began to walk towards Ruddy and the others at the stream. To get to them I had to pass the man. When I came near, he reared suspiciously, but without the authoritative menace of a few minutes before. The women had gone back to their laundry and the children were tumbling in and out of the clear, shallow water again; but I had the impression that their activity was contrived. Ruddy waited for me, with his head lowered and half-turned.

"Well, Ruddy," I said. "We're off now. See you again in a few months, eh?"

"Yes, Teach," he muttered sulkily. We looked at each other furtively and quickly: the trapped, melancholy glances of dislike and accusation which people exchange when they have shared humiliation. He shuffled and rubbed his hand irritably across his face, as if wiping off a smear. Then: "Jesus Christ, Teach," he said, "I sorry, you see. I sorry dis happen to you down here." His voice became plaintive and faintly indignant as though he were trying to justify some unavoidable sin of omission. "Dem only come here fe' cause trouble." He gestured with timid disgust to the man. "Me don't want any business wid dem, I tell you."

"You're right," I told him. "I'm glad you didn't interfere, Ruddy. He's taken up a little too much ganja and he's not safe. It wasn't your fault, man. Don't worry about it." He looked at me again and his face pulled briefly in a diffident, grateful smile. "I didn't know you had any of Sheba's Sons down here," I continued. "How many of them in the district?"

"Oh God, Teach," he said, grimacing. "Too damn many. Dem start a settlement a few months gawn in de bad land back of de swamp." He pointed inland across the stream to the scrubby, grey-green tangle of sea-grapes, *macca* and thornbush that began where the massed, foetid vegetation of the marsh ended. "Dem come sometimes fe' buy fish from us." I won-

54

dered how little Ruddy and the village were getting for their fish, but knew that it would be no kindness to ask. It would only put him to the necessity of lying to save himself another mortification. "Dem keep demselves to demselves," he explained insistently.

"Yes," I said quickly. "I understand." The unaffected esteem and fondness we felt for each other—that special regard which seems to flourish when two men of widely divergent skills find a common ground for their talents—only emphasized our discomfort. We shook hands shyly, like partners who have failed to honour the full spirit of an unwritten contract. I turned and walked back towards the station wagon. "Come again soon, Doctah," Ruddy said heavily. "Sure," I called back over my shoulder. "I'll be down in a few months."

The man was waiting for me as I came back. I didn't look at him but went straight past to where he had shattered the tank. Slowly and carefully I began to scrape dirt over the jagged fragments, using the edge of my sandal like the blade of a miniature bulldozer. I didn't look up when I heard his sharp, laboured breathing behind me.

"Den why you come down here fe' boder me, sah?" he said fiercely, but now there was something baffled and diffuse in his animosity. As if he sought the answer to some overwhelming question to which I really had the answer.

"Man," I said deliberately, still keeping my eyes on the careful scraping of my sandal, "I didn't come here to bother anybody. It's you who treated us bad. You know how much this tank cost?"

"I shoulda bust your head de way I bus' dat," he said, with the same mechanical, indecisive heat. He pounded the end of his stick on the ground between us, like a dried actor stalling for time.

"You could do it now," I said. "I couldn't stop you."

"I gwine remember your face," he said. "When de day come an' de righteous word is given, I gwine remember your

55

face." For a moment he seemed to fasten on the promise of these words with the oblivious concentration of an earthquake survivor clutching to some worthless object he has salvaged. "De day," he continued, "when Israel's children of Africa return to deir own land." His eyes were lustreless now, and his head wavered; he reached at the air before him with a vague searching gesture as if a flung line had fallen short of his fingers. When I turned away he did not even glance at me. As I climbed into the front seat beside Lois Gay and she started the engine, the man came back to himself with a galvanic jerk. He looked about wildly and then came leaping to my window, with long, frantic strides.

"Remember what I tell you," he stammered, pushing his head through the frame of the window. His face was brilliant with sweat and his fingers hooked over the door in the convulsed squeeze of electric shock. "Remember what I tell you," he repeated with that driven and bewildered urgency. "All of you trouble black people too much an' deny us our kingdom. . . . Wait! Wait!" he shrieked as Lois Gay let the clutch out and the wagon began to move. "I don't finish . . . . Wait!"

Then the sweating, vivid face was suddenly snatched from the window, the heavy wagon accelerated; I heard his stick clang on the side; and looking back I saw him fallen on one knee in the dust of the narrow road, flourishing the huge *coco-macca* with a sort of spent, despairing fury, and laughing.

III

We got back to the university just after dark. For a while, across the bleached, shadowless plain of limestone and scrub beyond Caymanas, until we reached the ample order of the sugar lands by Catherine River, the wagon was shrill with banal, excited discussion. And listening to their young, hurt voices, I realized that perhaps what they sought was not an explanation but a way back to innocence. They had been brought up suddenly this afternoon against a purposeless and indescribable spirit of destruction: something at once cruel, greedy and insignificant, outside the explained conflicts of race, class or commerce, and far older and more obstinate than these. From now on each would carry, like the scar of an old accident, a persistent, insidious doubt. They would never be quite certain again that the polite contrivances which hold even a changing society to understandable terms might not be shattered in a moment by a force careless of any laws, theories or ties.

But as we drove deeper among the familiar patterns of cultivation and villages in Braganza parish, their spirits began to bounce back into shape. I made Lois Gay stop in the little market town of Serena and I took them into the beer parlour next to the grocery. Sitting there around bottles of strong, gassy beer while the juke-box sprinkled us with comforting, synonymous trivialities, they all seemed to forget what had happened. Even Patrick Henry lost his sick, dazed look and took Betty Donaldson off to dance on what appeared to be about a square foot of floor by the juke-box. When we left, the men carried more beer, and by the time we pulled up outside the science block at the university, they had managed to make Ian Macpherson a little drunk. The lights were on in the dining-halls on the far edge of the wide campus so we unloaded the specimens quickly and took them into the laboratory, going through my office which had a door onto the veranda.

"I'll manage from here," I said as we put the jars and boxes on the long bench at the end of the laboratory. "You'll want to go and get cleaned up and gowned before dinner."

They went outside, and I heard them laughing and teasing Macpherson as they climbed into the wagon again and Lois Gay drove them off to drop them at the various halls of residence before she took the car over to the motor pool. Her father owned a garage in Barbados and she drove with the same accomplished confidence that she brought to the lab bench; whenever we went out on field work, she assumed the role of chauffeur in the way that the only woman at a tea-table pours.

I switched off the row of lights we had turned on as we entered and went back to my office. There were seven first-year essays on the desk and I picked them up to take back to my flat. I drew the door to behind me, shaking it after the Yale lock had clicked, and went down the broad, shallow steps of the veranda. A hot segment of moon had begun to show over the mountain ridge on the other side of the dry river gorge below the university lands, like a huge, polished seed being squeezed slowly from the centre of a fruit. Above the black paper cut-out of mountains there was a soft lemon glow that diffused slowly, like a pale stain spreading through dark water, into the lavender sky and blonde stars of early evening.

Half-way across the cool grass of the wide, empty campus I stopped and turned my back on the long crescent of lighted windows in the residential buildings. I returned the way I had come until the square mass of the science block suddenly appeared with that hazy, limp look of all buildings emerging from darkness, as though they were erections of canvas instead of stone.

I opened my office door again and felt my way across the room, through the door into the laboratory and down the wall to the light switch. The fluorescent tubes flickered and then blossomed abruptly with that heatless, steady glare. I went to the open shelves at the end of the laboratory and reached down the big record book in which we entered all field expeditions. There was a tray of gummed labels on one of the lower shelves, and I took a wad of these also. Then I carried the book and labels across to the bench where we had put the day's collection. The essays were still under my arm, and the little canvas holdall with my swimming costume, towel and rolled-up cloth hat hung from its strap over my shoulder. I lifted my arm and the essays fell on the bench; tilted my shoulder and the bag

58

dropped to the cement floor. The clock above the lectern said half-past seven, I remember, and when I next looked at it, it was pointing to half-past nine. On the wide, formica-topped bench before me the jars and boxes were drawn up in single file, labelled, and between them and myself was the record book with my signature at the end of the report. When I read the report over it was like reading the words of a stranger who somehow had written exactly as I would have done.

The snug, used tiredness which filled me seemed also to have given me that relaxed clarity of perception you get after the first drink at dusk. I swung round on the stool, leaned my back against the edge of the bench, and lit a cigarette. The smell of the laboratory, sharp and artificial, made up of formalin, acid, fixative and dead flesh in alcohol, reassured me as if I had been away for a long time. With a sedate, tethered contentment, I looked along the wavering glints of serried bottles, tubes, jars and flasks until they faded among the deep shadows at the far end of this functional cavern. It was difficult to realize that I had been in Cayuna only two years: this big, ugly room seemed to fit around me like a sett around a badger. I thought, without regret, of the brisk, clinically efficient Midlands university from which I had applied and, rather to my surprise, been accepted. "Yes, you ought to take it," old Tollgrace had said when I went to see him in the grey, ironmaster's Gothic house that always smelt of wet felt and yeast for the home-made wines we suffered for his sake. "You'll never do anything here. Responsibility at your age might push you into doing something original. Because of your blasted pride, you know, Mahler. You'll feel you have to live up to your exalted rank. Otherwise," and here his heavy hand, corded with grey-blue, old man's veins had flourished, not moralistically but with a sure impartial assessment, "otherwise you're bound to spread your talents thinly and entertainingly among your contemporaries, and finish up whimsically old before you're fifty. So get along to your wretched little colony and let's hear from you.

Where did you say it was?" "Cayuna," I had told him. "Oh, yes; West Africa, isn't it?" "No," I said, "West Indies." "Same thing. They're all Surbiton in the sun. The only difference is that you can't get to London for a few bob."

Now, as I put the collections log back in the case, I was whistling: the notes swirled, rich and liquid in the pressing silence, high up against the ceiling. I crossed to the long, wide shelves on which we kept the demonstrations and experimental animals and fussily tested the catch on the guinea-pig cages. At this time we were still sharing the laboratory with the botanists; a frontier, on which both sides kept a balefully suspicious eye, being drawn half-way across the laboratory. In my first year at the university, someone had failed to drop the hook properly on a batch of guinea-pigs. During the night the gluttonous little brutes had escaped, crawled along the shelves and gorged their way enthusiastically through the dicotyledons prepared against the next day's examinations. The plants had been flown out from England specially; and when their gnawed, useless fragments were discovered the next morning enough had been said by the botanists to precipitate one of those vicious, spinsterish academic feuds that smoulder like a combusted coal-heap until a really important issue fans intrigue and spite into a roaring flame. For weeks a dark, silent war of ambush spread across the university, involving more and more allies. And then Ovando, the Principal, had stopped it by a brilliantly timed questioning of some half-promised appropriations for the whole Science Faculty. This had re-united us all.

There was dew on the grass when I left the building again and a cool, vagrant breeze flicked across the campus from the mountains. In the union on the bluff over the river, the students' steel band was practising and the plangent drone butted steadily into the yielding texture of the night. It was monotonously arresting as a pulse beat: the unworked rhythms of a people who have only realized music as a social adjunct and

60

not yet as an art. A group of four or five couples passed me, materializing with that floating, footless glide of those seen by moonlight: their voices caught my attention lightly, like cobwebs on the face, stretched into the darkness, and parted with the same gentle elasticity. There was a dulled ache along the back of my neck and head, but I felt vibrant and quick. Hungry too, but it was, of course, too late to dine in the bachelors' mess at the common room. Suddenly, with an exclusive, comfortable anticipation, I wanted to be with Bernice. I began to run across the grass, crushing the dew up among my dusty toes through my open sandals. At the flat, I dropped essays, holdall and clothes in an impatient line between the door and the shower, kicking off my sandals as I stepped under the spray. It took me five minutes to dress and go out to the little car I was gradually buying. All the way down the long, shallow hill into Queenshaven, bursts of remembered music seemed to gather themselves like small waves inside me and break out uncontainably.

Freude, I sang,

> *Freude, schöner Gotterfunken*
> *Tochter aus Elysium.*

IV

She was preparing a drink for three men who looked like sailors; at least they had that air of transient but utter possession sailors and cats assume in any strange place so long as it's comfortable. I went to the end of the bar next to the door leading out to the back rooms. The dark polished slab under my bare forearms clung lightly to my skin, like a piece of oiled silk, and the long, brightly lit mirror and the stacked bottles flung transparent reflections deep into the surface of the glossy wood. Bernice stopped mixing the drinks and stood with the misted shaker held against her and called, "Cherry!"

The girl who served the tables and washed the glasses looked up from the corner of the room where she was chatting with two men, caught Bernice's nod in my direction and came over to the bar quickly. Bernice watched her intently while she took a bottle of Danish beer from the big chest of cracked ice by the cash register behind the bar. "Not that glass, Cherry," Bernice said. "Take the one I put in the frigidaire." She continued to watch until Cherry had poured half the beer into a glass that was grey and sticky with cold; then she turned back to the sailors.

"Thank you, Cherry," I said. "Have something."

"I'll tek a Green Stripe, Doctah," she said.

I put a five shilling note on the bar and she took it, slid it into the till of the cash register and rang up the price of my imported beer and her cheaper, local brew. Then she took change from the till, put the price of her drink into the pocket of her apron and brought the balance back to me.

"I'm hungry," I said. "You have any patties or hard-boiled eggs left?"

"Miss Bernice leave dinner for you, Doctah," she said and added with a bland, unambiguous complacency. "She say to me, 'Cherry, Doctah comin' down tonight, so leave some o' de cawn beef an' de green banana an' spinach for him, eh.' You want me bring it fe' you here, Doctah?"

"Yes," I said. "Yes, please."

She went into the office behind the bar space and came back with a plate under the meshed dome of a fly cover. There were five slices of reddish-brown corned beef on the plate, and three phallic, grey-green boiled bananas with a pat of butter on each, and a heap of the virulently green, broad-leafed Cayuna spinach.

When I was starting on the third slice of beef, Bernice came along the bar from the sailors. Immediately Cherry took her tray and left through the lifted flap in the bar.

I was using a fork only and now Bernice took my left hand,

62

which rested on the counter, between both hers and studied it with a still concentration, her fingers moving lightly over the back and palm. Then she squeezed it slowly and rocked it gently on the cool wood as if she were memorizing the shape of an object she was about to relinquish forever. Then she raised her tranquilly intent face, smiled at me and poured the rest of the beer into my glass.

"Hullo," I said.

"Hullo, mister," she said softly, and smiled again with that pensive yet absent tenderness. "You going to stay?"

"Yes," I said. "May I?"

"You know that."

"Yes," I said, quite seriously, then joining the unhurried intimacy of her mood: "Thank you for leaving dinner for me. How did you know I was coming down?"

"Oh, I just know. You don't come for a week now."

"Five days, Bernice. I have to work hard for what they give me at that place."

"I know," she said. "I glad you come though." She circled my wrist with her fingers and frowned on my arm. "How come you have so much hair? The hair on your arm longer than some men have on them head." She tugged gently at one of the hairs on my forearm.

"It's just the way I am," I told her. "You should have seen my father. He had so much all over his body that in summer he didn't have to wear a jacket."

"No," she said, like a child struggling between its own common sense and the authority of an adult's assertion. "No. You joking."

"Well, yes," I said. "I was exaggerating a little."

"Miss!" one of the sailors called. Bernice let go my wrist and went over to them. The two men in the corner had gone and Cherry was standing half-way up the bar, leaning her back against it. She gave me a tired, friendly smile and nodded a question at my glass. I nodded back and she came down the

63

bar, through the gap and took another bottle from the ice-chest. When I had finished this I got up from the tall stool and walked through to the lavatory in the back. It was the smallest of four rooms around a little hallway. The other rooms were the office, a storeroom, and a saloon with one large round table where parties sometimes drank if they wanted to avoid the open conversations of the bar. At the end of the hall-way there was a flight of wooden stairs, turning back on itself at the landing and leading to the rooms above the bar. I went up these stairs and into the bedroom and took a book from the little bedside table, turned on the bedside lamp and lay across the foot of the bed. The book was a very long, elaborately con-trived detective story; it had been washed up into my hands in the manner of such stories, and I kept it at Bernice's to read in small sections when I was waiting for her like this; I tried to keep each development in my head, like moves in a chess game, building a gradual summary which I would consider from time to time, strolling to work, or in bed in the mornings. Here, in this room between Queenshaven's commercial quarter and the waterfront, the night noises of the city were curiously sub-dued, as if occasionally one of them—a stab of music from the band at the big tourist hotel, a rattle of distant shouts, the hiss of tyres on the road, the clattering, headlong roar of anchor chains or boom cables—had left its origin, paced through the warm, thick night, called softly under the window and returned quickly to its own home. The room was very warm and close and smelt of her powder, the trapped petrol fumes of the day's traffic, the heavy must from the sugar sacks and rum vats in the warehouses, the sour brine and hot oil seeping across the town from the docks.

A little after midnight I heard the clang of shutters and the chink of glass as she and Cherry closed up downstairs. And a few minutes later her deliberate steps on the stairs. I shut the book and rested my forehead on my crossed forearms, my eyes closed.

64

"You tired?" she said. The mattress dipped and sighed as she sat on the edge next to my head.

"No," I said. "I have a headache. Here." I took one arm from under my forehead and rubbed the palm of my hand up and down the base of my skull.

"You sick, Stefan?" she asked quickly.

"No. Not sick. We were out in the sun all morning. I just feel as if I had a heap of lead shot under the skin, here. It's nothing."

Her large soft fingers dug into my neck, gripped where the trapezius muscle joined the neck, and worked with slow, confident firmness up the back of my head. Soon the dull, congested distress began to fade, as if being carried downstream on a rush of cleared blood.

"You don't know how good that feels," I said.

"You really feel better?"

"Really."

She stood up and the springs pushed the mattress under me. I heard the faint rasp of her zip and the susurrus of her dress being taken off. When she sat next to me again I lifted my head, my eyes still closed, and wriggled round until my face was pressed against the *cous-cous* and warm flesh scent of the cotton petticoat that covered her broad stomach.

She took my face between her hands and turned it upwards to her. I opened my eyes and smiled with the lazy satisfaction of a man lingering deliberately on the last step before love.

"You know something?" she said simply. "You beautiful."

"Oh God, Bernice!"

"Why you say that?" she asked as if mildly surprised. "You don't like hear me say that you beautiful?"

I laughed, not with embarrassment, we were too close for that any more, but to declare my conventional protest.

"It's not that," I said, "but any man feels foolish when he's called beautiful."

"But if it's true why I can't say it?"

65

I put my hand up and stroked her face and pushed my fingers among the coarse, stiffly permed curls. She bent over and kissed me.

"You want us make love now?" she asked.

"Yes," I said.

3

I

Lying beside Joan's sprawled body, I watch the curtains swell briefly before the mountain breeze. They turn slowly against the moonlight with an air of curious, shy purpose, as though they had only waited for the daytime world to sleep before resuming a gentle, silent dialogue with the other inanimate beings of the room. Couldn't one, then, reverse Berkeley and postulate a reality of things that only emerges when we lie in it unconscious? A separate life of still, inconceivably tender communion between the matter we choose to regard as dead or mindless?

I raise myself on one elbow and look at Joan's face. It is the face of a stranger, filling me with a quiet ache of sadness and desire. I study it with something like awed care, almost guiltily, as if I were trying to violate the peace of a really sacred privacy and solitude. In the confusing glow of filtered moonlight all the lines and claw marks of experience have been smoothed away, and the face I examine has the elusiveness and self-sufficiency of an inscription in some vanished tongue. If there were only some way in which I could lift this stranger lovingly from sleep and discover her secret in the waking world. But a touch here is enough to commit murder: even too direct a gaze has the force to destroy this fragile and disturbing creature I can never know. I feel more profanely intrusive than I did an hour ago, when her face beneath mine was slack and open with delight and she gasped my name until the name itself died in an amazed, shuddering wail.

I get from the bed carefully. Not that there is any need for moving cautiously. After love Joan slides to a dark, mid-ocean floor from which she can be dragged only with difficulty. Going over to the window and pulling one curtain aside, I look out into the white, carbide glare of moonlight on the garden. Everything, the grass, trees, hedges, even my neighbour's roof across the road, has been blanched by the moon, and I gaze into a veiled, tremulous world withdrawn from the sharp, utilitarian definitions of the day. It will be another four hours at least before the first bright thinning of the sky above the mountains.

I feel as though I stood in the beating heart of a riddle. The faces and events that have drifted to me from their own world are accidental clues, brief lights by which I try to discern some unifying explanation. We all attend on the past with this great hope: the expectation of some precipitated image in which all that we endure will be made clear.

When I was making love to Joan an hour ago, it was of Bernice that I was thinking. It was not infidelity to the woman who has astonished me with happiness, but rather a kind of instinctive honour paid to a time renewed for me this afternoon by Oliver's unanswered question, and to the woman in whom that time seems most real.

II

During the first few months after I came to Cayuna, I used to drink in the bar of the Palm Bank Hotel. It was a place to which I had been taken and it was pleasant enough to become a habit. The young professional and commercial men, and their women, use it and you can always be sure, on a Saturday morning, of being asked to join a group. They are a gossipy, flirtatious, endemically hospitable people. Among them, I find, the essentially coarse colonial mind has been sharpened and made flexible by two factors in their lives: the rich *pot-au-feu* of race that simmers in their genes and the almost ideal size of a city just large enough to foster those conceits and eccentricities that can develop only in a capital yet just small enough to make anonymity impossible. It is the human heart that is passed from hand to hand here and examined with a practised, minute relish. (And like every society whose main entertainment lies in evaluating the intimate experience of its own members, it is under the authority of women.) Every desire, every involvement, every device of self-assertion is sooner or later blown about the island on a prevailing wind of eager, unabashed scandal, producing, by a kind of cross-pollination, a spirit tolerant of all the climates of passion. Before long, in those days, I had begun to know a number of people for myself, apart from the more restricted set that came to the university, to the flats and houses of my colleagues.

Then one afternoon, I had to go down to the docks on business. A shipment of apparatus which we needed badly had arrived from Canada and been held by the customs. Several telephone calls had only deepened a confusion that now seemed to have acquired a life of its own far more complex than the original, probably mechanical, obstructive act on the part of one man. When I reached the little, hot shed just inside the dock gates, the name of the officer responsible had long been forgotten, even the reason for the delay—the diamond bit of the Archimedes drill—was now merely the first stitch in a splendid tapestry of forms and declarations. For two hours I explained, signed, gave sworn assurances, trotted the scorching streets between the dock and two offices at opposite ends of Queenshaven. Finally, with the air of reluctance and melancholy resignation officialdom adopts when it is forced to release something for actual use, they agreed to clear our equipment. Apologetically, trying to give the impression that I was only a

69

conscript in an outlaw band, I gathered the heavy parcel and left. Sadly, like priests witnessing some incorrigible perversion of fallen man, they watched me go.

I carried the box out to the car and manœuvred it through the door and on to the back seat. By now it was nearly dark; the offices had closed for the day, and the street lamps twinkled wanly in the rose-grey haze of dusk. I felt mildly poisoned by the forced labour of the afternoon, and knew that I would be unable to read or even talk intelligently until my mind cleared itself of the leaden fantasies of the customs house. As I turned up from the waterfront, I began to look around for the first tavern.

It was like this, by an accident of impulse, that I first met Bernice Heneky.

III

Later on she was to tell me: "You is always going to need a woman. The first night you come in here an' I look at you, I know that. . . ."

"But every man needs a woman, Bernice. There's nothing strange in that."

"No," she said, shaking her head with amused impatience. "You don't understand. I don't mean to say that you *want* a woman. I mean that you *need* woman. The same way a baby need milk. How long since you grow to manhood that you ever have to go without a woman?"

With Bernice one always had the sensation that truth was a common but enduring commodity, like the salt on a table between two people sharing a meal. It was not something one rationed, or even regarded: you simply passed it between you.

"Never for very long," I admitted. "Except once for a while during the war when there were none where I was."

"I know," she said. "It write on your face." And again she returned to the disturbing image she had used. "The first

70

time I see you my breast did hurt. Like I did have milk an' no child to feed."

When did she say this? It must have been early in the "dog-days" between our first meeting and the disruption of her father's emergence. Once, a long time after, Oliver, with the surgical, dispassionate callousness of a writer honing himself on a friend, said: "Of course I envy the real sensualists like you, Stefan. You have a mongrel's instinct for snatching juicy bones of fulfilment from any garbage the world tips over you." I didn't tell him that Bernice had said it before him, perhaps with more precision and force.

Her bar, Long John's, had become at the time when I first discovered it, an informal, tacitly recognized club for most of the journalists, artists and younger politicians in Queenshaven. Here they could relax those rigid public attitudes of en-thusiasm or indignation which constitute the professional penalty common to all three trades, as interrupted sleep is the price doctors pay for their unique satisfactions. They could exchange their accumulated disillusions without hypocrisy, and by unspoken agreement very little of what was said over the iced lager or the rum-punch was ever leaked to the innocent world they all served. "Look at them," Oliver said fondly one night after we had started to become close. "Like a lot of old whores with their corsets off, having a good scratch after the last client has gone." But this was some time after I had started to go there. At first I was only one of the assorted lay-men, sailors, soldiers, waterfront workers, taxi-drivers and the like, whom the others accepted as background noise but seldom adopted into their loosely knit, almost familial circle.

Yet if they enjoyed having a cosy, neutral talking ground on which to meet, there were upwards of two dozen bars or taverns in the district that would have done as well. Places where the rest of the middle-class men went only occasionally and the middle-class women not at all. It was Bernice who really stood at the centre of the snug, undemanding welcome that fitted like old slippers whenever you went into Long John's.

To call her a maternal figure would be trite. Particularly in a country where nearly every woman, of whatever class, begins to assume matriarchal lines before she's adolescent. . . . No, what we all recognized, I think, was an innate, undefended compassion. It was part of her, like her broad, heavy body. There was nothing sentimental in it, for she was incapable of lying, but it responded to any distress, however well deserved or secret. Nor could she play the stock barmaid role of pseudo-philosopher and guide. Her commentary, like her perception, was limited to the immediate. Most of the talk around her was not so much outside her capacity to follow as outside her scope of interest. I don't mean that it bored her, but that her attention was given to the individuals who spoke. This was not a pose. I have often sat and watched her study the face and mannerisms of a stranger with the same fascinated calm and fidelity of concentration she would employ as she studied my hand or the lines of my body. And I used to feel a twinge of churlish, tight-fisted jealousy until I told myself, angrily, that she did it with the same compulsion as a sculptor defining the true shape hidden in a marble block. Perhaps had she not been uneducated, or rather if she had been untroubled by a half-education, she would have realized all this in paint or stone. But that part of her imagination had been too badly stunted by the narrow moulds of her schooling. What had been left was her unpretending, unconscious delight in the fact of another. And what the callowest or grossest of us sensed was that we somehow acquired an indestructible significance in the clarity of the loving appreciation.

Tangibly her nature showed itself in indiscriminate, ultimately anarchic charities. Catering, as she did, for notoriously casual managers of money, it was to be expected that she would often have to give credit. But while most of them used this fairly there were others who probed her vulnerable centres with the instinctive accuracy of killer wasps. She would not allow this in respect to drinks past a certain point: she couldn't if she was to replace her stocks and satisfy the big rum company from whom she leased the place. But as far as food went, she submitted helplessly, for that was her own sideline and the company was uninterested whether she served it or not. Frequently she would feed one of the painters or newspapermen for three days and then he would be in funds again and that would replenish her supplies against the next man who had to be carried. It was characteristic of the whole understanding she had created. Except among a few who had learnt that she could never refuse food. "You shouldn't do it, you know," I would say after she had named some of the most persistent, whom we all knew. "They're the takers. They smell out people like you, and they'll use you up then go on to somebody else." "But if they hungry," she would reply, "what I'm to do? A man can't work hungry." "Of course they're hungry," I would tell her. "They're hungry because they've spent the money with people they respect more. People who won't let themselves be taken. They'll only end up despising you, and resenting you when you have nothing left for them to use." "But, Stefan, how they can 'resent' me, as you call it? I don't do them anything." And she would look at me with mild bewilderment. She could not really understand the more ambiguous relationships.

I like to think too that it was at Bernice's I first met Oliver. I don't quite know why; in a society as stratified as Cayuna we would have been bound to meet eventually. But it was here one night that I looked up and caught him watching me with that tentative, half-questioning smile which sometimes marks the obscure premonition we have of future rapport.

He was with a large group at one of the tables and for some time I had been trying to follow, without appearing to, their rapid, allusive argument. Caught eavesdropping like this, I could only smile back slightly, with a sort of facetious contrition, and nod. For a second we both remained like this, as if

73

vaguely tantalized by the nearly inaudible strains of a familiar tune distorted by distance. Then he rose and came to the bar where I sat.

"Doctor Mahler, isn't it?" he asked.

"Yes," I said.

"I'm Hyde of the *Newsletter*. Somebody pointed you out in the street the other day. I've been down in the small islands or we'd probably have met before. How d'you like it here?"

"Very much," I said. "A senior lectureship at my age is wonderful luck, and there's a lot of blank spaces to be filled in if a man wants to do research."

We were, I think, feeling our way with deliberate shyness, or caution, using platitude consciously until we were certain that the impalpable augury we had both recognized was a real promise.

"Will you have a drink?" I said.

"No. My turn first as host. You're Austrian aren't you?"

"German," I told him as he ordered two whiskies from Bernice. "At least I was. I was naturalized after the war."

"I see. Have you ever been back?"

"Once." I raised my glass to him.

"But it wasn't a very good idea was it?"

That was the first time I saw Oliver following the trail of someone else's experience. He did it with an arbitrary direct-ness, as if assuming a phenomenon that was no longer yours. It was strangely beguiling.

"No," I said. "It wasn't a very good idea. I couldn't seem to connect with what I saw."

"Yes. What was it like?"

"Hard to say," I told him.

"Were you bitter or. . . ?"

"God no. That's not it. It was something quite different."

"Put it in a picture."

"Well . . . it was like seeing two of everything. You know, streets, men and women, houses, and the present set of people

74

and things which I wanted to touch and take up with again were always blurring into a past set of people and things. It was like living in one of those dissolves you see in a film. . . . Look. I'm only a scientist. I'm not very good at putting this sort of thing into words."

"You're doing all right," he told me, and laughed. "All you need is practice." And then he looked around the room, his small, terse face quick with a sly, tender irony, and said: "You'll get plenty of practice in this country. We spend our whole lives here agitating in the spaces between an intermittent reality. I do hope you cultivate a translator's style, Mahler."

"I'm not sure I understand that," I said.

"Neither do I," he said without affectation. "But it's a clue I feel I ought to hang on to."

It was Oliver who, with a random observation, made me realize that Bernice wanted me.

This must have been two months or so after our first meeting, early one Saturday evening when we had come back, sticky with a crust of salt and dried out by the sun, from an afternoon's fishing in the harbour off Careen Point. We had hired one of the boats from the market pier at the bottom end of Catherine's Street, and when we returned it was almost without conscious decision that we found ourselves in Long John's before going home. During the afternoon we had beached for a while because I had never been to the rambling, scruffy fringe of hills around the western side of the harbour. These, except for the naval station at Careen Point, had remained uninhabited since the days of the Arawaks and swarmed with iguana. It was a seared, olive-drab territory, remote in a still, unexploited depth of time from the dense, sweet mountains and the city across the bay. The hills were almost rainless because of a freak of contours and all life inland from the shore seemed to be wrapped in tough, dull leather and have been caught in the perfect balance of stasis. You had the feeling that

75

here birth was deposited sluggishly, like layers of sediment, and that death, even death in competition, was a regular, imperceptible crumbling away, like the erosion of the hills themselves. The iguanas were pantomime dragons, with an enchanting, cartoon ferocity of countenance that would suddenly become pathetic as we advanced and they turned, frilly combs quivering, to scuttle heavily across the paths into the dingy green of the scrub. Singly, they got out of our way with the dim desperation of fat old backwoodsmen crossing a street in the rush hour; but when we came on a colony, they remained still, gummed to the grey, sun-soaked rocks in plump heaps, drowsy drunk with the security of their collective euphoria. I had scrambled and quested across the tilted folds of limestone until Oliver became mutinous; then we had returned to the boat.

But as we sat at the bar in Long John's and the first beer cooled us, I began to itch abominably. Soon I was scratching at clusters of red, angry bumps on my wrists, forearms, calves and ankles, anywhere that had been exposed.

"Midges," Oliver said. "Or sand-flies." He looked with deep interest at my inflamed skin. "They're bad out there; they can give you hell. I knew an English girl once who was taken to a picnic out by Careen Point and she got bitten so badly she ran a temperature for three days."

"They don't trouble you, I suppose?"

"Not much," he admitted cheerfully. "I've been bitten too often. What's it you call those animals in Africa that have been exposed to *tsetse* fly and recovered? Oh, yes. 'Salted.' If you're born here you get 'salted' against sand-flies."

"A-a-h!" I groaned in a sort of luxurious anguish, as I scraped my nails across the back of my knee.

"If your fingers aren't clean, you might infect yourself." Oliver offered as I explored another area of irritation.

"Thanks," I said, "I hadn't realized that. God, it must be wonderful to have your breadth of information."

It was then, as I scrabbled at my limbs, that Bernice came to our end of the bar carrying a little brown bottle and a roll of cotton wool wrapped in blue paper. Absorbed in currying myself, I hadn't seen her leave the room.

"Why you don't try a little of this, Mister Mahler?" she said smiling at me and then at the grinning Oliver. "It will cool them down."

"What's that?" I asked.

"Just a little witch-hazel. It good for cuts an' insect bite."

"Thank you," I said. "That was very thoughtful of you."

I took the bottle, soaked a wad of cotton wool with the witch-hazel and eagerly dabbed my bites. It took half the lotion and another wad of cotton wool, but when I was finished the hot itching had cooled to an occasional prickle.

"Thank you," I said again, giving the bottle and roll back to her. "I was going mad. That feels much better."

She only nodded and went towards the office with what I had given her.

"Better?" Oliver asked.

"Yes," I said. "But you weren't much help."

"She likes you, you know," he said, and I remember the exact gesture with which he took the little black cigar from between his teeth and pointed it towards the open doorway of the office in which Bernice's back was framed.

"Who likes me?"

"Bernice." The bar was empty except for three men at the other end talking loudly about the night's boxing, and Oliver did not even have to lower his normal, conversational tone. "She likes you a lot, man. I've watched her. Not just now, but a couple of times when we've been in before."

"Nonsense," I said, warm with the absurd elation we can't escape when another confirms, however wrongly, our attractiveness. "She likes everybody. She's one of the nicest, most comfortable people I've met in Queenshaven, but she doesn't

77

like me more than you for instance. I only come here once a week anyway. Sometimes not even that."

"I'm telling you, Stefan. You could have her any time." He looked with casual assessment at her back, and added indifferently: "It's a pity she's old fowl now. Ten years ago she'd have been all right. Bad luck, eh? You came too late."

And then as Oliver, completely unconscious of his superficial brutality, said this, it was as if all the deeper appreciations of Europe within me surged to protest: a submarine upheaval whose effect on the dry, adjacent surface was registered only as a tremor, a shivering of the vision in which I seemed to look at Bernice for the first time.

Not that I looked at her with love, or even desire. In this moment of silent indignation, I saw her only as another victim of that crude and tedious limitation to the Caribbean scope: the sexual snobbery of the West Indian male. Pampered, flattered and indulged from birth by their women, the men of Cayuna, I had recognized early, are all sexual aristocrats, with that discreet, insipid respect for the accepted or proven which so often characterizes aristocratic taste. They cannot comprehend and have no reverence for the more subtle assumptions of Aphrodite: nose-tethered tighter than stud bulls to a hierarchic scale of desirability, they regard with vague astonishment any heresy of the imagination.

So it was that, as Bernice came back from the office, I looked at her not as a possible lover, but with the disinterested care of a judge considering an appeal from a lower court. . . . The smoke screens the heart can lay! It is by these haphazard and converging lines that we come into love. Her kindness to me, Oliver's astute eye and indifferent dismissal, my smug conviction of a more flexible experience: who is to tell at what point they met and became critical that night? . . . Love is the supreme pragmatist.

Up to then, I had thought of her simply as a rarefied equation in the higher mathematics of race and cross breeding: the

78

African splay of her nose, sharpened by an almost Semitic bridge; the cannon ball skull backed by a long, dolichocephalic droop; her remarkable skin, neither brown nor fair, but a strange copper-grey. Her large milky green eyes belonged to no place I could think of but the Caribbean. But now, as I smiled at her and nodded to our empty glasses, I saw that she was beautiful. She had the rare and withdrawn beauty of something that has been wonderfully made and used to a point just short of exhaustion. Metaphor will not do, but I was thinking, then, of an ageing vineyard, with its sculptured, exacting contours, and contrasting it with the facile luxuriance of a young garden. It was in this moment, I think, that I began to imagine what it would be like to want her.

IV

We live in a world of incalculable pressures: everything bears on the other and we struggle through chronology as through the escape hatch of an aeroplane drowning in an enormous sea. Only the artist, with his lightning stroke of inspiration, is able to establish a still pattern of meaning. The rest of us fall in love.

For a little while at least, with a new love, the senses close like a huge fist around reality. . . .

It was such an uncomplicated passage, really on her part, from my first imagined deed of possession into the act of love with Bernice. Afterwards, when I thought of my designs for a calculated seduction, I would feel a qualm of shame, like a man caught cheating in a card game between honourable friends.

It happened two or three nights after Oliver stirred my interest with the comment he had probably forgotten within an hour; and I went back to Bernice not with any tenderness but with incurable, almost abstract optimism of the sensual: the hope that in the next embrace, the next adventure we shall plunge through to some final revelation. Anyway, that is what we tell ourselves: there are other explanations.

I had waited until I had no lectures the next morning, so that there would be no need to go back for sleep, and I arrived at the bar about half an hour before she closed. She greeted me with a look of faint curiosity, for I seldom came down during the week; but there was also, in her solicitous efficiency as she served me, a personal warmth and pleasure that seemed to me, with Oliver's words in my mind, a repetition of something I had sensed before and not taken in, as a noise that hauls us from sleep is always familiar when we wake.

When Cherry had begun to gather the glasses from the outer tables, I said: "Miss Bernice, are you tired?"

"I always a little tired at this time," she said, "until I sit down an' have something to eat an' read the paper."

"It would be nice if you'd come and have something to eat with me?" I said. "I'm hungry too and I'd like to have some company."

"Come an' eat with you?" Her voice was hesitant, almost politely embarrassed, as if she were asking a newly introduced acquaintance to repeat his name.

"Yes," I began. "When you close up," I was going on to say, but at that moment three late customers came in. They were two Cayunan sergeants from the regiment and a gigantic English sergeant-major. The sergeant-major was very drunk and walked between the other two with the slow precision of a man shot through the stomach but determined not to fall. His glazed eyes fixed on me with the righteous, cosmic fury that never deserts a good sergeant-major, and he swayed stiffly, a fraction to each side of a rigid perpendicular, while the two sergeants bought a bottle of rum. One of them slipped the bottle into the front of his bush-jacket and then they both took him out like two brisk jeeps manœuvring a massive field piece across a parade ground. Bernice came down the bar to me, frowning gently; then, as I watched her closely, she gave an odd little shake of her head, lifted it and said with undissembled, quiet gratitude: "Yes, Mister Mahler. Thank you. If you will wait till after I close I would like to come with you."

"Oh, that's splendid," I said. "I hoped you'd say yes. I'll have another beer while you're getting ready."

She brought another bottle from the chest, reached my glass from before me and poured. When the glass was full she did not pass it back to me immediately but kept it before her, looking down at it and frowning again with that still, equivocal reflection. She raised her head suddenly and her lips twitched in a gentle, bantering shadow of a smile. "I will go an' change my dress," she said. "Cherry! You can start closing up now, eh."

I drank a little of my beer quickly, poured the rest and took the glass over to one of the outer tables. Sitting there, I passed the contrived advances of my evening before me in a sort of parade: they seemed unspeakably sheepish and shabby, like deserters winkled from the cellar of a brothel. The unillusioned, indulgent teasing of her smile nagged implacably at the anticipation with which I had started. As Cherry rang the heavy bar into the brackets on the door, I knew that all the easy heat of an idle desire was gone: that I had been unmanned by a sudden awareness of aesthetic propriety more crushing than any ethical code. When I heard her in the passage and stood up, I was determined to atone for the vulgar, inquisitive greed that had so nearly compromised her integrity and gentleness.

"You lock up good, Cherry?" she asked.

"Yes, Miss Bernice," Cherry said, and yawned.

"Right then. I see you in the morning." She looked at me and nodded slightly to the passage behind her. "Let us go this way, Mister Mahler. Through the side door. It's easier."

I had parked my car in the lane beside the bar, so it was only a few steps across the grit-sprinkled sidewalk from the door. She climbed in and I shut the door on her side and went round to the wheel. "I thought," I said formally, "that we could get

81

a chicken up at the Star Garden. In one of the booths." "Yes," she said, folding her hands about the handbag on her lap and settling back against the padded plastic with a small, gratified sigh.

We drove through the deserted streets in silence. There was no moon and the bluish pools of light around the lamps looked raw and tawdry like patches of mange in a dense fur. On the harbour road, the great bay was as lost to sight as the water at the bottom of a well. I wanted to say something light yet intelligent that would acknowledge the worth of the composed honesty beside me; but a sluggish unease had fogged my mind. Just before we reached the Star Garden at the head of the harbour, she said quietly: "I must call you by your Christian name now, but I not sure how you say it." "Stefan," I said: of all the things that might have broken the silence, this had never occurred to me. "It's just like your Stephen, only it's German." "Stefan," she repeated. "An' tell me something else." "Yes?" I said. "Sometimes I hear Mister Hyde introduce you as Doctor Mahler an' sometimes as Mister Mahler. How is that? You is really a doctor?" "No," I heard myself explaining with the relaxed fluency of one old friend to another. "Not a medical doctor. It's just a title, a . . . a degree you get when you write a paper." "Oh," she said, and laughed softly. "I see now. I never knew say you could be called 'doctor' unless you heal people. Which one you like to be called?" I laughed too: "I don't mind," I told her and on an impulse of generosity I added a fiction, because I knew it would amuse her. "Once, on board a ship, I was asked to deliver a baby because my name had 'doctor' against it on the passenger list." "No!" she said, shaking with new laughter. "What a thing to happen to a man, eh? What happened then?" "Oh!" I reached into my invention, found an embroidery, and prudently discarded it. "They went on bad when I told them I wasn't that sort of doctor. But she had her baby all right. Some of the married women on board helped." Even then with Bernice, I realized that, like an

82

uncluttered child, she would go straight to the logical nub, and I didn't want to disappoint her by leaving a loose end.

I turned into the driveway of the Star Garden: a mechanically frenzied, joint explosion of hot-green, neon glare and harsh, vapid music, splitting the soft, cool deeps of night between the jagged wall of hills and the road. This garish, gimcrack pleasure garden was something like a temple—for only the senses are really worshipped in Cayuna—and here all the classes of the city could mingle casually, across the lines, in a catholic, nightly ritual of dancing, music, drink and lust. Most of it consisted of an enormous cement floor, open to the sky, and two or three hundred sheltered tables impartially used by the freelance whores of Queenshaven, men on their own, and parties who came for the band which was very good in the undemanding, dextrous style of music to which one listens only with the body. In the back yard there were a number of discreet booths and alcoves, made of closely latticed wood or palm leaves and set on the hard, acid earth under the coconut trees.

Bernice and I went down the long veranda past the rowdy, pungent dance floor and out into the yard at the back. I chose one of the booths by the fence and we waited without speaking until the girl came to take our order.

Now that I could no longer excuse my attention by letting it wander dutifully ahead of a moving car, I was stiff and inept again: acutely conscious that I was hardly providing the sexual interest any women taken out has the right to expect. She sat opposite, her hands together in the middle of the little table, looking at me with a tranquil, courteous expectancy. Then, as I sketched the meaningless smile with which we try to inoculate our awkwardness, she smiled also, without embarrassment, as if from a separate, private moment of pleasure, like someone smiling over a book, and began to talk.

I remember very little of what she said that night, except that every so often, nowadays, I find myself using some item of information about the island I didn't realize I knew. But then that was the content of most of Bernice's talk. In her company you were presented with specimen after specimen of rich anecdotal ore, dug from the brute mass of the island's experience. She had a prospector's instinct for unregarded fragments and yet she never used them as I, for instance, did when she told them: put them in a crucible to obtain their moral residue. Her involvement was with the various textures of life, and her delight was in the fact of discovery. After this, she passed on. The refinements of tragedy or satire were, I think, beyond her: she saw only the pain or the occasions of laughter and excitement. Her judgement, like her offerings of kindness, was irremediably anarchic.

By the time we had finished our meal that night, I had forgotten my conscience and clumsiness. I had more vivid stories and incidents about Cayunan life to digest than I comfortably could; and now as she leaned back and sipped the last of her beer, I wanted to celebrate her entertainment. To show the same sort of grateful appreciation that one would for anything faultlessly performed and happily shared.

"Bernice," I said, "d'you like champagne? D'you think we could get some here?"

I was already half-turned and pressing the button of the electric signal between the booth and the bar.

"Champagne!" For the first time since we had left her place she looked disconcerted, even alarmed. "But. . . ." she said. "Lord, man! That's only for weddings an' things like that. . . ."

"Do you like it?"

"Of course I like it. But it going cost plenty. . . . I mean. . . ."

She floundered in a genuine distress, then suddenly looked pleased and kept quiet. The girl who had served us tapped at the swing door and came in.

"You have any champagne?" I asked.

She put her head to one side thoughtfully, then: "I t'ink a nex' bottle leave into de fridge, sah," she said.

84

"Good," I said. "Bring it for me. But don't bring wine glasses. Bring two of the beer mugs, and see if you can get ones that have been on the ice."

When the wine came, it was not any brand I recognized; but it was very cold, and drunk from the chilled mugs it had a clean, volatile fineness of flavour that felt novel and exhilarating after the coarser demands of spirits and beer to which I had become accustomed. I was suddenly held by a transformation of gaiety, as pure, in its way, and as ephemeral as the little bubbles shooting up the side of my glass.

"Champagne," I told Bernice, "is the dandy of wines. It's a damned useless drink, really. Completely frivolous and dressed for show. But it does it so well that you can't help admiring it."

A blankly puzzled look came to her face, and this struggled with the experimental smile of one who acknowledges your effort to amuse and makes a polite gesture in return.

"I was only joking," I said. "There are some people who seriously talk like that about wine, and I was imitating them. Wine is for drinking."

"It's very nice," she said solemnly. "*You* really like it, eh?"

"Yes." I recharged our glasses evenly with the last of the wine. "My father used to own a vineyard. You know, like a man here owns a sugar estate and makes rum."

"True. Then why you don't work with him? You have a brother who does that?"

"No."

"But your father still runs your place?"

"No. He's dead."

"I sorry to hear that."

"Oh, it was a long time ago."

"But your mother is still alive?" she asked hopefully.

"No. She's dead too. She and my father and my sister were killed in an accident."

"Then you don't have nobody?"

"Some cousins in England," I lied. "And I have lots of friends."

I hoped she would ask no more questions, and she did not; she only shook her head with fatalistic commiseration, and finished her wine.

We returned to her place through the sleeping town. It was now about two in the morning. The houses and shops down the long harbour road, caught between the feeble radiance of the street lights and the blackness behind, looked like frail, grey tents stranded in a shallow tide. All the way down from the Star Garden the streets were empty, except once when two policemen emerged from the shadows of a side road, as featureless, above the smeared glitter of their buttons as a primitive's picture of twins in a guilt myth. I felt content and secure within a double ring of my own high-minded revisions and the festive companionship she had evoked.

I drew carefully up to the kerb by the side entrance from which we had left and pushed down on the door handle. The door was already half open, and I had one foot already on the pavement, when she leaned across and put her hand on my shoulder.

For a moment I could do nothing but sit still and wordless, with the door held open and my sandal resting on the gritty sidewalk. I was seized by an untidy paralysis of the will and feeling, like a careless borrower with all his debts called in at once. It was as if her unambiguous declaration had suddenly revealed all my smug resolves in their real nature: spurious and pharisaical conceits more contemptible than the presumptuous carnality with which I had begun the evening. And yet, as the pressure of her hand grew more insistent and I turned to kiss her, it was with the ignominious protest and resignation of a man who sees the cherished fictions of a peace treaty being emptied by the autonomous drift of war.

"It's late," I said in a limping voice after I had kissed her.

"Perhaps I'd better go. You'll want to go to bed and. . . ."

"But you not coming up?" Her even voice frayed with confusion, and I realized then that nothing could justify a refusal. Her sincerity and my deceits had committed me to responsibility as the contradictions of a paradox commit it to truth.

"If you want me to," I said.

"Of course I want you to stay," she said, almost indignantly. "I couldn't let you go like that." She got out on her side briskly. "Make sure you lock the car good," she added through the window. "Plenty thief down here this time of night."

Climbing the stairs behind her, I was choked by an irrational excitement and terror: like a boy following his first unpurchased woman into her room. In those firm, solid kisses she had given me in the car, in the sway of her broad, ready buttocks, I discerned something quite different from the genial, graceless experiences of the past. A premonition, perhaps, of that great hammer-blow of fate which shatters the hygienic glass walls of our liberty and nails us to an inconsolable search for truth. . . . There are moments which must be gulped in their entirety, like oysters, if we wish to savour the process of growth.

I paused at the door while she went over to the lamp on the bedside table. The dark was heavy with the thrilling and inimical odour peculiar to the room in which a woman dreams and prepares herself: a smell at once complex and wild, such as might lie in the den of an heraldic creature, rocking the delicate balance of the male imagination with its profound synthesis of artifice and atavistic strength. She switched on the pink-shaded lamp and turned. I went up to her slowly and took the hand she held out to me. We sat on the edge of the bed, searching each other's face with the elaborate attention that is not really a scrutiny but a preliminary form of caress. Then I kissed her again and put my hand on her breast.

A quarter of an hour later she said: "What's wrong? Something bothering you?"

"No," I said.

87

"You don't like me?"

"Yes of course I like you. This just happens to men sometimes. I'm sorry."

We were lying naked under the sheet in the dark.

"Don't worry yourself," she said and patted my chest and shoulder as one would gentle a horse. "I know how men stay sometimes. Just lie quiet an' don't worry."

I was cold and weak with the panicky rage of one trying to finish a problem against time, who sees the blurred form of a solution and cannot quite bring it into focus.

"Just like *La Ronde*," I said, because silence was unbearable.

"What you say?" she asked.

"It's a play. There's a man in it who has this happen to him. He tries to make himself and the woman feel better by referring to another book, just as I'm referring to *La Ronde* now."

"I see," she said uncertainly.

"It makes people like me feel much better if we can find a situation in a book to quote in support of whatever is happening to us," I told her. "It's not a very good way to live because it makes you self-conscious and insulates you against real feeling, but we don't seem able to help it."

And as I said this, I saw myself join the chain of hallowed popinjays who have suffered amorous frustration to redeem us from the sin of solemnity. I shook in spasm after spasm of genuine amusement at my laborious attempts to shore up a humiliated ego and at the curt revenge the body takes for the mind's pretensions.

"Why you laughing?" she asked, and I felt her stiffen cautiously and draw away.

"Not at you," I said, putting my hand firmly on her broad back and pulling her close again. "I'm laughing at me. God, I'm a fool, Bernice. You know what I deserve? I deserve to have it cut off and put in a museum as a warning."

"But what you mean?" She heaved in the hoop of my arm, raising her head from the pillow as if trying to read my face in the dark. The movement rubbed her stout thigh across my groin and brought a sour, musky puff from her armpit and suddenly my body, liberated by laughter, was wrenched and twisted by a shock of desire so intense that it almost hurt. With an astounded groan I pushed at her shoulder, forcing her on to her back, and trembling avidly I sought the warmest thicket in which all men have been hunted to a welcome death. A giant hand gripped me in the small of my back and hurled me face down into an endless, cushioning dark that reverberated with the echo of a hoarse shout.

v

Women of profound moral force often seem to be informed by the living tissue of some great epoch. I mean that their possession of history is so often a vivid, organic attribute, quite unlike the laboratory brackets with which men have explained the seasonal changes in a single climate of life. So that sometimes with one woman whom you love you may return, through the sudden lift of her head, to the miraculous agony of an exposed nerve that was the renaissance; or, with another, you may hear in the beloved voice the unique accents of wit, precision and superb energy that described rococo; and a third in the full fig and confidence of her best clothes, sleek with the residual warmth of her last tumble, is not only herself but true daughter to the Wife of Bath or those magnificent burgher women whose lush fertility swells from the canvas of Rubens and the early Rembrandt.

I should like to add one or other of these traditional splendours to her memory. But of course I cannot. There is no history in Cayuna: only politics. There is no established trust fund from which all the heirs are allotted, impartially, their respective incomes. Everyone is engaged in an immediate competition for a rightful inheritance. . . . Jealous siblings who wait for their unreconciled ancestors to lie down and die.

So when I remember Bernice she emerges with a peculiar integrity: her scrupulous, experienced body and a mind quick with the desire to understand and console. . . . But I am indulging the European mania for rational definitions. Nothing can be safely understood until it is flayed, stuffed with analysis and niched in the museum of the mind. I must accept her as she accepted me, without reservation, giving me the comfort of her flesh and spirit as she would have given me bread.

"I love you, you know?" she told me, towards the end of the first month after we had gone together. Her voice was gently emphatic, as if she were reassuring me about a fact which, in my justifiable preoccupation with other, more important matters, I had overlooked. "I love you, Stefan. I never meet a man like you before." She said it without a hint of the reproach or demand that, almost ineluctably, accompanies a woman's declaration of love.

I have been luckier than I perhaps deserve. She caught me at one of those moments when the heart and soul seem to have been cut adrift from the past and we go nudging down a tide of new pressures, following, very often, the tow of a current of which we are not even aware on the surface of things. At such moments, the direction of a whole life waits on the first comer who assumes command. Or perhaps, in the vague, unacknowledged terror and distress we feel, we are ready to live for a while on the strength and confidence of another and to set a course to the magnetic north of their personality. Something like that. We are the sum of those who have filled our confusions.

And, indeed, with Bernice it was a sort of nourishment that began to take place. As if some half-starved corner of myself began to come to its full capacity under her care. So that sometimes now I become aware, on a rush of stinging gratitude, that all I know of kindness, responsibility and honour in love was learned in those scattered hours in a small, warm room above the sleeping city. She prepared me as carefully for the

90

demands of love as we prepare a child for the adult world. I only realized this when, looking at her, I felt a throb of guilt for the inevitable break. The eroding circumstances that surrounded us—the difference in our ages, the fatal inferiority of her education, the very attitudes of our society—would gnaw the foundations of any attempt to establish something permanent and public. I remember feeling an unreasonable, angry humiliation at this moment, as if we had been both used by a pitiless force that cared for nothing except it own brief display.

4

I

It must have been a week or so after the sad, ugly collision
down at Caymanas that I came back to my flat to find a message
pinned to my door: *Miss Honky fon to Ring her back*. The note,
I knew, must have been written by the porter, and good
manners demanded that I play all the changes on "*Honky*"
before asking him who had called me. It was several minutes
later that I discerned "Heneky" in it as I would have guessed a
word spoken by a cleft palate. In the eighteen months since we
had been lovers Bernice had never telephoned me; as in those
eighteen months I had only twice had occasion to introduce
her, so that her surname was a shadowy appendage to our intimacy, remembered more from the licence above the door of
the bar than from use. I went along the veranda to the extension
telephone that served all the flats in my block.

"Hullo," I said. "Bernice?" I had not known her number
and searching for it among the tattered, doodled pages of the
directory, she had seemed insubstantial, like a casual acquaintance; but now, as she replied, a curious, utilitarian quality
seemed to enter our relationship.

"Stefan?" she said. Her voice was clipped by apology, yet
quick and determined. "I sorry to trouble you now. . . ."

"Don't be silly," I said. "What trouble? I was coming down
in about an hour anyway." (This was a Saturday morning.)

"I know," she said. "But I want to beg you a favour."

"Of course. What?"

"I want to go to the country. To see my father. He's sick an'

92

I just hear an' no bus going that way until late. Take me up, please, Stefan."

"For God's sake, Bernice, don't ask me like that. Of course I'll take you. How soon d'you want to leave?"

I heard her laugh softly, as if relieved, and she said: "When you come down. Thank you, Stefan. It nice of you to offer like this. I know how you busy. . . ."

"Bernice!" I said.

"Yes?"

"I'll get angry with you in a minute. You have no business treating me like that. I'll be down as soon as I've changed."

She laughed again, with the comfortable appreciation of a woman who has been caressed in passing.

"All right," she said. "I see you soon, eh?"

I rested the receiver for a moment, picked it up and dialled again.

"Operator," I said, "I'd like Admiral's Bay 43. . . . Yes. A university call. Staff flats."

There was a dead pause before a mutter of sound like the sinister whispers from a distant battle: organized technology and climate in Cayuna sway in a constant guerrilla warfare, and outside the Queenshaven itself, technology's daily losses are heavy. Three clicks stabbed my eardrum like blunt nails; then there was an exhausted but victorious buzzing.

"Hullo. Andrew Fabricus here."

"Andrew," I said. "Stefan. . . . Look, I won't be out until late tonight. After midnight, probably."

"Oh, hell." His manifest disappointment was as reassuring as a handshake. "You mean you won't make it in time for dinner? Anything wrong?"

"Nothing. Some business that's just come up and can't be dodged."

"You really earn your money, don't you? Now don't hang about after you've finished. Come straight out. Shall I keep some dinner for you?"

93

"Yes," I said. "You do that."

I put the receiver down and entered my name on the pad suspended by the telephone for registering long distance calls; then I went back to my flat. As I packed my holdall with a few clothes for the next day, I thought of the curious, camouflaged occasions of happiness that surround us. Having to miss Andrew's dinner, and perhaps the party afterwards; the obligation abruptly wished on me to take Bernice to the country: these together should have been an irritating dislocation to a week-end I had anticipated. Instead they made me feel quietly satisfied. Intrinsically they were worth nothing, like banknotes; but they were backed by the solid specie of Andrew's disappointment and Bernice's confidence. For the first time in many years, my absence left a hole in the pattern, as my presence was sought to fill a need.

II

She was waiting for me at the side entrance. "I saw you from the window," she explained before I had got from the car. "Lord, Stefan, I sorry to do this to you. I know how you did look forward to going over to Admiral's Bay."

It was the first time I had ever seen her agitated or uncertain and it increased the sense of prosaic and uxorious protectiveness I had felt when she had spoken to me on the telephone. I crossed the pavement to her side, and we stood in the shadow of the lintel while the Saturday morning crowd drifted before us: everyone, even the bank messengers and the draymen driving the huge, glossy Jamaica mules, moved with an air of deliberate and contented relaxation, like people casually putting a room straight. Work in Queenshaven on Saturday morning tends to become a subtle *aperitif* to the week-end's leisure.

"What's wrong, my dear?" I asked her. "You said something about your father. Is it serious?"

She fiddled with her handbag and said in a strained voice:

94

"I don't know. I just hear that he was sick an' I don't know if anybody stay where he is can look after him good." She looked up at me with contrite resignation. "It far, you know, Stefan? Clear up in the St. Joseph mountains. At a place call Gran' Dum. You know it?"

"No." I smiled, and scolded her fondly. "But I'll find it. And don't apologize again for asking me. I want to take you."

"Really, Stefan?" She gave a little sign, as if someone had just relieved her of a heavy suitcase on a long, hot road. "You want a drink before you go?"

"No. We can get one on the road. D'you have anything to take or are you coming back tonight?"

"I not sure; but I taking this." She bent down and reached inside the door to bring out a small, scuffed attaché case. "And there's a basket with some things," she added. She carried the little case across to the car and I followed with the round hamper. "Careful," she said, "it have things in it to spill."

She was sitting stiffly in the front when I had finished fitting the hamper into the corner against the arm-rest of the back seat with the little attaché case laid flat to hold it on the free side. She glanced at me as I climbed in, smiled flickeringly and leaned forward with a tense start, as if her mind were already far ahead on the road to the St. Joseph mountains and her body had tried to follow it.

"Relax, Bernice," I said. "I'll get you there in good time. He'll be all right. . . . I didn't even know you had a father. You've never mentioned him."

She made a gesture like a punctuation mark, for convenience, then: "Yes," she said, as if answering a question.

The road out of Queenshaven to the west of the island leads through the main business sections: diverging straggles of office blocks, stores and warehouses which, in their insensible, vicious hastiness of design, their drab, brutal purpose of mere shelter or concealment of gain, have less dignity than the brothel district of an occupied town. Most of commercial

95

Queenshaven looks as if it had been bought as a job-lot from some squalid confidence trickster on the run. Only the sun, which cleanses while it frays, and the flamboyant energy of the people which hardens the air like a battle roll of drums, give any significance to this part of the city. As I drove Bernice out that morning I wondered how I would ever again be able to live among the pallid, cautious masks of a landscape without coloured faces.

I did not speak to her again until we were on the long straight of road across the flat land behind the western fore-shore. On either side of the road were the slum shacks: built from old cardboard cartons, beaten out kerosene tins or abandoned truck chassis covered with sacking, they were strewn across the sour earth, between bilious pools of rain water, like sodden gobbets vomited by some enormous stomach: scrawny chickens tapped mechanically at the ground about the shacks, and several pigs, lean and dog-like as the swine in a medieval book of hours, plunged the stubby rapiers of their snouts into festering mountains of garbage. Driving past quickly one had the impression that the people were not so much clothed as badly bandaged in grey rags.

She was still bent forward, like a woman sitting on the edge of a chair to listen eagerly; I took my left hand from the wheel and put it firmly on her shoulder, pulling her back.

"I'm not going to drive any faster than this," I said, "so you might as well lean back. Besides, if I stop suddenly, you'll go straight through the windscreen."

"What?" she said. "What you say, Stefan?"

"What's wrong with your father?"

"I don't know. A man come to tell me that him sick. Him never look after himself, though, an' I worried."

"What does he do?"

"He is a preacher."

A preacher! I didn't know that, Bernice. Why have you never told me about him?"

96

She glanced at me once and then looked away again. "I don't know," she said. "I just never think to tell you."

"What's he?" I asked. "Church of England or one of the Nonconformists?"

"Nonconformist?"

"Yes, you know. Like Baptist or Methodist or Moravian."

"Oh," she said. "Like that. No. Him not any of those. Him have his own church."

I had been in the island long enough not to be surprised. God, in Cayuna, is hardly jealous and is added to daily life not as a duty but as an essential ingredient whose value is much the same under whatever label. When I first came out, Father Montesi, one of the American Jesuits, whom the university borrowed as a part-time lecturer, had told me that some of his most devout parishioners in the deep hills behind Queenshaven would often alternate their attendance at the Catholic church with a visit to a brisk revivalist sect that had formed recently in the neighbourhood. Nothing he could say, he had added, would convince them that the same God was not being worshipped in both places, with equal validity. "If they get up too late one Sunday morning, Doctor Mahler, to walk the four miles down to St. Peter and St. Paul, they'll trot along to the Brethren of the First Emmanuel and back to their lunches, happy as a bunch of kids coming from confirmation." He had drunk feelingly from the beer I was giving him in my flat, and added: "Sometimes I wish I was dealing with honest pagans, or unreconstructed atheists like yourself. All this cheerful enthusiasm for religion is worse than a Reformation."

So now, when Bernice told me of her father, I only said: "Oh, I see. What's his church called?" Asking her because it was an addition to what I knew of her, and because religion in Cayuna had a relevance, like climate, that it did not have in the world of linked suburbs from which I had come.

"The Pure Church of Africa," she said, and I had the feeling she was defining it with exactly the same emphasis as she would

97

have said, "He work in a bank," or "He is on the railway."

"The Pure Church of Africa?" I said. "I haven't heard of that one. What are its special beliefs?"

"All sort of things." Her tone was hurried, almost evasive. "I don't really know. I am Baptist, myself. What church you go to, Stefan? I never ask you."

"None. I don't believe in God."

"You don't believe in God!" She became direct and animated for the first time since I had picked her up. "But how you mean, Stefan? Everybody must believe in God."

"Not me. He just doesn't exist for me. I'm not even interested enough to think about it."

"I don't believe you." Her voice was not shocked. What I had said was simply outside reasonable exchange: as if I had told her I was unconscious of the sun. "You mustn't say things like that, Stefan, man. God will punish you."

I smiled to myself and put my hand on hers; she took it and held it against her cheek for an instant; then she let it go and stared thoughtfully at the flat cane-lands through which we were passing.

At Saragossa the road branches: one fork leading straight north through the gap town of New Stamford to the coast; another north-west across the tilted shield of the cattle-lands into the citrus hills and bauxite beyond Shelford; and a third taking you west over an arthritic finger of limestone and into the plain of Braganza, with its enormous, bristled fields of cane, brick-pink dirt roads through each estate narrowing between bottle-green walls like exercises in perspective, slab-bodied milky Indian steers, sun-faded houses with deep verandas crowning knolls above the massed spear blades of the cane, long olive buttresses flung down from the blue mountains to the north, and all suspended in a silvered brilliance of light beneath the eye-watering blue sky as behind glass.

By the time we reached Serena, my eyes were gritty with the

effort of squinting and my throat felt as if it had been lightly dusted with pepper. I stopped outside the little grocery and bar. We went in, and I ordered beer and a plate of sandwiches.

"Try to eat something, dear," I said a little later. She was looking down at her hands on the table as they played with the catch of her bag; one half of a sandwich with the middle nibbled out lay on the plate beside her and she had taken only a little of her beer.

"I not hungry," she said slowly.

"Eat," I urged. "I know you're worried, but it won't help your father for you to upset yourself."

She raised her head and gave me a quick, uncomfortable glance. "It not that, Stefan," she said and looked down at her hands again.

"What's wrong?" I asked. "Come on, dear. Tell me."

"It hard to say," she said, hesitantly at first, then with embarrassed resolution: "Look, Stefan, me love, I want to tell you about my father so you'll understand when you meet him."

"I think I understand now," I told her.

"How you mean?"

"I mean he isn't going to be very pleased to see me. That church of his. . . . He doesn't like white people very much, does he?"

"How you did guess that, Stefan?"

"Oh, by the name he gives to his church, and by something that happened to me last week down at Caymanas. I sort of added them together."

She looked up quickly, her face suddenly concerned and questioning. "What happened to you, Stefan? Why you didn't tell me before?"

"I don't know, really. Perhaps I hoped that if I didn't talk about it, it would go away."

"What happened?" she insisted.

I told her about the Son of Sheba and what he had said to me and how he had broken the tank.

99

"Stefan!" She covered my hand with hers. "Lord, I sorry that did have to happen to you. Why you didn't tell me before, man? Not all of them are like that, you know? Only a few of the bad ones who like to frighten people."

"Is your father one of Sheba's Sons?"

"I not sure."

"You're not sure? But. . . ."

"No." Her voice was dulled now with a curious melancholy, and she looked away as if ashamed. "You see, my father an' me had a bad quarrel, Stefan. The last time I go to see him he curse me an' tell me not to come back."

"Why?"

"Because I wouldn't join him in his church, so he call down a curse on me an' say that I betray his God for the God of my mother, an' that I will perish with Babylon."

"Your mother was white?"

"No, but she was fairer even than you. She's dead now."

"Then how long is it since you saw your father?"

"Oh, a long time now." She shook her head and looked up with a nostalgic little grimace. I realized how selfishly I had used her: there was something mean and tasteless in my knowing so little of what had been endured by this woman who gave herself so generously.

"Do you think you ought to go?" I asked her gently. "I mean he didn't send for you, did he?"

"No. I don't even know what he's doing up in Gran' Dum. He always stay in Queenshaven. But I must go to him, Stefan. Suppose he's sick bad an' nobody up in a little place like that to look after him."

Her face, to which years of adventured passion and ungrudging response had given a still glow, like the surface of a jade piece stroked for generations by knowing fingers, was bright with hope, and a little unsteady: the face of a child in whom no rejection can yet teach love to be cautious, only apprehensive. As I studied her bent, pensive head, I thought: she will

100

know every disaster of the spirit except envy and remorse.

"Yes," I said, rising, "there's that to it. Are you going to finish your beer? No? Well, we'd better get going, eh?"

She rose, giving me as she did so a brief, grateful smile, as though I had supported her in an unpopular opinion.

III

We crossed Braganza and drove into St. Joseph's parish by mid-afternoon. At the edge of the great plain to the south we could see the heat haze above Caymanas hanging in the air like finely ground pearl dust. The road from the mountains joined the highway just beyond Logan's Town and I turned north on this, guiding the little car carefully along the ruts in a surface thick with loose stones. Soon we began to climb steeply, in a series of sharp curves cut around the rims of huge, limestone pits packed with bush and trees and along the ridge backs leading into the real mountains. A narrow, khaki river pitched into and out of view as we followed each swoop or rise of the track, and green folds of land opened wider and wider below us until we began to skirt the moist, bluish wall supporting the peaks. The air was cool, smelling of juniper, and twice we drove through swirls of mist drifting down the mountainside. Then the road turned an acute shoulder and up ahead we could see the roofs and walls of Gran' Dum scattered among stands of banana, ginger and yam vines. A broad ramp of forest rose behind the village to a crest of two sugar loaf peaks; and between the peaks a belt of water fell straight as the flow from a tap for about five hundred feet against the sky until it vanished behind the tree tops below.

The village was at the end of the driving road. I drew up in the little square that was not really a square but a widened space where the side of the mountain had been cut further back. The children had already began to scamper down the tracks from the huts, and three men came on to the cement veranda

101

of the shop that was built against the hillside where we had stopped.

"Good afternoon."

"Good afternoon, sah. You come from far?"

Bernice and I got from the car and entered into the strict ritual of polite exchange and the unabashed frankness of curiosity (in itself a form of good manners) that one learns to appreciate in the small hill villages of Cayuna: an eager but punctilious tasting of new experience which the visitor should not try to hurry or avoid. Then Bernice asked where we might find her father.

"Reveren' Heneky?" one of the men said. "Now I don't know dat I know him. Him live here, ma'?"

"No. Him visiting."

"Ken, you know a Reveren' Heneky?"

"No," Ken said. "I don't t'ink say dat I ever see him. Who him stay wid, missis?"

"I don't know," Bernice said. "Is a man down in Queenshaven tell me say that he is here an' that he sick. He is me father, you see."

"O-oh! I see."

"Wait now," the third man, a slow, heavy half-coolie, said. "Wait. I t'ink I remember now. I did hear say dat a Missa Marcus Heneky did visit wid Mass' Howard. Yes. I hear so."

"It far from here?"

"No. Not far. But you will have to walk. One o' de bwoy dere will show you de path. Nat'aniel!" One of the younger boys trotted over from the car. "Tek dis lady an' gentleman up to Mass' Howard's place."

"Thank you."

"Not at all, sah. Walk good."

We crossed the square and followed Nathaniel's bobbing rump up one of the tracks leading down from the mountain.

5

★

I

What did I expect to find that afternoon as we followed the child Nathaniel up the track between steep patches of cultivation and through a wide tunnel of tree ferns? Some battered and absurd old fanatic, his mind made dense and dangerous as a bullet by the sealed force of his conviction? Or something more perplexed: one of those stranded in the wake of injustice like men fallen from a surging battle who call out in a fellowship of pain for the places where they will be restored?

I must have projected some such banal silhouettes on to my imagination as I held Bernice's hand to steady her on the path which was treacherous with loose stones and a slick of mud.

Her palm was damp and her fingers rigid on the back of my hand, and when we turned a bend in the path and saw the little house at the end of a grove of plantains, she let go quickly. I fell back a few paces and she went ahead with the tense determination of someone advancing on an uncertain dog. Nathaniel looked back at us and said, "Here it is, missis," and ran down the short path under the plantains calling, "Mass' Howard! Mass' Howard! Visitor come fe' see you." There was a flight of three narrow wooden steps leading down from the veranda, but he was just at the age when some arboreal nostalgia seems to inspire a boy to take the most irregular route between any two points. He swung himself to the veranda rail with a bounce and a twist, balanced across it on his little round belly and called for Mass' Howard again.

A voice answered from the back of the house, footsteps sounded on the uncarpeted boards and a man appeared in the doorway. He was small and dark brown and brittle. His striped shirt, small-knotted tie, metal sleeve bands and flawlessly creased trousers looked as though they had been sewn tightly about him, like the clothes of a fussy, inexpensive doll, and as if they would never, for as long as he wore them, acquire a single characteristic sag or wrinkle. He walked with a mincing, doll-like stiffness, his little bony elbows stuck out at precisely equal angles from either side, moving in time to his steps.

"What you say, Nat'aniel?" he began as he came to the doorway, and then as he saw us at the foot of the steps, he stopped, and the too neat, mannikin face became pinched with puzzled suspicion and curiosity.

"Yes?" he said flatly and warily. "You want to see me?"

"Good afternoon, Mister Howard." Bernice's voice was hurried, almost deferential. "I sorry to trouble you, but I hear say that the Reverend Heneky is staying with you an' that he is sick, an' I come up to see him."

"Who I must say want to see him?" Howard asked with the impersonal but inflexible challenge of a sentry who has learnt that even innocence of purpose may be only a camouflage for the entry of treason.

"I'm his daughter," Bernice said. "Tell him that Bernice come to see him." She looked at me, and I had the feeling that she was trying not to see me as a piece of contraband, something not so much criminal as shameful; like the banned book, or the undeclared phial of perfume found in a packet of sanitary towels. "This is a friend of mine," she continued in a humble, explanatory tone. "Him did bring me up from Queenshaven in his car."

"All right," Howard said. "I will tell him." I listened to the jerkily precise footsteps as they tapped across the floor inside.

104

"Maybe I ought to wait for you in the car," I said softly. "I mean your father won't want a stranger about the place if he's sick."

Relief and something like gratitude showed on her face for a moment. She opened her mouth and nodded, and then, decisively, made a firm line of her lips and shook her head.

"You stay here, Stefan," she said.

"That's what I think, really," I said. "I just didn't want to cause any trouble."

"Trouble?" she said unhappily. "What trouble? After all, I not ashamed of you."

"I'm not ashamed of me either," I told her. "A lot of people tried to make me ashamed once, but the inoculation never took."

A little wrinkle formed between her brows and she said in a faintly surprised voice: "What you mean, Stefan? What inoculation you talking about?"

I patted her arm. "It's a long story," I said, "I'll tell you later." I smiled at her encouragingly and looked up at Nathaniel who was still balanced across the veranda rail. Now he was see-sawing his body on the fulcrum of his solar plexus, absorbedly teetering his head and feet to the extreme limits of balance. "Hi!" I called. "Nathaniel." He clambered down with the exuberant facility of a small ape and came over to us, hesitant with sudden shyness. I reached into my pocket and found a shilling by touch. "How much Paradise Plums cost now?" I asked. "I don't know, sah." he said, speaking to the ground. "Go on," I told him. "You must know, man." I pressed the shilling into the warmth of the small plump palm. "Thanks for showing us the way," I said. "Now use that shilling to get something for yourself and the others. We'll know the way back." He glanced once at the coin in his briefly exposed palm, grinned at us and scudded up the path; as he vanished round the turn, we could hear him begin to yell to the other children, then the ululation of the voices closing in on him and the diminishing rattle of comment as they went down the track to the shop. I clung to the sound of their going for as long as I could, and from the corner of my eye I could see Bernice doing the same, her head tilted slightly to hear better as she smiled faintly. Then the tack hammer knocks of Mister Howard's heels sounded in the house and we both turned to face him as he came to the door.

"Him say come on in," he said in the same bleak, grudging voice, and moved to one side as we mounted the steps to the little veranda.

"Thank you, Mister Howard," Bernice said, and then shyly: "Tell me. How him stay? Him really sick bad?"

"Him don't good," Howard told us, and now, for the first time, his voice lost its distant chill and became vibrant with a touching gravity. The finicky precision of his small face became larger, more untidily generous with the warmth of his concern and self-importance. "I did do me best for him, but him won't agree to go an' see a doctor." He shook his head with a sort of awed exasperation, as if referring to a being beyond real criticism or comprehension. "*You* know how him stay," he said to Bernice.

"Yes," Bernice said, "I know."

"Well," Howard continued, briskly, almost amiably now, "come on then. Him at the back of the house." He made a careful, rigid gesture at the doorway and followed us closely as we stepped through into the little parlour.

It was much like the living-room of any other small settler's house I had visited since coming to Cayuna: rigorously cluttered with furniture, gleaming as much with patient accumulation as with polish. But on the walls, in this case, instead of the customary Hanoverian images and meaningless landscapes from an unrelated climate, there was a large photograph of the Ethiopian Emperor, with two green, yellow and red flags above the frame, their sticks crossed, the cloth spread flat, and a loudly coloured relief map of Africa on which Addis Ababa

106

was symbolized by a huge, gilt Star of David. On the third wall, facing this, was a framed text in twelve point Baskerville: *For the hurt of the daughter of my people am I hurt; I am black; astonishment hath taken hold on me.*

"This way," Howard said, and led us through to the little dining-room behind the parlour. There was a sideboard of mahogany stacked with blue and white Victorian china, and small, obviously imported dining-table and chairs. Against the exact grace and limpid glow of the old mahogany piece, the table and chairs were spurious and strident, like cheap patent leather beside old morocco. On the wall above the sideboard was another photograph of the Ethiopian Emperor riding into his capital on a white horse. A door opened out on to the back veranda, and beyond the doorway one could see the hillside planted with yam and ginger, and a white stream cutting across a corner of the field, with high grass along both banks. Howard turned and waited for us to follow. He had suddenly assumed an attitude that was at once ceremoniously severe and intimate; the expression of a chamberlain preparing you for the privilege and mystery of an audience. I gave Bernice's elbow a little squeeze as we stepped on to the narrow wood-floored veranda. She shook her arm free and frowned at me.

II

This evening, before we left Oliver, I looked again at what he had written on Marcus Heneky. Our wives had withdrawn suddenly, as if on some inaudible, coded signal, leaving us and retiring to the ritual of oblique gossip with which women wryly console themselves for the greed and inconstancy of the male heart. Andrew, Oliver and I sat drinking in a sort of un-admitted gloom: Andrew and I resentful of the blanket implication of guilt we shared with him, yet oddly, almost defiantly sympathetic. It was very uncomfortable, because nothing had been openly conceded yet, and for a while, until the wives left the room, remarks passed between us all like referred cheques. I picked up Oliver's article again, with relief, to insulate myself with this spent disturbance from the disturbance beginning to mutter on our common horizon.

But half-way through what Oliver had written I put the review aside.

"Oliver," I said then.

"Yes?"

He was huddled at the far end of the big sofa, looking at the curl of smoke from his cigarette, his face lonely and stubborn.

"I'll tell you what you missed about Marcus."

"Really!" He leaned forward quickly. "Good. I knew you'd come up with something, Stefan." He smiled teasingly. "You're wasted on animals, you know. Why don't you come and work for me? What did I miss?"

"His fidelity."

"His *what*?"

"All right," I said. "His honour, then. Call it what you like. None of you have got that somehow. You've all made him so negative, a sort of political indigestible with an obsession."

"Well, wasn't he?"

"Yes, but there was more to it than that."

"Don't tell me you two are still on about old Heneky," Andrew said. He was at the other side of the room under the big standing lamp, going through the folio of Post-Impressionist reproductions I gave Sybil at Christmas. Andrew knows next to nothing about art but he is willing to be told what he ought to like. He put the folio on the floor beside him and rose and came over to us: a big, heavy-boned man, with that vivid, bronze flush under the skin which one sees in the old whites of Cayuna whose ancestors had the genetic good sense to take a little of Africa into the blood. "What else is there to say about him?" he asked us now. "A poor old lunatic bred by the sort of injustice we've had here for three hundred years. . . ."

"Still have," I said.

"Still have, if you like," he said. "But don't pretend he was anything more."

"He was," I said. "It's not easy to put into words, but when you knew him you felt it."

"Felt what?"

"A sense of purpose. Choice, maybe. You know, there are some men who feel that the pain of this world is one pain. Who try to assume it, struggle with it and free us from it. Marcus Heneky was like that."

"God Almighty," Oliver said, "you Germans are all the same. Jew or Gentile, you're all romantics. Look, Stefan: Heneky had one idea and he limited it to one race. Africa triumphant. You can agree he had a lot of justification for feeling the way he did, but no more. He felt that the turn of the black man had come round. The only thing that I still haven't got clearly is the man himself. What made him unique, I mean."

"That's what I'm trying to tell you," I said. "The triumph of Africa and the black race was only the external part of it. A . . . a sort of symptom. He wasn't just a common little fanatic, for all his limitations. I tell you: that old man belonged in another class altogether. Perhaps he didn't even know what moved him or what he was really trying to do, but it was there all the same: the necessity to erase another bit of the lie that makes slaves of us."

"I've lost you," Andrew said. "What lie?"

"It all depends," I said. "It varies from time to time and place to place. In Heneky's case the lie was that the black man was faceless. What he had to do was try to change that, to give the black man the sort of vision of himself that would make him free. And make the whites and the browns free, because they were shackled to the lie too. But it wasn't just a matter of giving the black man a vote, or a ministerial portfolio, or an equal income. All those things come into it, but there is something else needed."

"What?"

"A territory the heart can occupy."

"You mean, you think that he was right in all that back to Africa nonsense?"

"Not right in your terms, Andrew. Not in your politician's terms. But true. A truth of passion, if you see what I mean."

"True for how many?" Andrew said with exasperation. "For God's sake, Stefan, how many people in this island, black, white or brown wanted any part of him? Look what happened, when he and his chaps were on the run. They didn't dare show their faces anywhere."

"That's not important. What we had all witnessed was the important thing."

"Oh, you!" Andrew said. "You're incurable."

III

But now of course in the clarity of this sleepless morning, lying beside my sleeping wife, I realize how indefinite what I tried to say earlier in the evening must have seemed. Particularly to Andrew who as a planter and politician must give priority to the tangibles of existence. Oliver too. He looked disappointed, as if I had promised more than I could deliver. But then he was wrong about me. My profession has made me uncertain about people. They don't fit into synonymous patterns as my fish or lizards do. The accumulated observation which one can bring confidently to a new example of a species one knows has so little to do with the way one must look at a man. All I can do, when I try to describe another human being, is apply the method in which I have been trained: the deliberate fitting of one piece to another, as I might work on the scattered bones of a vanished animal. And I am not sure that the result is any more true to life than the wired skeleton is to the hunting, mating, subtly coloured beast whose mere shape I have reconstructed.

So what I remember of Marcus Heneky, beginning on that afternoon as Bernice and I followed Mister Howard along the veranda, is really a gaunt frame for the living tissue. What a lot of reality must have decayed and been absorbed by time since that afternoon. All I am left with are the indestructible, osseous fragments.

He was lying back in a deep chair, wrapped closely in a frayed dressing-gown made of towel material, and his eyes shifted from Bernice to me, then back to her with the intent rapidity of a man following a fast rally in a game on which he has a large bet. I remember that my chief feeling was curiosity; I wanted to meet the man who could arouse such a reverence of love in both Bernice and Mister Howard. But mingled with this was the primitive apprehension and jealousy one feels when you first meet the father of your mistress: however old she is, however independent of his authority, you have taken and used his flesh; he knows her, as you will never be able to even approximate, in the naked helplessness of her babyhood; she has worshipped him with a total commitment of which her love for you now is only a shadow; even the first tremor of sexual need had its fulfilment in him. The lover is always a usurper instinctively trying to justify himself to the lawful king.

"Well now, daughter," he said. "So you come up to look for the old man," and hearing that bright, cruel voice, I realized how frail all my assumptions about him had been. It was the sort of voice that, hearing it in a crowded place, one turns eagerly to see the speaker. And if I call it cruel, it was cruel only as a sword is: an instrument that might compel from you all your respect, intelligence of attention and courage of response. Quite simply, it was the most beautiful voice I have ever heard (the most beautiful I am ever likely to hear) and if the man to whom it belonged was impressive enough, with his great square grey head, wide, hungry nostrils and long obstinate chin, it was the voice that set your imagination echoing. It had none of the patient training and artifice that goes to make the singer's voice, although he could range it, like all of us, across the scale of passion. It was, you felt, the tempered product of an astonishing forge.

"Hi, papa!" Bernice said shyly. "I hear you sick an' I come up to see what I can do. I know say how you never look after yourself."

All the splendid, maternal composure to which I had become accustomed had vanished: she looked pathetically, almost ludicrously, girlish. No, not girlish. In that moment she reminded me of a woman at one of those abominable fancy dress parties where adults have to come as children. And then, beneath her embarrassment and uncertainty, I could see an eagerness of love and solicitude and hope of acceptance so intense that I felt a jealous distress numb my stomach. No one else in the world, I realized then, would ever be able to trespass on what seemed to come from her and palpably envelop that spare, muscular old man in the chair before us. I had known this before but only as we anticipate a possible thirst during a cool drink. For a second she hovered before him; behind me Mister Howard breathed audibly and crisply, and I wondered if he had suffered, for old Heneky, the same foul blow of jealousy as I for Bernice. Then Marcus Heneky's cold, assessing glare was brightened by a slow smile; he chuckled and gestured—it was an oddly artificial movement, like a freemason's sign, and somehow I knew that it went back nearly fifty years, to a child. Bernice gave a sudden little sigh, as if a spring had been suddenly released inside her, bent over and kissed him and rested her cheek against the top of his head. The brown face by the black were startling in their resemblance, as family likeness seen for the first time always surprises.

"Old man," she said. "How you do, eh? You sick bad?"

"Cho!" he said impatiently. "A little fever. It soon pass off. So you come an' look for me." He chuckled again. "You don't hear what I tell you the last time?" He was holding her hands tightly and his eyes never left her face. The mockery in his voice was so tender and intimate that I felt like an eavesdropper.

"I can always go back," Bernice said, and tossed her chin at him gently. "You don't deserve I should come up after the things you tell me."

He frowned, and I remember my instant recognition, conviction rather, of the possibility of anger behind that frown. It was as different, I knew, from the facile petulance of the choleric as the pent turbulence of a volcano is from the heat of a stove. I watched him closely, fascinated and troubled by this brief stirring of prophetic wrath, and curiously enough I didn't compare it, even for an instant, with the frenzy that had seized the Son of Sheba down at Caymanas Marsh. He had been a fugitive driven into a corner of his mind. What ravaged Marcus Heneky's face for a second that afternoon after Bernice had spoken seemed to come from the centre of a more enduring inspiration. . . . Or am I attributing to my perception then what it understood later? Hard to be sure now: even three years can falsify the sum of a moment's experience. I only know that when Marcus Heneky's face cleared and he grinned again at Bernice, I relaxed like a runner after a false start. He shook his head slightly.

"Don't worry yourself about that now," he said. "That pass. The black man was bothering me that day you come to see me. Bothering me bad with his sin an' blindness. . . ." He paused and for the first time since we had come along the veranda looked directly at me, then up at Bernice again. "And who this?" There was no hostility in his voice: only the weary resignation with which one waits for a piece of disagreeable news.

Bernice said quickly: "This is Doctor Mahler, papa. He is a good customer of mine, an' he was kind enough to bring me up to see you. You know how the country buses stay. I could never have got all the way up here if Doctor Mahler didn't offer me a lift."

She looked at me sadly, and by this time I had known her long enough to understand the shame and hurt she was feeling for her necessary equivocation. With Bernice honesty was never an obligation: it was an appetite.

"How d'you do, sir," I said, "I'm sorry to hear you're not well," and I put my hand out to shake his.

In the nearly imperceptible hesitation before his hand was slowly extended to join with mine, in the sudden doubtful flicker across his steady gaze, I thought: so that's it, old man; we've both been wounded in the same accident; just as you'll never completely believe that a white man can call you "sir" without patronage, so I'll never be quite sure that any Gentile of my world doesn't make a reservation when he meets me; we both demand proof; and that's silly dangerous; it's an invitation to the world to hurt you again.

His hand was uncomfortably warm with fever, and when I looked closely at his face I could sense sickness behind its hard lines.

"So you're a doctor," he said in a soft, cold voice which conceded nothing but the words. "You work at the hospital in Queenshaven?"

"No, sir. I'm not that sort of doctor. I teach at the university."

"He teach science, Papa," Bernice said suddenly with unpretending pride. "He teach ... what you call it again, Stefan?"

"Zoology." To Marcus Heneky I said with a carefully impersonal concern: "I'm not a medical man, Mister Heneky, but I really think you ought to be in hospital. I know enough to see that."

"You hear now!" I had almost forgotten Mass' Howard, and his explosive interruption startled me. He went up to Marcus Heneky. "You hear what him say. . . . I glad you tell him, sir. Now you'll believe you sick an' should go an' see doctor. . . . Thank you, eh, sir."

He bobbed before the older man with a sort of scolding

veneration. His fussy little body and anxious bullying should have been comic: instead they had an affecting dignity.

"Cho, Howard!" Marcus Heneky said. "You is an old woman. A man have a little bit of fever an' you want put him in hospital."

"Then if you get sick bad what we goin' to do?" Howard said excitedly. "You know is you we count on for all what we have to do. . . ."

"Howard," Marcus Heneky said brusquely. "I thirsty. You have any of the coconut water left? Bring some for me, no? An' bring some for me daughter an' her friend here."

"Just the thing," Mass' Howard said. "Some leave into the pitcher to keep cool. I will get it directly. Miss Heneky, a chair for you, ma'am." He took an upright wooden chair from its place against the wall and held the back daintily, with his finger-tips, while Bernice sat close to her father on his right. "And you will take a seat, Doctor Mahler." He smiled at me as he passed another of the light chairs across the narrow veranda: my judicious advice to the old man had been my credentials: temporarily, at least, I was an ally. "I won't keep you," he assured us and hurried off with his dapper strut along the veranda to the tiny kitchen at the end, by the door leading into the dining-room.

"He don't have a wife, papa?" Bernice asked in a whisper.

"Eh? What you say?" He had been studying me from under the iron-grey tufts of his brows, without cordiality, but with the frank curiosity of the very intelligent. Now he turned his head to Bernice. "What you say, me child?"

"Mass' Howard . . . him don't have a wife?"

"No. He did have one, but she die."

"And no daughter?"

"She gone to America."

"Then no woman in the house to look after you?" Bernice said reproachfully.

"I'm all right, I tell you. Howard looking after me good."

"I think Bernice is right, sir," I said severely. "I don't mean to interfere, but at your age you shouldn't neglect a fever."

The heavy head, square and formidable as a lion's, turned back to me, and again I came under the scrutiny of that cool, openly interested gaze in which, now that he had relaxed, I seemed to catch the light of a sardonic and disconcerting gaiety.

"But you say you don't have doctor's training," he said, "so how you can know whether it's just a little cold breeze I pick up an' take a chill?"

"How long have you run your temperature, sir?"

"Oh, a few days now. Not long."

"Papa," Bernice said. "That's not true. The man who come to tell me that you sick, said it was ten days an' more."

"Who come to tell you?" he asked with a sudden harsh intentness. He leaned forward, his hands gripping the ends of the arm-rests and his body drawn together: it was like watching the concentration of purpose in a big cat before the leap. Bernice blinked.

"It's one of the men from the church," she said. "He know say that you is my father an' he come an' tell me how you write to them and say you sick. He is a good man that. He was worried 'bout you an' think I ought to know."

"Oh, I see." Marcus Heneky eased himself back against the canvas slowly. "What the man's name was?"

"Ralston . . . Ralston something," Bernice said. "I can't remember now. He is one of Sheba's Sons does a little work sometimes for the beer company when they have the big barrels to handle. A big strong man."

"Oh, yes," Marcus Heneky said, and the evenness of his voice sounded to me deliberate, like that of a man who doesn't want to show how much a steep flight of stairs has tested him. "Ralston Edwards. He join the church a while back."

Mass' Howard came from the kitchen carrying a tray with full glasses and a plate of crackers and cheese. After serving us, he watched like an anxious housewife until we had taken the

116

first sip and nibble: the coconut water had been mixed with condensed milk and a dash of rum and was much too sweet, but the squares of cheese had been sprinkled with drops of a red sauce hot as lava, and with that prickling on my tongue I managed to swallow the drink convincingly.

"Well, you decide yet?" Mass' Howard asked Marcus Heneky. "You goin' to take good advice an' go down to see doctor?"

Marcus Heneky shrugged. "I will think about it," he said.

"Tell me, Mister Heneky," I said, "have you had any pains in your arms and legs since you took sick?"

"Little bit," he admitted. "How you did know that?"

"I thought so," I lied firmly. "My guess is that you have rheumatic fever. You know what that can do to the heart if it's neglected. You'd better come back to Queenshaven with us, sir."

He turned to Bernice. "I suppose you going' to tell me the same thing," he said. "You can't wait to see the old man on his back, eh?"

"Go on," Bernice said, "you know you sick bad. If you don't come with us willing, I goin' to make Mass' Howard an' Doctor Mahler march you down the hill like a criminal."

"All right then." The old man surrendered with obvious relief: he had refused to acknowledge the usurping flesh, but now he could tell himself we had forced him into it. "I know say how you can carry on when you want, Bernice. I'll come back to Queenshaven with you." He put his hand out to her.

Bernice gave a sniff of tender, mocking laughter and their hands touched briefly: as two people belonging to a forbidden faith might exchange a scrap of precious dogma in the street.

Sometimes now when I think of that silent exchange and of the sudden, astonishing light in her face, I realize how little we can ever know of another. To understand Marcus Heneky, I would have to know what he gave to Bernice as a child: with what unrecorded treasures of gentleness and security he had

117

surrounded her so as to earn, after nearly fifty years, the still unqualified love she revealed that afternoon. At least, though, I understand her honesty: she must have learnt to lie much later than the rest of us.

IV

We took Marcus Heneky back to Queenshaven almost immediately. He and Mass' Howard left us for a while after he had agreed to go, and the blurred murmur of their conversation drifted back to us from the bedroom at the front of the house. Then they came out and Marcus Heneky said, as if he were conferring a great favour, "Well, I ready now, child." He was dressed in very old, very clean brown linen and wore a square black hat that looked as though it had been laboriously hollowed from a block of rusty iron; Mass' Howard carried a fibre suitcase and a blue blanket folded over his free arm.

On the path down to the car, we saw how sick Marcus Heneky really was: he stumbled several times and by the time we reached the little square, his breathing was heavy and uncertain. When we climbed into the back of the car and Mass' Howard made a shawl of the blanket about his shoulders, it seemed to invest him suddenly with an enormous tiredness as much as with warmth.

"Now stretch out your legs, papa," Bernice said: it was typical of her instinct for small kindness that she had not tried to help Mass' Howard settle her father.

"You want a cushion for your head, Marcus?" Howard asked. "I can run back up the house an' get one." Reluctantly he ceased to make the last unnecessary adjustments to the blanket. He straightened and stood forlornly by the car. "What about the cushion then?" he repeated.

"Cho, no," Marcus Heneky muttered irritably, then his wonderful voice strengthened with dramatic fury. "I don't know why all of you have to carry on as if I'm a woman in labour." His eyes, glazed by fever and fatigue, brightened and he looked at me with the same challenging and incorrigible gaiety I had seen up at the house. "White man's car is comfortable enough for the old black man, eh, doctor? Him should be glad to even get a lift, eh?"

"I'm not doing this for you, you know," I said. "I'm doing it for me: because the Bible says he that gives is twice blessed."

His lips twitched. "So you sharp, eh?"

Bernice turned to Howard. "Thank you for looking after him, Mass' Howard."

"I no must look after him," Howard said. "If we don't have him, who we have?" He put his head in at the window. "Get well and come soon again, Marcus."

"Go with God, Brother Howard, an' remember the Lord is my rock, and my fortress, and my deliverer."

"I will call upon the Lord," Howard replied, "who is worthy to be praised. Go with God, Brother Marcus."

Each of them put the other into God's care with an utter yet matter of fact deference, as if recommending a humble traveller to the powerful and benevolent leader of a caravan. They held hands for a moment, looking at each other, then Howard stepped back and Bernice got into the front seat.

"Good-bye," I said to Howard and held my hand out.

"Go with God, doctor." He shook my hand. "I will pray for you," he added, gently, like a surgeon offering the comfort of an operation to a hopeless case.

I went to the driving side, waved to the interested loungers on the shop veranda above the square and got into the car. As we drove off Howard lifted his hand slowly, and until we turned the bend in the road, the driving mirror reflected his prim, tense little figure, poised in the middle of the cosy square, with the hand still raised as if waving good-bye to a ship from the jetty of a remote island.

During the drive back to Queenshaven, Marcus Heneky

slept most of the time. The only conversation we had was at the beginning, before we had come out of the hills, when Bernice said: "But, papa, what you were doing all the way up here, in a little place like Gran' Dum?"

"I was uttering the true word of divine purpose, child," he said.

"You have a big congregation up here?"

"No." He paused, and then added in a tone of quiet bitterness, "Babylon an' its forces reign in these hills. Only Howard an' a few brethren know the Living God an' the way of redemption for the black man. . . ." His voice fell, trailing suddenly from its musical certitude, and I glanced back quickly. He had sagged against the padded upright of the seat; his skin was dull and sweaty, and he wore the impatient grimace of a man struggling with an irrelevant but enormous distraction. I stopped the car, reached over the back of the seat and took his wrist. It was hot, far hotter than I liked to allow for even with fever, and as I held it, he began to shiver. I took the thermos flask of water from the shelf under the dashboard, opened the flap of the cubby-hole before Bernice and felt for the box of luminol tablets I always carry if I'm going to be away from home for more than a night. Bernice was half-kneeling in her seat, her hand on the knee of the shuddering old man, her eyes narrowed: her face when she looked at the little box of tablets was full of pleading hope.

"They're only to make him sleep," I said. "I don't know what's wrong with him, but if he can get a little sleep between here and town it'll be a good thing."

I got out and went to the door on his side; he was struggling out of his spasm, driving himself into clarity like a flagellant whipping himself into a state of grace. But as he looked at me, his will surrendered again to the dry heat inside him; his eyes became unfocused and his voice wavered from the misty shallows of delirium. Broken phrases, fragments of passionate significance, were carried to us on the sluggish currents of

120

fever. . . . "Zion . . . and the angel standing in the sun . . . the white horse of the great king . . . when true Israel is restored. . . . Fire. . . . Babylon falling to the ground. . . . But if the heart is corrupt, the people shall know oppression. . . ."

"Take these, Mister Heneky," I said loudly, putting two tablets into his damp palm. He looked at them stupidly for so long that I was about to put them into his half-open mouth. Then he raised his hand shakily and grazed on his palm with flaccid lips, like a horse on short grass, and I quickly put the flask-top of water to his mouth. Some of the water dribbled down his long chin, but he swallowed most of it noisily.

"What we goin' to do, Stefan?" Bernice asked in a small, squeezed voice.

"Get him to Queenshaven as fast as we can. Don't worry. He'll be sound asleep before we've gone five miles. The motion of the car will help."

It is easy to sound assured and competently in charge when you are not involved: the lines of fear which had crumpled Bernice's face like a badly tied parcel began to fade as I spoke. And when, a few miles further on, she settled round in her seat, she said almost happily: "You was right. Him fast asleep now." She leaned to me and put her arm across my shoulder and kissed me on the cheek. "Lord, Stefan. You is a good man, you know!"

In the hospital yard, three hours later in Queenshaven, we had to shake her father awake. Between us, we supported him, drowsy and protesting, into the reception room. The benches along each wall were nearly empty: it was past the regular examination hours but too early yet for the first flotsam of night emergency cases to have been flung up from the streets of the town. I pushed the bell button as we entered and helped Bernice lower Marcus Heneky to the bench.

"How're you feeling now, sir?" I asked him.

"So so, boy," he said indifferently. He was awake but still caught in the drug's effect. I went to the button again and pressed it, hard, keeping my finger on it until I heard the unmistakable, menacing hiss of starched skirts and rubber soles in the corridor outside. One half of the swing doors flew back and a tall sister entered, her coif spread behind her head as if stiffened by her electric discharge of reproof.

"Were you ringing that bell?" she asked in a voice that would have cut glass.

"Yes, sister . . ." I began hurriedly, but not hurriedly enough.

"D'you realize that this is a hospital? And that we're busy? You will observe there is a notice above the bell which says. . . ."

"I saw it, sister, but we do have a sick man." I jumped on to her pause for emphatic breath as though it had been the first rock fording a stream. "I think you'd better look at him."

She withered me with a final, awful glare of warning and turned to Marcus Heneky; the immaculate skirts uttered a severe whisper as she bent close to him. She turned her head to me and said, "Typhoid," in a minatory tone, as if I were responsible for this too.

"Typhoid!" I said. "Are you sure?"

"Of course I'm sure, young man." The lean face could not have been more outraged if I had questioned her chastity. "D'you think I don't know typhoid when I see it. . . . Two in a bed we used to have them over in St. Clare in the old days," she explained with nostalgic relish to Bernice. "They used to have to bring 'em in trucks when it became really epidemic. . . ."

"Of course it isn't the same nowadays," she said to me with a sigh half an hour later. "What with aureomycin and all that, typhoid's nothing now. Still, it's a good thing you got him here when you did. He must have been a walking case for over a week."

We were smoking illicit cigarettes in the deserted corridor outside reception while I waited for Bernice. They had allowed her to take Marcus Heneky's clothes up to the ward and to wait until he was settled in. And now that she had

122

established the proper relationship between medicine and the laity, the sister had unbent. Watching her tip the ash from her cigarette surreptitiously into the fire bucket was slightly unsettling, like hearing a priest or an elderly schoolmaster swear.

"You're sure he'll be all right?"

"Right as rain, my dear." She sucked with innocent gluttony at her butt and exhaled two slow trickles. "I don't think it has affected the intestine yet. And if that's all right, we'll have him up and about in no time."

By now, I thought, she must offer reassurance or commiseration from the same impregnable fund of detachment: life would be too destructive otherwise.

"Well," she said, "I can't stay here all night talking to you. I must be off."

"Good night, sister, and thank you."

"Good night, Mister. . . ?"

"Mahler. Stefan Mahler."

"You're Doctor Mahler from the university? The one we asked to get us those frogs from Caymanas Marsh?"

"I suppose so. I hope they were satisfactory."

"Yes, man. They take the cancer grafts better than anything we've used yet. It's not my department, but one of the sisters in surgery was telling me about it. Why you didn't say who you were?"

"It never occurred to me, and those frogs were nothing. I just happened to be down that way and to know where to find them. It was the boys in the village you should thank, really. I gave them a penny for each one in good condition."

"Well," she said again. "If I'd known."

She smiled, bullied a pleat into precise alignment, and trudged off under the subdued light of the corridor, the white delta of her coif tugged by her brisk displacement of air.

Soon after she had left me, Bernice appeared at the end of the corridor, coming from the stairs that led to the male wards on the second storey. She walked slowly down to me with that

123

long, deliberate step, which because of the slight roll it gave to her body, always reminded me of a sailor taking his first promenade after a long voyage. I met her half-way and she smiled with the weariness of released tension.

"Them allowed me to see him for a minute," she said. "They say they're going to start giving him . . . that thing . . . what you call it?"

"Aureomycin. It's the latest thing. He'll be through the worst in a few days with that."

"Lord God," she said and let out a long, shaky breath. "When that sister say 'Typhoid', I think say me heart nearly stop. You ever see what it can do to a man?"

"That was the bad old days," I told her. "When it had to run its course and they had to pack you in ice. But not now. Don't worry."

"I know." Her eyes widened with realization. "Suppose say something didn't tell me to go to him?"

"I'm glad you followed your mind. I like your father. I wouldn't like to see anything happen to him."

"Really, Stefan? You really like him? Him treat you hard today, you know."

"Not really," I said. "Come on, I'll take you back." On the way back through the mauve dust of the first of the evening, she giggled, suddenly and weakly, like someone who survived an accident and whose enjoyment of small things is close to tears.

"What?" I asked.

"Nothing," she said, and giggled again.

"Go on. Tell me."

"Him is a hard old man, you know." She touched her handkerchief to her eyes. "You know what him tell me after they put him to bed? Just before I leave?"

"No."

"Him tell me to tell you that the lift you give him is the first thing for a long time him ever take from a white man an' don't

124

pay for." She gave a gurgling laugh. "Him say to tell you that he will pay for the petrol, both ways, as soon as he get out."

Long John's was full when I pulled up at the entrance in the lane: by now the tyres seemed to just brush the kerb as if sliding off a production belt into a mechanically allotted groove. From inside came the ebb and surge of male voices sliding back and forth over each other like the alternation of stones in surf.

"H-mm h-mm," Bernice said. "Big night tonight. An American gunboat come in today." Her remark was immediately underlined by a twanging arpeggio of obscenity from the corner: it sounded like a ritual chant between the gritted teeth of a boy passing his initiation test. I thought: Americans sound artificial when they swear; good cursing ought to be a symbolic manure from the bowels, as it is in Europe or Cayuna. A slight dark sailor on a crutch stumble-hopped round the corner from the front entrance and began to cross the empty street like a lame jerboa. Two other sailors, one fair and hardly pubescent, and a massively sinewed Negro, pursued him with placatory cries, scooped him up carefully, crutch and all, and bore him back across the street.

"I must go in now," she said. "Is only Cherry in there, an' a girl help us sometimes when we have a rush. Come an' eat before you go."

"No, thanks. I'm hungry, but not very, and they'll have kept something for me."

"I so sorry I spoil your party," she said ruefully.

"You haven't. I'm glad I had to do this. I'm sorry it's your father who's sick, but I'm glad you wanted me to do something for you."

I was afraid that she was going to thank me again and I didn't want that. She had received so little from me: my practised, vigorous member; the novelty of my origin—no novelty to her who heard confession daily from the half a hundred nationalities who used the port; a few presents; and a somewhat old-fashioned courtesy, a finesse of manners which was little more than a device for inconspicuous survival I had learnt early in life. Whenever I said to her, "I love you", it was a lie which she accepted with the same unillusioned gratification of a woman seeing her face made more attractive by cosmetics. She could already see to a time when I would no longer need her, and although we never talked of this, I would occasionally surprise her looking at me with a pensive, tender resignation, as if I were the photograph of someone long dead.

Now she said: "Kiss me, then." And as I leaned across and our lips touched, we were both gripped in one of those sudden, almost alarming spasms of desire so different from the mounting heat with which two bodies ordinarily prepare for each other. Her back arched and her arms round my neck tightened like shrinking wood. "Oh God, Stefan," she said thickly, "come up for a little."

We went up the stairs to her room in a stupefied haze, hand in hand, leaning shoulder to shoulder in a trembling anguish close to exhaustion. When we toppled across the bed we had not even kicked off our shoes, and when a few seconds later we each touched the other's face, it was with gentle, exploratory fingers, as though amazed to find the familiar contours unchanged.

v

Take the road east from Queenshaven: on your left the huge peaks of the Blue Range, on your right the nibbling sea: stretched between them a long ribbon of plain, crammed from the shore to the foothills with sugar and banana. Thirty miles deep in this Eastmoreland plain, Andrew Fabricus holds a few hundred acres of sugar, acquired the year before I came to Cayuna. I have never seen him except as a planter and, more recently, a politician. Sometimes I think he is the only completely happy man I know.

"Of course he used to be much more interesting," Oliver told me when we became close enough to open up our friends between us. "It's a pity you'll never meet him as he was a couple of years ago, when he was business manager for the *Newsletter*. He had such a lot of nice jagged edges then."

"You could hardly call him sleek now," I said.

"No," he admitted. "Not sleek, but safe home. Smug as a bride. Two years ago, when he was still hoarding like a bloody squirrel, full of guilt and frustration because he wouldn't marry Margaret until he had a place of his own to take her to, hating his old fraud of a father for selling Fabricus Head before he could take it over, he was sensitive. Man, I used to dip him into situations like a piece of litmus paper whenever something came up and I wasn't sure of my judgement. I'd ask him something and he'd look at me with those great sleepy bull's-eyes and say, 'Well, I don't know, Oliver, but . . .' and come out with an opinion that went to the middle of the business like a bullet. Now he's as ripe as a grape with realized ambitions. Joining the Radical Party was the only thing he needed. Once he'd done that and taken Eastmoreland for them, he was able to put that Calvinist conscience of his out to grass."

"The thing is you're jealous," I said. "He's got more of everything than you: more talent, more money, more confidence, more people who love him. He's happier than you . . . and much nicer," I added fondly.

I was thinking of this conversation as I went up the steps to the veranda of Andrew's house that night after leaving Bernice. Watching him as he came to meet me, I realized that here was a man who had made peace within his own terms of competence and within a scope that any other man had to respect. Even seeing him superficially like this, as he smiled at me in the half light of the steps, gave an impression of unshakable calm: the ponderous yet discriminating responsibility on which all achievement is raised.

"Well, it's about time," he said. "Come and eat before you start circulating."

It was a big, noisy party, but intimate, as parties tend to be in Cayuna where there is seldom any need for introductions, and where allusive comment among one group can be decoded by nearly everybody without explanation. The stereo speakers of the big set in the corner moaned some shallow endearments and the bright skirts of the women swirled around legs that moved with the precise, instinctive provocation of the Caribbean. A happy, small brown man I didn't know said, "What can I get you?" as Andrew and I threaded ourselves through the gaps across the floor. I told him: "Whisky and water, please." And by the time we reached the folded back doors at the other side of the room, he was there, holding a glass. He put it into my hand with the practised casualness of a trainer passing a flask to a road racer, smiled cordially and vanished. I didn't see him again for the night.

Margaret Fabricus and Oliver were in the dining-room, at opposite sides of the long, densely gleaming mahogany table which is the only possession Andrew salvaged from the foundered past at Fabricus Head. Their faces were troubled and thoughtful and when we came in they both looked round with the remote stares of people forcing their attention back to the present moment or company. Then Margaret said, "Stefan!" and got up and tilted her cheek for me to kiss and tucked my hand under her arm. "Sit there," she told me, pointing to the end of the table where she and Oliver had been sitting. "It won't be a minute." She went to the far door and called out: a maid's voice answered from the back of the house, and Margaret said: "Doctor Mahler is here. You can serve now."

"Hi!" Oliver said as I sat.

"And hi to you too."

"So you got here finally."

I leaned back in the high-back end chair and listened to the steady, singsong pulse of voices, the throb of vulgar music and the sudden counterpoints of ice against glass in the room beyond. The white hot consummation, almost like a death shudder, that I had shared with Bernice an hour before had left me stranded in a gorgeous passivity; all sensation seemed to enter through a lubrication of sweet, thick oil: it was not happiness, but rather as though, for an accidental moment, I floated at the still centre of experience, without even an active image to follow.

When the maid brought my tray, Andrew and Oliver rose and drifted out, and as they went through the doorway I could hear Oliver say something in a worried grumble.

"What's wrong with him?" I asked Margaret.

"Oh," she said, "Joan's back." There was a half bottle of hock on the tray and she took it and poured a glass for me, her face frowning and intent as if it was an action that demanded strict concentration. She put the sweating bottle down, took the glass, sipped it and passed it to me. "She flew in this morning. We didn't even know she was coming until she showed up this afternoon." She sighed, with a sort of impatient tenderness. "Of course, she was drunk then. But nothing to what she is now. She's got to the deceptive stage. You know, when she'll hold a serious conversation for fifteen minutes without understanding a word she's saying."

"No," I said, "I don't know. I don't even know Joan."

"Good Lord!" The incisive, subtle face—so much like Oliver's except for its milk chocolate skin—creased with her amused apology. "Of course. I keep forgetting you haven't been with us for very long. Hasn't Oliver ever told you about her?"

"No."

"Well, you'll be seeing a good bit of her from now on." (Prophesy, I sometimes feel, is one of the commonest elements in our casual speech.) "She's Joan Culpepper, Oliver's sister-in-law. By his first wife, that is. The one that died. She's been in England from before you came out." She paused and shook her head resignedly. "It's too long to go into now. But she's our problem girl. Like Oliver used to be our problem boy a long time ago. Only he got over it."

"Yes," I said. "I know he used to drink. That's this Joan's trouble too, I take it?"

"God!" she said astringently, but still in the same voice of protective and understanding tolerance with which Cayuna discusses the casualties of passion. "Man, if that was her only trouble. She's had all the troubles you can mention: husband trouble, man trouble, scandal trouble." Her amber voice, the voice of the educated Cayunan, had slurred, unconsciously, into the thick, peasant tones with which all Cayuna emphasises a drama from life. With something like reluctant admiration, she added: "When that woman goes to make a mess of things, she really does a finished job."

"What began it all?" I asked. "Or was she just that way from the beginning?"

She gave an accommodating, nearly indifferent shrug, and I realized how old and futile an inquiry this must be to her.

"Bad luck," she said. "She chose the wrong man for a start and stayed in love with him too long. She used to be married to Ian Gordon. . . ."

"You mean the fellow who runs the schooner company?"

"That's the one. Can you imagine anybody choosing *that*?"

"Not you," I said, "and not Sybil, but I can imagine some might."

"Well, Joan did . . . and when I think of the men who'd have walked fire to marry her. But that isn't what's made her the way she is now. It was bad luck . . . two pieces of bad luck combined. She stayed in love with him too long and when she couldn't even pretend she was getting anything from him, she tried to get it from the bottle."

"That was choice," I said. "She could have left him and tried her luck again."

"Yes, but alcohol doesn't make her sick. The way too much

of it does me. It only makes her foolish. Man, Stefan, you haven't seen her drink. She could match you or any of the men out there and leave you unconscious. But that's what I mean by bad luck. An accidental strength of constitution that saves her the sort of normal hell of a morning after. If it wasn't for that, perhaps she would have made the compromise with disappointment. . . ."

She had begun to pursue the elusive scent of behaviour with the same abrupt transition to detachment that I had learned to expect in Oliver's talk, and I understood, then, the nostalgia he so often expressed for the days, before her marriage, when she had worked with him on the *Newsletter*. And it was at this moment that a voice called with a jocular plaintiveness, "Margaret! Margaret!" and a plump, vividly sweating man in a shirt like a sunset appeared in the doorway, trotted into the room, seized her hand and led her out. She looked back over her shoulder and made a grimace of cheerful haplessness and I raised my gnawed leg of cold chicken in mock salute.

Perhaps I remember my first sight of Joan that night because Margaret's dramatic voice had prepared me for her. Now, I only have to call the Fabricus dining-room deliberately to mind, like a mnemonic, for her to appear: the heavy, liquid shimmer of the Chinese silk dress, the gold locket, no bigger than a half-crown, askew up against her shoulder, the pathetically rakish strand of hair across her forehead, the fugitive, foolish insolence of drunkenness in her eyes. Perhaps her unexpected, noisy entrance wrenched my luxuriously drowsing nerves into receptiveness, so that now she is fixed in the exact detail, the unnaturally emphatic colour of a dream, while other, more recent moments of sudden, memorable vision are comparatively blurred. Certainly it was not with any love, but simply with the self-satisfied tolerance of the sober for the drunk that I first saw her that night.

I had nearly finished eating, and comfortably taut with good food I was beginning to anticipate the rest of the night: four more drinks, I had decided, maybe five, but no more because of the wine, a few dances, the usual end of the morning talk, and then I'll sling the hammock in the yard between the garage wall and the breadfruit tree instead of sharing a room with whoever it is staying over until tomorrow. A woman's voice sounded loudly as she made some hilarious, jeering but in-audible remark in the passage leading to the back of the house; two sets of footsteps, one light and unsteady, the other heavier and slow, and looking round I saw Joan Culpepper as she lurched gracefully through the doorway behind me. I was sure it could only be her: the women in Cayuna as a rule are too fastidious or too sexually engaged to get drunk, and there is seldom likely to be more than one the worse for liquor at any party. She was followed, reluctantly, by a very young, un-blemished looking boy and I knew him also: Hippolyte Vogier, one of the university students; not from my department, but from the history school. I wondered what he was doing here and then I remembered having seen his elder brother, Jerome, one of Andrew's political colleagues, in the drawing-room as I passed through. His mouth and chin were smeared with lip-stick and he had the mazed, empirical look of a man reprieved just before the order to fire. With no more effort than it took to see that she was drunk and aggressive, he frightened and full of chagrin, I was certain of the scene they must have en-acted somewhere in the long grass behind the house: her vio-lent, selfish fingers, his flattered excitement shrinking into an older terror.

I wanted to comfort him, for it had happened to me too. The memory returned, shocking as a thorn beneath a finger-nail: myself at fifteen and the grim little Viennese, three years my senior, permanently and dangerously drunk with loneliness and disgust, a fortuitous last message, like myself, posted from the death chamber of Teutonic Jewry; her small breasts squirming under her blouse like two ferrets in a bag; the angry, myopic lewdness of her eyes as she dragged me down to gratify a desire as private and hallucinatory as greed.

Now, as my unexpected presence registered on her clouded perceptions, Joan Culpepper smiled—the flabby, indiscriminate *camaraderie* of the drunk—and swayed quickly over to me.

"Well, well," she said gaily, "who have we here? No, don't get up." I was pressed between the padded, fragrant slope of her hip and the arm she had thrown about my shoulder. Hippolyte came up and looked from her to me, a speculative hope beginning to clear his stricken face. I smiled at him and winked; he winked back, with an elaborate and conspiratorial worldliness like the bravado of a child crying inside itself.

"Hullo, Hippolyte," I said heartily. "Introduce me, please."

"Oh, sure, Doctor Mahler." He spoke hurriedly, as if he were anxious to seal a bargain. "This is Joan Culpepper. Joan, this is Stefan Mahler. He's from the university."

"Hullo, Stefan," she cooed in a clownishly wanton voice. She bent her face close to mine, frowning with the effort of proper focus. Then she looked round, pulled the nearest chair to her and dropped into it. Carefully, as though she were landing an aeroplane, she slid her cheek to rest against the fist of the arm she rested on the table. From there she continued to study me with a laborious, happy concentration. "I don't know you," she said finally.

"Yes, you do," I protested in the briskly soothing voice we reserve for the petulant sick and the drunk. "We've just been introduced. And Margaret told me about you before you came in. You're Oliver's sister-in-law."

"That reminds me," she said suddenly and severely. "Where *is* that little bastard, Ollie? He's been dodging me all night and I won't put up with it. No, sir, he can't get away with that. Not with me, he can't." She flung herself back in the chair and looked up at Hippolyte with remote yet kindly dismissal. "Hippolyte, why don't you go and find Oliver for me? And tell him to bring me a drink when he's coming," she added as

Hippolyte hurried off. "The little brute," she muttered. "Trying to dodge me. After all I've done for him."

"Who?" I asked. "Hippolyte or Oliver?"

"Oliver, of course. D'you know I used to take that little bastard home to sleep with me?"

"Really?"

"Yes, really." Her voice hardened with the facile hostility of her condition. "But not what you think. We used to go out drinking together after Cecile and the baby died and he'd get all cold and lonely and I'd take him back to my place and hug him till he went to sleep." She looked at me reproachfully, and added in maudlin, forgiving tones. "It was just like hugging a Teddy Bear. Don't you think he looks like a Teddy Bear?"

"No," I began, "I've never ..." but she had already dropped the subject in the manner of the befuddled, like a baby dropping a toy into oblivion.

"Tell me about you," she said. She leaned forward intimately, and I began to hope that Hippolyte would find Oliver and that Oliver would come soon.

"There isn't much to tell, really."

"You're not Cayunan?"

"No."

"England?"

"Now I am. But I came from Germany originally." I glanced towards the doorway.

"For God's sake," she said, with a sort of weary contempt far sadder than anger. "If you want to go that much, go on. I'm not keeping you." She put her hands flat on the table and pushed herself to her feet. And as she stood there, teetering slightly on the support of her arms, Oliver and Sybil came in.

"Ollie!" Joan cried and flung herself on him, and indeed, wrapped helplessly for a moment in her jovially voracious, silken and uninhibited embrace, he did look like a Teddy Bear. She hugged him closer and bending her lovely dark head began to smother him with ripe, happily incestuous kisses.

134

"My little Noll," she said and looked back at me with a warm smile as if I had brought Oliver for her. He wriggled free and grinned at her, holding her at arm's length with practised, gentle firmness.

"So there you are," he said. "What have you been doing? I thought you promised to stick close to me."

"Joan," Sybil said, "come and help me put a face on. I've hardly seen you since you got in this afternoon."

"All right," Joan said brightly and much too carefully. I thought: here come the tears. I had watched them gathering while she was talking to me and had dreaded they would break before Oliver arrived. Now as she surrendered herself to Sybil, she suddenly became listless and looked at us with a wavering, faintly incredulous despair.

"Come on, dear," Sybil said decisively, and putting an arm around her waist led her off.

"Sorry about that," Oliver said gloomily. "I didn't know she'd found you until Hippolyte came and told me." He gave a little dry chuckle. "What the hell did she do to that boy? He looks stunned. It's my fault. I should have kept her under my eye but she gets very cunning when she's had enough. I didn't think she was going to pick on poor Hippolyte though."

"What will she do now?"

"Oh, she'll go to sleep. One more drink and she'll call it a day. Damn it! She's not really like that, you know." He looked at me almost angrily.

"Why did she go to England? Did she go for a cure?"

"Lord, no, man. It was an idea we all had. That if she got a job there and had to look after herself, it might help." He sighed. "Well, you see what a good idea it was. She's back and just the same."

"Maybe she couldn't find enough people in England to care whether she got drunk or not," I said. "It's no fun breaking things if you can't count on somebody to weep over the pieces with you."

"You're sounding very moral and pompous tonight. What's wrong? Did she make a nuisance of herself?"

"No." The marvellous trance in which my senses had rested was beginning to fade under the pressures of food and wine and the quickening tempo of the party outside. A shiver of pure irritability jangled inside me like a discord. "No," I snarled at him. "She didn't make a nuisance of herself, but she's one of the emotional parasites. People like that practise an imperceptible cannibalism. I know. You wake up one morning and find yourself drained. And they're irresistible. The only defence you have against them is being bored. Oh, come on, Oliver. I'm going to get a drink and enjoy myself."

I was glad, when I woke the next morning, that I had taken the hammock into the yard. The air smelled like the heart of a new lettuce and I could see the flesh-textured sky behind the mountains and the rose stain of the sun uncertain as the tide of blood in a blush. Above me, the last stars guttered on the lifeless mauve like cheap rhinestones. I rolled to the edge of the hammock: the cars of those who had stayed over crouched in the thinning mist, strange pachyderms, as if humped above tucked under legs and heads. Then I was properly awake and rolled my weight over the edge of the hammock, until it tilted and dropped me feet first. Inside the house, the stale, prisoners' odour of sleep between walls. My little holdall was in a corner of the drawing-room, beside a divan on which Hippolyte Vogier lay in a flattened, twisted fashion like a man killed instantly as he charged. I took the towel from the case and went from the house and across the wet, tickling grass of the lawn. The dark green cane leaves were olive in the first light and the mountains stirred under a lilac dust: the narrow dirt road through the cane to the cove ran straight and bluish as the road in a dream. I was barefoot, dressed in the sweat shirt and shorts I had worn for sleep. In the time that it took me to walk the two hundred yards between the house and the beach, the ground became tepid and the steel-coloured water seemed to heave against a close transparent skin of pale fire. And it was because of this dazzling play of light on the cove that I didn't see Joan Culpepper until I had dropped my towel on the coarse brown sand and begun to tug the sweat shirt over my head. Or rather, that she saw me and gave a warning whistle. It came to me, limping round the ubiquitous echo of sound low across water.

I looked about and then saw her arm lifted and the flat gleam from her decapitated head on the silvered platter of the water.

"Here!" she called. "Look, I'm sorry, I didn't know anyone else was going to be up. I don't mind if you don't, but I'm naked."

Her voice was friendly but cool, rolling in slowly as if clutched at by the surface.

"That's all right," I shouted back. "I always swim naked myself at this time."

She waved a casual acknowledgement and turned and swam slowly, parallel to the beach, the round dark wet stone of her head bobbing gently.

I stripped and waded across the pebbly shallows, until the water became chalky green and I could no longer see my feet. Then I flung myself on to my belly and sank, with the smack of the surface like needle points all along my front and the chill that was not really chill but only a contrast to the warmth outside freshening the pace of my blood. I surfaced slowly through increasing light and followed her. She turned when she heard my splashing, pushing two slow ripples from her undulating arms until her feet found the bottom. About a yard from her, I let my own feet sink to the pebble studded sand. She nodded pleasantly, without constraint, as if merely recognizing the agreeable use we had both found for this hour.

"Sorry to have disturbed you," I said. "If I'd known you were coming down, I'd have waited."

"Why?" The cordial voice inflected faintly with a polite surprise. "There's plenty of room. I woke early and I haven't been able to do this for two years so I came down." She paused, moved her hand gently through the water and added simply, "May I apologize for embarrassing you last night?"

"You didn't. I didn't think you'd even remember."

"Of course I remember. I made a squalid fool of myself." The admission was made with an austere, laconic humility that begged nothing, not even the amnesty of agreement.

"Oh, everybody has a little too much sometimes," I said hypocritically. "Particularly if they've just come back."

"Haven't they told you?" Again the unaffected note of surprise, like an even inquiry. "It's not sometimes with me. I drink too much as often as I can. That's why I came back. I couldn't afford it in England and I was missing it too badly."

"I see."

"But anyway it's not very interesting." The courteously attentive, unsmiling face before me was unshadowed by even a hint of self-pity, and she uttered the words only as one draws a convenient line under an exhausted topic of minor importance. "Well," she said. "I think I'll go in now. I wonder if you'd mind looking south until I've dressed. Then I'll leave it all to you."

"If you wait for me, we can walk up together. I've about had enough. I only do this because it sets me up morally for the day."

She laughed softly and briefly, for about as much time as the feeble pleasantry deserved. When she laughed, the dry point lines around her mouth and nose showed mercilessly.

"All right," she said. "I'll give you a hail when I'm ready."

The deep shining chest, the colour of a walnut's meat, and the darker face disappeared suddenly. The surface sagged and whorled and I felt her foot thud against my skin as she turned underwater. Her streaming head appeared with a sullen flash

138

fifteen feet away and she swam to the beach without looking back. I allowed the creeping undercurrent of the cove to carry me and I considered her with the same mild, aesthetic regret I would have felt for a good picture damaged by carelessness. Only physical accident, of course, could ever spoil the long spine and the limber pelvic frame I had seen the night before. And by the same token, she would always have the sooty black eyes, just widely spaced enough to lull a man with an impression of generous appetite and good nature. But her skin, the opalescent, waxen skin of the tropics, would coarsen, as already the beauty of her face had begun to run down those fault lines at the corners of her mouth and nose.

"All set!" The amiable, circumspect voice called from the shore as I dragged down the lazy current. I turned and saw her sitting on the beach in shorts and a shirt, buckling a sandal. As I butted into the shallows, she swung round and remained sitting, gazing at the mountains across the plain and hugging her shins. The sun was well clear of the mountains and their true colours had come to the surfaces of things.

"No shoes?" she asked when I joined her.

"No. Why?"

She shook her head and said in the chiding tones of a responsible hostess, "You should know better than that by now. It's not safe on a cane-piece road. Cattle pass up and down all week and if you cut your foot it could mean lockjaw."

"I've done this every time I've come down."

"No, seriously. You shouldn't. Even a dildo prickle would be enough. I'm surprised the others haven't warned you."

"They're never around to warn me. They're always asleep. I tried to get Oliver up once, but he carried on so."

"Oliver!" she said, and shook her head with a sudden crooked little smile, at once enormously proud and tender. We were in the narrow road between the walls of cane and now she reached into the little airline bag she carried and took out an orange.

139

"I brought this along," she said doubtfully, "but I forgot to bring a knife. You wouldn't have one, would you?"

"No, but I'll flay it with my claws, like the beast that I am. Give it to me."

She said, "How do I look? Does last night show very badly?" lifting her face candidly to the sun and looking straight at me without trickery of appeal.

"You look all right," I told her. "Your eyes are a bit blood-shot, but that could be the salt." And I continued to strip the blazing yellow rind of the orange she had given me.

"Good," she said. "I didn't want to look too haggish when that Vogier boy sees me this morning. It wouldn't be nice for him." I broke the orange into halves, the sticky thin juice squirting like the mist from an atomizer and filling the air between with scent that tickled. She took her half with a dutiful nod of thanks as we walked on, adding in a tone of passionless assessment, "I've got that much pride left, I'm afraid."

The mountains seemed much nearer now than when I woke, as though they had folded back darkness like a hinged door and crept out to sun their slaty blue hides on the green plain. The bell of the little Moravian church in the foothills clanged a brusque, unadorned summons, strict as judgement day in the soft air. A bright, gauzy plume of smoke rose from the yard behind Andrew's house, and even the house itself (one of those indestructible, modern Cayuna bungalows so ugly that you feel they must be deliberate parodies) seemed to have settled into the little hill against which it was built and to lie in a sabbath glow that was near to shapeliness. I found myself wondering how a woman like the one who walked silently beside me could have loved or married a man like Ian Gordon, a coarse-grained, decorative animal in the unique colonial mould, never exposed to the stimulus of competition nor even criticism.

Sybil, Oliver and Andrew were on the veranda as we climbed the steep lawn to the house: Oliver in pyjamas on the

140

top step, drooped over a cup which he held in both hands, and looked into without enthusiasm; Sybil and Andrew, dressed, in two light chrome and canvas chairs behind him, regarding him with obvious amusement.

"You know what you look like," I told him, climbing the steps. "You look like that bird in the story who got caught in the badminton game."

He raised his half-asleep, scowling face.

"I'm further along the evolutionary scale than what you are," he said. "Any of you. My metabolism is different. If I had my way nobody would get up till after midday."

As she passed, Joan reached down and pulled his ear gently and he caught her hand and looked up, his face suddenly alert and fond: for about a second, they seemed to exclude us all. Then she let his hand go and said, "I'm going to wash the salt out of my hair." She went inside.

"Where's everybody?" I asked, sitting on the top step with my back against the pillar.

"What did I tell you?" Oliver said with great energy, looking round at Sybil and Andrew. "I knew it. As soon as I saw him striding along there, I said he was going to ask where everybody was, as if they were being sordid and degenerate. . . ."

"They're stirring," Andrew said, "and Meg's seeing to breakfast. Hungry?"

"Yes, man," I told him, and leaning close to Oliver said distinctly, as if speaking to a half-witted foreigner, "There's nothing like an early swim to bring the best out in you. I feel as if I could write *The Origin of the Species* now."

He looked at me steadily. "You're evil," he said at last. "Plain evil, Mahler. Were you ever in the army?"

"Yes."

"I bet you were the sort who got up before the bugler and shined your shoes and made your bed and *walked* to parade or whatever you call it."

He rose and shuffled across the tiles into the house.

141

"Is he really like that," I asked Sybil, laughing.

"Not really. It's just a legend he has built up so that I won't be tempted to talk to him in the mornings." She hesitated, gave me a quick, thoughtful glance and said quietly, "She's a strange one, isn't she?"

"Who? Oh, Joan. Yes, she's strange all right. Coming up with her a while ago I could see why you people feel the way you do about her. There's a . . . what's the word? . . . A sort of rectitude about her. But quiet. Much too quiet. As if she's afraid she might demand too much from you under false pretences. And it's not the usual exhibitionist way. It's as if she's a prisoner under a sentence that's much too harsh. Only she's the judge too. And the judge and the prisoner are in agreement. The one gives justice but no mercy and the other doesn't whine. But maybe I'm being sentimental. Perhaps it's all calculated to attract attention."

"You don't really think that, do you?" Andrew asked anxiously. "About her doing it to attract attention to herself, I mean?"

"No. It was one of those thoughts that pass when you're trying to define something, and I just said it."

"You should have known her in the old days," he said then. He bent over and rested his forearms across his knees; his heavy, symmetrical face—already growing the uncomplicated, patriarchal lines of his occupation—was suddenly serious. "She's not really like how you saw her last night, you know, Stefan."

"That's what Oliver told me. I wish you both wouldn't go on as if you have to sell the idea of her to me. I quite like her already. Man, if she's your friend, then she's mine too. You know that."

"Yes, I know that. It's only that you saw her at her worst last night, and it's not easy to get over first impressions sometimes. But she isn't just a mixed-up drunk who can't keep her hands off a good-looking boy."

142

"I never thought that. Or if I did, I realized this morning that it wasn't so simple. You needn't defend her to me, Andrew. I take people as they come. I've had a lot of practice at doing that."

"I'm sorry *I* didn't know her before all this business started," Sybil said. "If I had, maybe I'd know what really goes on inside her now. I don't like feeling responsible and protective about anybody, the way we all feel about Joan. It's not good for either side."

"Yes," Andrew said, as if breaking a silent exchange with himself. "She really was a girl then, Stefan. Before I went to the war. After I came back even. Before she got herself all tangled up with a shoddy piece of goods like poor old Ian."

"You were in love with her?"

"No. . . . Well, yes. . . . In a peculiar way. A lot of us were at one time or another. Ever since we began to notice that a hair-ribbon wasn't the only difference between a girl and a boy. But it wasn't simply that. . . . She had a quality that's hard to describe. Even when we were children." He made an irritable, searching gesture, and looked at me as though I had asked him to find something put away, at an inconvenient moment. "I can't put these things the way Oliver can, but you ask him if I'm not right. . . . She had this odd quality of feeling. If anything happened to hurt somebody she knew, she felt it with passion. Not like most people feel sympathy, in the head. It really hurt her too. I don't mean physical hurt, you understand, but the sort of damage people do each other when they're cruel or cowardly or just careless. And she had this same ability to feel good for you, to really take pleasure in whatever good had happened to you. She didn't make a fuss about it; you just knew that she had the same glow you did." He stopped, with the expression, half-ashamed and half-defiant, of someone surprised in an intimate, necessary act. "How d'you put these things into words, eh?"

"Go on," I said, "I know what you mean."

143

"I remember once," he went on, "that Oliver and me and the rest of us like Johnny Gort and Carl Brandt used to know a chap from the country who won a scholarship to the college. This was before Cayuna began to get civilized, when people used to walk round the colour business as if it was a dirty secret. Anyway this chap was black and his old man had a little dry goods business up at Turn-Around, and the son had won this scholarship. That sort of thing. But he could do everything in any game about ten times better than the rest of us put together. You know, one of those people who think at twice the normal speed and make their bodies and their hands do whatever they think. And he was nice with it. Not only nice, he was the sort of boy whom other boys centre around. Just enough of a bully to be respected, but funny as hell and ready to start the things you think of but don't dare. Well, we took him up. He was always at my place, or Oliver's, or at the Gort's. And of course everybody was glad to meet him. In that way. After a game, or on a Saturday morning to listen to jazz records. Then one day Johnny Gort gave a hell of a party for his sixteenth birthday, and this chap came round on his bicycle that afternoon to lend Johnny some boxing magazines he'd collected, but of course nobody had told him anything about there being a party. . . . He came half-way up the drive, I guess, and stopped when he realized that it wasn't just a few people listening to records, and Johnny went down the driveway before he could turn round and talked to him and took the magazines because there wasn't anything else he could do. And then this chap rode off. He looked back once. I don't think he meant to, but at sixteen you can't help a thing like that. . . . We all felt pretty uncomfortable but carried on as if it hadn't happened until we forgot it or put it aside or something. It was just one of those things. For everybody except Joan. . . . She'd been dancing with somebody when it all began and she just left him and went and sat in a corner for about ten minutes after it had happened, with her eyes shining, not cry-

144

ing but the way you see sometimes when the tears can't come. All of us kept looking at her and pretending not to. Then she got up, went over to Johnny and said, 'But, Johnny, you couldn't have done that,' and walked straight out of the house, down the drive and out of the gate. She didn't even go to collect her handbag. I can remember the way she spoke to Johnny. She wasn't accusing him, really. She just couldn't believe it yet. And the way she looked when she walked past me: sick, as if she'd caught her fingers in a door. . . . But you know something else? I think that Joan left that damned party not only because a boy she hardly knew had been hurt so rottenly, but because she felt that she had no right to enjoy herself anymore; that she was somehow responsible because it hadn't occurred to her before that he hadn't been invited. . . . You see what I'm getting at?"

"Yes, man. You can tell a story. You have an eye for the details. What happened then?"

"Nothing. We all felt embarrassed. Confused, really. Especially Cecile, her sister. The one Oliver married, who died. She was furious. I suppose she thought some of what Joan had done would rub off on her. . . . But I only told you about this because I was involved and I've always remembered it. It's like having a negative of the real photograph. . . ." He looked at me interrogatively, as though asking me to confirm his metaphor, and I nodded back. "I mean, ordinarily, she was something quite special. It wasn't that she was the best looking girl in our set. She's a handsome woman, but Cecile, for instance, was just goddam beautiful. When *she* married a little shrimp like Oliver you could hear a lot of men asking why all over Cayuna. But that woman inside there now could make you feel like you were opening a present. . . . You know what women are like, Stefan. Before they're married. You take a girl out and fool around and she likes it, because it's flattering and part of the business of selecting. She likes you, too, but whatever she gives is in return. . . ."

"Well, thank you, Andrew," Sybil said. "That was very nicely put."

"Oh, you know what I mean," he said. "That's just the way it goes. I didn't mean there's anything wrong in it."

"She's getting at you," I told him. "That's part of the game too. She knows you weren't referring to her. Go on."

"Joan wasn't like that, though. When you went out with her, she gave you the impression that your enjoyment was the most important thing. . . . I mean that she was enjoying your pleasure and happy that she could provide it. No, that's not it, but I can't put it any better. . . . God, she was a sweet girl, Stefan."

"Sweet!" I said. "She sounds a walking disaster to me."

"How d'you mean?" He gave a blink of confusion, as though I had played a silly practical joke.

"Just what I say. And I'm speaking from a sound instinct of self-preservation. That sort of unguarded intensity is bloody dangerous. Like a shotgun with the safety-catch off. You never know who's going to get sprayed."

"I don't understand you. I don't understand a word you're saying."

"Sybil does," I said. "Don't you, Sybil?"

"I suppose so," she said. "I've known her the last four years. Since I met Oliver. And she was well on to the way she is now, even then. But I can still get an idea of what she must have been like. Only what you call 'intensity', I call her damned innocence."

"Yes," I agreed, "that's a much better term for it."

"That's a new name for it," Andrew said. "She has slept with half of Cayuna since Ian chucked her out, and he had cause enough to do that then, poor bastard. He had more horns than a cattle pen."

"I wasn't thinking of that," she said impatiently. "I meant the sort of incident you described, and the way she must have given herself to a *nyamps* like Gordon. Only children should be allowed to feel like that. Because when an adult does, parti-

146

cularly a woman, and things go sour, or somebody fails her, then she begins going to hell in a hand cart."

I said idly, "Have you ever painted her?" thinking that, if she had, the penetrating astigmatism of her artist's eye might have caught a clearer likeness than Andrew's words or hers: idly, too, because I wanted to conceal from myself how fearful I had suddenly become that my place might be taken by this stranger for whom they all seemed to have such an obsessive, fraternal regard.

"Only a charcoal sketch," Sybil said, and pulled a disparaging mouth. "Soon after I met her. But it didn't come out good. I got her all wrong because I wasn't looking at her properly." She grinned, as though mocking herself kindly. "I was crazy mad with jealousy the day I sketched her and determined not to show it until I was good and ready."

"Jealous? Why?"

"I'd just found out where Oliver spent his nights sometimes when he got drunk and didn't come home. . . ."

"Oh, yes. She was going on about that last night."

"It was when I was doing the mural for Reception House and I'd asked her to model for the octoroon mistress in the ball scene, before I found out about her and Oliver. I nearly went for her while I was doing the sketch. I was just waiting for her to say something, the slightest hint that would really set me off. When she didn't, I decided on a big dirty row the next time Oliver didn't come back. I had it all planned. Big drama. Anyway, about a week later, it must have been nearly four in the morning and Oliver hadn't come in. I didn't have a car in those days, so I walked all the way from Harbour Road to her bungalow at Saviour Spring. Can you imagine! Me one and God at four o'clock in the morning, going up that road like a lunatic. I didn't even stop to ask myself what I was goin' do if he wasn't there. But of course he was. Nearly asleep on the divan in the drawing-room, but talking and talking as if he would never stop, with Joan holding him the way I'd hold a

147

baby. She was drunk too, but a funny sort of steady drunk with having to take care of Oliver. She didn't even look surprised when I came charging in—they'd left the front door open—but just smiled at me as if she was trying to comfort me and went on holding Oliver. He didn't even know I was there. Then he started to be sick so we took him into the bathroom and held him until he was finished and washed his face."

"And then?" I asked.

"Then we put him to bed between us. I was nearly dead from that walk; I'd really knocked foot, you see—and the next morning I made Joan drive us back to my place so I could get them something to eat."

"And you weren't jealous after that?"

"No, man. It sounds funny, but I was grateful. Whenever Ollie took off and didn't come back I used to lie there hoping he was with her and not on a bankside some place. I knew she could give him something I couldn't. At least, she could add to whatever I could do, and I wasn't any more jealous of her than I would have been of a doctor."

And yet, a few minutes later, when we were all sitting down to breakfast at the long, beautiful table (which made the inept proportions of the room appear extrinsic as one would hardly notice an ugly frame around a masterpiece), I looked at Joan Culpepper across the table and felt again that odd sense of having no reference point. She had pinned a big woolly white towel about her head, and her face seemed to have little to do with the woman Andrew and Sybil had described to me, quite other than the face I had seen the night before. It was not sad or emptied, but still. Even when she smiled or chatted into the merging cross-currents of talk, she never appeared outside that expression of gentle deference: I longed to see her animated, like the other women, by some imperious and reassuring use of sex.

Part Two
RETURN

6

★

I

The most sinister effect of exile by violence is the growth of a grubby and insidious egotism. With its severance from all the old sources of nourishment, the self becomes a bed-ridden stranger for whom one is unwillingly responsible. Merely to keep it alive requires an incessant attention to sordid details, a numbing routine of watchfulness and broken sleep.

This is an area of experience that not even Oliver understands, really, when I have tried to explain it to him. How could he? Not even Joan. How could she? They were both brought up to a life in which family, friends and the very air they breathe fit like a skin, whole, without a break in the supple tissue. They understand an inflammation of the part, but not its slow, independent starvation. . . . An hour ago I came back from the window and lifted the sheet down from Joan's curled up, naked body. I put my hand on the bottom of her belly and caressed her gently until, in the moonlight, I could dimly see the face of consciousness coming up from sleep, like a face itself nearing the surface from the opaque depths of a pool.

"Stefan?" she protested drowsily.

"Who else?"

"You!" she said, still protesting but with a counterpoint of smug resignation. "You're greedy, aren't you? What's the time?"

"Just gone three."

"Oh God, Stefan. Why aren't you asleep?"

"I was thinking."

151

"About what?"

"About you."

"That's nice. You ought to be sleeping but I'm glad you were thinking about me . . . my sweet greedy old darling." And, a few minutes later, in a voice from the back of a winding cave, "It's nice sometimes when you're sleepy, isn't it? Are you asleep, darling?"

"Nearly," I lied, and listened until I heard the even sighing of her breath against her pillow. . . . Would she understand if, tomorrow morning (this morning, really) I told her that the desire with which I woke her was not for her, but a moment of celebration which I wanted to share? But I can't think that she would: certainly not in any words that I could find to tell her. Without some appreciation of the invalid years, my attempt to explain would only confuse her. As Bernice, even, was always a little bewildered when I used to call her My America! My new-found-land! and try to describe what it was she had begun to do for me. But then she lived within a splendid simplicity of fleshly confidence, an unconscious relish for the immediate and tangible, an eclectic acceptance of each moment good or bad: her wonderful kindness was the instinct of a resilient heart, and like some tough hybrid she could have flourished in any climate. Unlike me, or her father, she never questioned her own reflection.

And perhaps this is what created between Marcus Heneky and myself a current of . . . not sympathy or affection, but of wry recognition: the fact that in each other we detected the same ailment and hurt of the psyche: we saluted each other with the distant yet intimate understanding of two veterans determined to survive the same campaign. . . . Strange the way we took to each other. Almost resentfully, as though attraction was a weakness. Almost as though we both regretted a false past which had to be redeemed and which would never permit us more than a cautious exchange.

I went to see him at the hospital a week or so after we brought him down from Gran' Dum, the day after Bernice told me he was well enough to have visitors. He was sitting up in the bed, his back propped against two folded pillows, and reading a periodical with an expression of mingled severity and thoroughness, like a judge hearing the evidence of a notorious criminal. Two Sons of Sheba were sitting, one on each side of the bed, following the quick scan of his eyes with the rapt participation of those to whom reading is not merely a skill but an enviable adventure.

He looked up as I stopped at the foot of the bed and nodded stiffly. It was a summary challenge rather than a greeting, and yet I had the impression that it was more the obligatory suspicion of a good custodian than personal antagonism.

I said: "How are you, Mister Heneky? I thought I'd come and look for you. Don't let me interrupt your reading."

The long, obdurate chin, faintly stubbled now with grey, sank a little further on to his chest, and in the shadows cast by his heavy, lowered eyebrows, I could see a moment's scintillation of that hard, cavalier gaiety I had noticed up at Gran' Dum. "I soon talk to you," he said and resumed his reading. The two Sons of Sheba swivelled their gaze from me back to him as if they were following an order in drill.

He was much thinner than when we had brought him, for even in these days typhoid fever is nothing to take lightly. His body in the drab hospital pyjamas had a faded, boneless frailty, as though blood, tissue and skeleton were restoring themselves slowly inside him; his grey tousled head and restless face were too large and graphic for the exhausted flesh to which they were attached.

We waited in silence while he finished reading. One of the beds next to his was empty and I took the visitor's chair and brought it over. The Son of Sheba on this side was a short, browny black man, with a face of sweet, calm idiocy to which his beard and long, plaited locks only added an emphasis of

153

gentle, pastoral holiness. He smiled at me benignly as I sat, and immediately returned his attention to Marcus Heneky. The periodical was an old, airmail copy of an English left-wing review and I wondered what they had found in it that related so closely to their strict, exclusive preoccupations. Then Marcus Heneky closed it, flung it to the foot of his bed and settled back into the pillows with an impatient twitch.

"Den what it say, Reveren'?" the man on the other side of the bed asked, almost timidly.

"What it say?" Marcus Heneky replied. I had forgotten the protean facility of his voice. "I tell you what it say, Ralston. It say lies. Lies from the heart of Babylon to confuse you an' weaken your spirit. . . ."

"Dat is what I tell de bredren, Reveren'. I tell dem, 'How a white man can know what happen in Africa?' But some of dem doubt say dat it true."

"Sometimes I think say that we was meant to suffer," Marcus Heneky said harshly. "What sort of people we? The white man write one little piece of false witness an' we ready to bow down before it like the children of Israel before the golden calf. I tell you, Ralston, an' you, Albert, that the day of Africa is near. That Zion's glory under the great Emperor of the black race is at hand. An' the white man and the brown man know this too an' will do all in them power to stop we. When them can't kill we or enslave we, them will lie. Tell the brethren that, an' tell them to pray to the one living God of Jeremiah for guidance among our enemies."

" 'Is not the Lord in Zion? Is not her kind in her?' " quoted Albert beside me, " 'Why have they provoked me to anger with their graven images and with strange vanities?' " His gentle, thoughtless face was raised, luminous with a contented adoration. Then he looked down and said humbly, "We need you, Reveren'. Is t'ree Sunday we don't hear de Word like you can preach it. You comin' out soon?"

"Soon soon, Albert," Marcus Heneky said. "Take courage,

my brother. If they did all have faith like you, is what a light we could shine into wickedness. . . . But wait," he added suddenly. "I don't introduce you to this gentleman here. Him is Doctor Mahler. The one I did tell you about. Doctor! These are two members of the church . . . Ralston Edwards an' Albert Craig."

We all exchanged nods, and again Albert gave me that smile of abstract, unclouded benevolence: Ralston looked at me steadily, with an open, careful indifference, then asked flatly, "You ever meet any o' we before, doc?"

"Yes," I said. "Once, down at Caymanas."

"An' what you t'ink o' we?"

"I don't know enough about you to say."

"Doctor don't want say," Marcus said with a steely playfulness in his voice, his face bland. "Him don't want tell the poor black people that them don't worth nothing."

"Oh no, Mister Heneky," I said cheerfully. "You mustn't say that, because it isn't the truth. . . . But I want to ask *you* something now?" I looked at Ralston.

"What?"

"Why did that one I met down at Caymanas try to tempt me into violence?"

I used the biblical syntax for my question deliberately.

"How that happen?" Ralston asked quickly, and straightened.

I told them about the day down at Caymanas evenly, without complaint or emotion. When I had finished, Albert shook his head in mild, sad disapproval; Ralston and Marcus Heneky looked at each other with unsurprised vexation and concern.

"Dat shouldn't happen," Ralston said heavily. "Dat not good. Not good at all. God never call man to waste what man make."

"No," Marcus Heneky agreed. "That was a bad thing. You see how Babylonian oppression can turn the weak to wildness an' shame." He looked at me with sudden, serious interest, as though seeing me for the first time. "Then why you never tell

155

the police 'bout this, Doctor Mahler? Them would catch the man for you, you know?"

"No," I said. "I didn't want that. It wasn't enough to lock a free man up for." I rose and put the chair beside the empty bed. "I must be going now, sir." I told him and gave him my hand. "I'm glad you're getting better so quickly."

He took my hand slowly, almost reflectively, his eyes never leaving my face. I shook hands with the others, gestured to him once more and turned to go.

"Hi! Samaritan!" he called softly, with a tight smile.

"Yes?" I said from the polished gangway.

"I never had no chance to thank you for the lift."

"Nothing to thank me for, Mister Heneky. I had to come back to town and there was plenty of space."

"All the same, I thank you. Come an' see me one time. . . . No, no, not here. At my place, when I strong again. Ask Bernice where I stay."

"I will," I told him. "Thank you."

I went down the ward between the beds and the stares of the other patients, impassively curious behind their sickness as the eyes of animals behind zoo bars, to the open, wide doorway. At the doorway I turned and waved to him again, and he lifted his hand slightly, still gazing at me with that truncated, thoughtful smile.

II

The Pure Church of Africa Triumphant, so Marcus Heneky was to tell me with utter conviction, owed its origin to a moment of strange choice: an experience quite outside any natural law. He no more questioned what had happened to him than he doubted the truth of Bernice being his daughter. Both were aspects of the same instinct of creation. . . .

He had been standing before the oven door of his little bakery in Morgan's Lane, waiting for that incalculable second when the bread has reached perfection, and he was suddenly snatched away.

For an instant he saw his soulless body, "like an empty flour bag", he said, lying on the floor before his oven in Cayuna and then he was hovering above a track in Africa on which a long coffle of slaves had halted while a white man flogged a prone, spreadeagled black to death. He described the slaver in extraordinary detail, down to the freckles on his sun-yellowed hands and the fact that he had a fiery sweat rash on his scrotum that brought him to the edge of madness by the end of each day's march. He could even imitate the white man's accent, his own soft, broad Cayunan vowels changing effortlessly into a nasal stammer unlike any modern English intonation I know. And he remembered, too, the smell exuded by the coffle as many of the slaves began to defecate or urinate with sympathetic fear of pain, and the fresh odours were trapped in the still, thick air between the trees under a blazing sun. The black, he knew, had been an incorrigible recalcitrant on the journey from the interior and had, at last, killed one of the half-breed guards with his chain while attempting to escape. His slow death was not only a punishment but an example. In that moment, Marcus Heneky had the freedom of both bodies. He could enter the white man who by now hypnotized by a sense of exquisite, almost fluid oneness with his whip, swung it with the precision and regularity of an automaton: or he could enter the black, a segment of whose spine now showed in a pink-white patch between two pulpy ridges of crimson flesh, but who, incredibly, still lived and was conscious. The moment of decision was beyond description, he said. As if a pair of ice-cold iron hands were stretching his bowels to opposite ends of the sky. It was not death he feared but pain. Then he entered the black, "like water into a glass". The pain was such that he no longer felt it *on* his flesh, but inside, as though it were distending what was left of his skin and would burst it, literally, and force his eyeballs across the clearing like bullets. There was no thought, only the sensation that he would disintegrate suddenly with an accumulation of anguish too great to be contained. He ejaculated twice before he died. That night he was born again to one of the women in the coffle whose labour had been brought on by her spasms of terror. When, many days later, they had been shackled in layers in the hold of the slaver and battened down, the slaves became really terrified: not the ordinary shrinking of the flesh, which is a commonplace like hunger, but a dreadful shrivelling of the soul faced with an incomprehensible journey in darkness. On the first occasion when they were brought on deck, they had been so relieved to see the same sun, and to be told, with rough, commercial good-nature by the slaver's captain, that they were only being taken across a big river to work—as they had done all their lives any-way—that their souls had filled again, but into the white man's shape. All except his. He had returned, through the centuries and many births, to the "empty flour bag" on the floor of the bakery. He had picked himself up, removed a batch of ruined loaves and known that from now he must devote himself to redeeming the misshapen souls of Africa's captive children. . . .

"You see, boy," he said to me that first afternoon I went to visit him in his shabby little house on the edge of the parched savannah under the drab, bony foothills at the head of the harbour. "You see how it stay? God put the truth of them-selves in the heart of each race: to search for an' love in His name. But your race now, the white man race, take mine away from his truth. For the heart of the black man never make the journey with his body. . . . You understand what I say?"

His deep eyes searched my face with a quenched, puzzled intentness, as if he still felt the torment of his harrowing vision and wanted me to confirm its meaning.

"Yes," I said, "I think so."

For a few seconds he continued to stare at me, then his square, lion's head dipped in a little satisfied nod.

"Yes," he said. "You understand little bit. That's why I tell

158

you all this. . . . It is God your white people take mine from. God an' pride. An' until both of these restore how the black man will ever know himself, eh? How him will ever find deliverance?"

"Deliverance?" I asked him. "You mean freedom?"

"Yes," he said simply, "but not what you think. Not freedom to imitate the white man like we do now. I mean deliverance from the past. That is what destiny is. That is why my race can't find our destiny. Because our past lie abandoned in Africa." He looked down at the bright, sticky linoleum cover of the little table at which we were sitting; a sudden, defiant tenderness had lightened his harsh, ardent face. "It is why Bernice an' me did quarrel. She don't understand. The white man's blood in her make her blind." He shook his head slowly, and added in a shy, defeated voice, "Is the sin I have. I did love her before God call me to witness, an' I can't stop love her now, even though she bow down to Babylon's idols."

When I was going he said, "If you ever passing an' have the time, come in an' look for me."

It was through him that I now began to meet those from the loosely articulated, estranged world within world of Cayuna. They all seemed to come to him eventually, pulled towards the broad rock of his certitude by hidden currents. Each of them, like a severed limb, twitching with impossible nostalgias of connection. Names and titles shaken like green fruit from an orchard of stunted, untended minds: The Sons of Sheba, Adherents of the Black Christ, Ethiopian Communist Federation Inc., The Brethren of Appointed Zion, The Society for the Salvation of African Israel. Differing in details of belief, they all shared the same vigil at the scene of a great historic murder as they waited for the sacrificed man to rise again. And they all came to Marcus Heneky to replenish a concept of themselves he explored for them in that purely compelling, intricate voice.

He was, I think, indifferent to the varieties of dogma with

159

which he was faced. To him, God was a question of attitude, and any external of custom that strengthened this attitude was acceptable.

"It is that we people have to believe," he said one Sunday morning before service in the church next to his house, and pointed at the wall above his pulpit, to a long silk banner, green, red and yellow in colour, with the text *One God, one aim, one destiny* embroidered in black thread. "It is that belief we will take an' overthrow your people, Stefan." He looked at me with open, sly mockery, as though inviting me to taste the essential comedy of our generous inclination in a world that had so irreconcilably opposed us. Then he stared again at the banner and added in a tone of immense weariness, "But it is to drive that into the black people. They think that God will give we ourselves for nothing. Without suffering." He turned and walked to the open side of the "church"— for it was only a large shed, its zinc roof supported by six wooden pillars, behind his house, next to the deep gully that bordered raggedly the tawny grass and grey-green *dildo* of the as yet unexploited savannah under the foothills. (Last week when I drove out to the airport it was under the bulldozers, being prepared for a housing development scheme.) "But why this, boy?" he asked, his back to me as he leaned against one of the pillars and looked out over the faded, shimmering savannah, too hot and airless for my class in Cayuna, too spacious and potentially profitable for his. "Why God can only bring His children to truth through suffering?" He swung round suddenly, his arms folded across the old, neat, brown linen jacket and waistcoat, his heavy head thrust to me in an eager, scenting fashion. "I'll tell you something, though," he said. "The day we answer that one, then we will know too much to allow any man to suffer again." He came close and put his hand on my shoulder and shook me with a sort of brusque, hapless consolation. "But by the time that happen, Stefan boy, you an' me is both long dead."

Later on that night I said to Bernice: "What an enormously complex man your father is. I think that's what all religious leaders must have in common. Different levels of meaning that need constant interpretation. I don't mean ordinary priests and rabbis. People want *them* to be all of a piece, like politicians. But if a man like your father is to attract followers, he must be difficult to read. Otherwise they feel they're not getting value."

"Him!" she chuckled fondly, but with an absent, maternal patronage because we were sitting in the middle of her bed, in our underwear, legs tucked under like yogis, playing cards. "That old man an' him ideas. Him will be the death of me yet. If I didn't stand up over him three times a week an' make him eat, him would fall down from hunger an' never know."

Since the day we had brought old Heneky down from Gran' Dum, I had begun to understand something of how completely these two possessed each other: they must have unconsciously sought their quarrel, I had decided, as the very rich and secure seek the appearance of simplicity or danger. Unrelieved luxury, even of love, can bore the instinctively adventurous. It was a relationship that gave me a feeling both of envy and obscure participation, like a one-legged man watching a friend perform some brisk yet uncalculated activity.

"How many?" I asked Bernice, holding the pack over the counterpane between us.

"Three," she said, and watched with still, lunatic anticipation as I floated the cards to the bed. Gambling, in any form, was one of her many unresisted passions: the only one, perhaps, for which she was ludicrously unequipped, because luck, like beauty in a courtesan, or good hands in a pianist, is a natural attribute of the born gambler; one for which no subsequent dedication can ever compensate. And poor Bernice, who carried the stud book in her head, knew the rules and elaborations of every card game ever invented, provided a substantial part of his income for the odious, darkly experienced little orphan boy who ran the illicit *peaka-peow* tickets about town for the

161

Chinese merchants, was always coming unstuck for lack of this donation of nature. It was enough for me to know that she had money on a horse for me to place my five shillings on another, any other. Fortunately for her, men in Cayuna won't gamble seriously with women, and she was forced to confine her card losses to the penny ante, two-handed poker she played with me, at which I monotonously won.

"Well?" I said, as she pulled a carefully unrevealing face over her cards.

"It cost you threepence to see me."

"I'm raising you. It'll cost you another three to see me."

"Oh, it like that, eh? All right, mister. Here's my three an' a next three." I thought this over for a histrionic few seconds; to give her pleasure; I was sure I had her outfaced. And she added: "Him is a good old man, you know? It just that ideas fill up his head an' won't give him rest. If only he never sell the bakery. If my mother was alive then she would have never let him. And if I did know say what was happening I would have call him down so until him change him mind. But is one day, I come back from delivering—is I used to drive the little cart an' mule we have—an' him tell me say that the shop sell, the flat above the shop sell, an' him going into preaching. Preaching!" She snorted without rancour, with the same genuinely ironic appreciation that so often exploded like an exhilarating booby-trap in her father's talk. "If it was only real preaching. But look at what it come to! All that foolishness about Africa. . . . What you have?"

"Full house," I said, tossing the closed cards down and beginning to pull the money towards me.

"Wait!" she exclaimed, with almost scared triumph. "Four of a kind, mister. That is all mine."

"You're joking! Here, let me see!"

"Hi! You think I would cheat you?"

"No, but I want to see this. I'd like to frame these, Bernice."

"Cho!" she said, handing me the cards and bending over to

162

scrabble for the money, her unbound breasts dropping solidly against the tenuous nylon of her slip. She flung herself back on the pillow, tossing her stout legs and rattling the money in her fist. I think she was really a little defiantly apprehensive about having won. The skirt of her slip fell in ripples and settled above her wide, able hips. She stretched her hand out—I was moodily shuffling the cards—and pulled me down until my cheek was resting on the broad, padded drumskin of her stomach. (Every so often now I catch accidentally from a sweating girl in a crowded store, in the sneaking air currents of a bar, the scent of that same nearly cheap, unsubtle powder with which Bernice used to dust herself, and it nibbles at my visceral memory as stingingly as a riff of forgotten vulgar music that once pulped against the background of a formative experience: as a reminder of Chanel returns me to that night in the *Residenztheater* when I woke to beauty against my sister's opulent breasts.) She waited in silence to see if I was ready, yet, to follow up her cosy invitation to love and then, rubbing my hair, she said: "All that African foolishness now. What him think say Africa have to do with we here? Is here we belong now, an' is here we must work an' pray God for guidance. Is only the wild men him gather round him, an' him, think different." She sucked her teeth in the indescribable Cayunan cluck that implies mildly exasperated yet sympathetic comprehension of folly.

"You know what?" I said, exercising a lover's privilege to tease affectionately. "You're a hopeless bourgeois."

"What that means?" Her voice was constricted and I knew she must have shifted her gaze from the ceiling and dropped her chin against her chest to look at me. She tugged my hair playfully. "Come on, what that means? Something bad?"

"It means you believe in respectability. You don't approve of the old boy's church because it isn't respectable, like all the other churches."

"Of course I like things stay respectable," she said axiomatically. "Is only a fair man and a bought woman can afford to not be respectable in this island." She sat up with a smooth heave of her powerful body, catching my head between her belly and the tops of her thighs. Almost without thought, I rolled over so that my neck rested just above the neutral territory of her knees. She wrinkled her forehead questioningly.

"What's wrong?" she asked.

"Nothing."

"Headache bother you again?"

"No, no. Tell me. Did your father love your mother?"

"Lord yes, man. When she did die, him just sit for three days like him did hope God would take him too. Him wouldn't even go near the oven. Him say that his sorrow would enter the bread an' hurt people. That is a man can love, you see. Like a woman."

"What would he have done if she hadn't died? I mean, you say she was so fair, she was almost white. He would have had a bit of problem there, wouldn't he?"

"I don't know. Him tell me once that God was merciful an' took her before giving him a vision so that he wouldn't be tempted to fall from the truth. But another time he say that the African blood in her would have saved her. He don't know himself, to tell the truth." She shook her head impatiently. "Him is so full of this Africa, an' how black man will only get justice there. I tell him say one time, 'Papa,' I say, 'a man feel like you, can speak like you, why you don't join with Mister Douglas an' the P.R.P? Him want justice too an' need support. Him will lead Cayuna into opportunity for all.' But him only shout an' say that Mister Douglas is a Judas steer for the white butchers. Is that really cause us to quarrel, for I know say what this island was like before Mister Douglas an' his party begin shake it, an' I know say, too, that everything, from a baby in a woman's belly to a whole country, need time before it grow into fullness."

I knew that she had an unqualified admiration for Eugene Douglas—leader of the Peoples Radical Party, one of those austerely handsome, leather brown mixtures, like Margaret

Fabricus, one sees in Cayuna—but I had not realized her concept was so articulate. I sat up and rested my back against the footboard and looked, with a sombre heart, at the half-naked woman whose fearless generosity had embraced my lust, my selfishness, my sophisticated pretences and informed them with her own incarnate gallantry of spirit. I thought: you must have sensed the incest in me, from the first; the way you know when one of your customers is embarrassed; you must have felt those two women who filled my childhood with their luscious, too demonstrative, fleshly proofs of adoration and for whose loss my sex was in permanent mourning. Yes. You must have known this in that practised heart of yours, although the idea analysed and stated would shock you; and now you have liberated me, made me independent of the highly charged, competitive, female attention which, like a little sultan, I enjoyed for my first ten years. I haven't dreamed about sleeping with my mother or Hannah since I've met you.

She looked up from her casual shuffling of the pack and asked, "You want another round? I feel like my luck turn."

"Sure," I said. "I still can't believe that you actually won."

"Good," she said and began to deal. "What's wrong, boy?"

"Nothing, Bernice."

"You have trouble up at the university?"

"No."

"Papa say any foolishness today that upset you?"

"No!"

"Then what? Is two hours you here now an' you not easy. You don't smile once. An' I so like to see you smile. You look so nice. What happen? You can tell me."

"Nothing is wrong!" I protested with the emphatic petulance of guilty concealment. "God's sweet sake, Bernice! How many times do I have to tell you that?"

For this was five weeks after I had been to the Fabricus party and met Joan Culpepper. And I was now in love with her and she would have nothing to do with me.

7

*

I

When did it begin? With every other emotion it is possible to define the moment, the circumstances of response. Admiration, hatred, contempt, pity, boredom, fear, even liking, all have their accessible reasons. Only love enters unobtrusively, furtively, and lodges to trouble you with its suddenly announced presence: like an uninvited, ruthlessly demanding guest ringing a bell for attention in a room you cannot find. A few months ago, at some reception, when Oliver made one of his rare surrenders to tipsiness, I overheard him disturbing one of those well-intentioned, determinedly liberal, wholesome and indefinably irritating Americans who wear their genteel seriousness like an academic gown: one is always tempted to cause them pain until one remembers their real decency, their unconstrained kindness, their enviable anxiety to be of use. "Love!" Oliver was barking at this woman. "Don't believe what you have been conditioned to accept. It's a venereal infection. Like syphilis. A side effect of capitalism and the mobile unit of society. It only came into existence when feudalism began to decay. A neurosis. A huge psychic hire purchase acquisition to keep up with the Joneses. I'm not talking about homosexual love," he added with quick concession as if she had pounced on an omitted line in his argument. "That's natural and healthy. Like the love of parents for children. But this business between men and women! We can't do without it now and it's more destructive than tobacco." He continued the sort of talk that, remembering it in the morning, one winces apologetically; but perhaps he was obscurely aware of one essence. Our intuitive vocabulary does speak of "making love", in a way that, for instance, we do not speak of "making hate", reminding us that this is the only act to which we give the name of the emotion.

So did I begin to love Joan when I found myself unexpectedly in bed with her that night I took her home to oblige Oliver? Or was it the next morning when I saw her in the raw, unarmoured sensitivity of my hangover? Or had it happened already, from the time that she staggered into my life at the Fabricus house?

I don't know. I only know that one morning I awoke in the tranquil and appreciative condition with which I usually returned to the day, and that by the next morning, at the same time, I had shuddered to a halt, was alerted by a novel need and hope which filled me with something like panic and for which I wanted no cure. . . .

That night I had to take a promised article down to Oliver. It was something he had talked me into doing—a layman's guide to the house insects of Cayuna—and I had left it until the afternoon before the *Newsletter* went to press.

At about six o'clock I drove into the city, parked in the empty street outside the *Newsletter* building, and went up the stairs to Oliver's office.

"My oath, Mahler," he said, half-way through the thousand or so words I had typed, "you write a weird, chromatic prose. No. I like. It's arresting. But one senses a *doppelganger* lurching around somewhere in there, my boy."

On the other side of the huge editorial desk, layers deep now in galleys and papers, he looked competent, contented and seraphically attractive, like a bland, worldly wise small boy doing a man's job and doing it well.

"It's because I'm just learning not to think in German when I write," I answered. "I don't at all when I talk, because I catch the flavour, but when putting down words alone, it all comes back."

"Isn't there some proverb that says 'a man who has two languages has two hearts'? I think that's it."

"I've never heard it, but it sounds just the sort of thing that becomes a proverb. It only means that a man like that can make twice as big a fool of himself as the monoglot."

He laughed and got up, leaving my manuscript on the tattered blotter-pad which was so ink-saturated I felt any new drop would run off it as off glass.

"Busy?" he asked.

"No. Why?"

"Come up to the House with me for a little. There's something I want to hear. Andrew's speaking."

"All right," I said. "What time are you eating?"

"Oh, when I get back. I'll nip out and get something. I won't be away from here until after midnight."

"Good. Then I'll eat with you."

We drove up to the House of Representatives in his car. In the streets, the sable and purple shadows had begun to lap against the walls, but the sky was green as a new leaf, and the lamps gave no more light than so many lemon ices on long sticks. There were only a few people, walking as if surrendered to random currents, or standing on street corners with an air of no purpose. The last workers had already gone and it was too early for gregariousness: the bars and parlours, when I looked in over the half-doors, were sparsely filled. A party of cruise-boat tourists passed us in a big, open taxi, on their way down to the Palm Bank Hotel probably. They gave an impression of boredom and anxiously resolute eagerness, as though they had long concealed the limitations of sightseeing but still attended on adventure with diminishing optimism. I smiled idly to myself, realizing how wrong I probably was about them.

When we reached the House, Oliver took me into the press gallery, settling himself expectantly on the edge of his seat and leaning his arms on the rail above the chamber. I sat back and let the debate fall on me as it came, because I was not really interested.

It was the last stages of a tortuously complex agricultural bill, and I knew as much about it as I had read in the paper: that it made it obligatory for the big buyers of produce and the large estates which took crops from the smaller farmers, to pay according to world prices at time of purchase and not according to local fluctuations, unless the local value was higher.

As we sat, Littleford, the opposition leader was denouncing every clause in the bill, with the intoxicated, happy rage of a man to whom the sound of his own voice is almost a sexual experience. I could see Eugene Douglas's brindled head, nodding over a newspaper in an elaborate demonstration of disinterest that was amusing because he obviously didn't expect you to believe it. As assistant to the Minister of Agriculture, Andrew Fabricus sat in the row behind the front bench. I thought he looked watchful, not tense, but hopefully expectant like Oliver.

". . . and, Mister Speaker, honourable members on both sides of this august and ancient house," Littleford was saying, "if we should permit, if we should so far betray our sacred trust to the people of Cayuna, who elected us to cherish their best interests, and permit this ill-conceived bill to become law, then we open the flood-gates, we surrender our homes, we bow our heads to a certain Communism and state-control." He paused, his genially rapacious face carefully raised and reverent. "My good friend, the Honourable Member for Eastmoreland One," he continued, waving a hand at Andrew, "has earlier this afternoon with his customary eloquence come to an inspired defence of this bill. He has assured us that it is all that is required for the small farmer to enter the promised land. We should have, perhaps, felt surer of his motives if he had seen fit to mention that his own estate, his own very efficiently farmed estate, is not large enough to maintain a sugar factory and that he sells his crop to the British Caribbean Sugar Association factory at Fabricus Head."

"Shame!" "Shame!" "Unworthy!" "Typical!" "Withdraw!" The inimitable parliamentary yammer spilled into the gallery.

"He's a swine, isn't he?" I whispered with amusement to Oliver. He smiled briefly, put his finger on his lips and peered down at the floor again.

"If the Honourable Member for Eastmoreland One objects to the implications of that last statement," the Speaker said, "then I must ask the Honourable Leader of the Opposition to withdraw it and apologize."

Andrew rose quickly.

"Mister Speaker," he said, and Oliver beside me squeezed his hands together in an odd spontaneous fashion. Andrew's heavy, archaic face was quite expressionless. "Mister Speaker, I am grateful for the readiness with which you remind the Honourable Leader of the Opposition that he might have found a happier way to suggest that I shall be among the many beneficiaries of this bill. But I have no objection. None at all. I only hope that he and his colleagues, and perhaps the citizens of the island itself, may feel that it is not irrelevant if I mention the fact that the sleeping partner in the recently registered London and Scottish Investment Company is my respected friend, the Honourable Leader of the Opposition." Most of the faces I could see had interrogative marks of surprise and anticipation. Littleford gave an angry shake and looked gloomy. "I mention this, Mister Speaker," Andrew went on, "because the London and Scottish Investment Company is, so financial circles in England assure me, a subsidiary of the British Caribbean Sugar Association, all directors except my honourable friend opposite are also directors of the parent company, and indeed it has nearly ninety per cent of its declared funds invested in the Association estates both here and in Jamaica. . . ."

"And that fixes that," Oliver said. There was no need for him to whisper against the squabbling, gobbling eruption from the floor. "Come along. . . . Unless you want to stay and watch Littleford wriggle."

"No."

As we went down the stairs from the gallery, Oliver burst into soft laughter, like a man impulsively tossing his hat.

"That Fabricus," he said. "And to look at him you wouldn't think he had enough brains to light a fire."

"This was a set hand, I take it?"

"Yes, man. But we didn't know Littleford was going to give Andrew the handle of the stick like that. Poor old thing. He must be getting senile. Five years ago he'd have smelled trouble and got out from under in time. Perhaps even made good out of it."

"How did Andrew know about the tie-up between the investment company and the big sugar boys?" I asked as we crossed the car park reserved for representatives and the press.

"He didn't. It was a pure hunch. Probably based on early training, when he was business manager for the *Newsletter*. He used to have to swallow some nasty secrets in those days when a woman called Ascom ran things. That was before my dispensation," he added going round the front of his car to the driving side; we both got in and he swung it out of the park. "Anyway, he felt there was something more behind Littleford's stand than just dutiful opposition. So he made a few inquiries in London, by cable. Paid for a few lunches and dinners, I believe. He doesn't say much about things like that, but Margaret thinks it must have cost him over a hundred pounds. Mark you, it's a grudge fight between him and Littleford."

"Why?"

"Oh, it's a long story, on the surface. I'll tell you one day. But there's something more, I'm positive. And it could only happen in a place like this. I think Andrew uses Littleford as a

sort of moral excuse for giving a lot of old prejudices an unconscious airing. You see a chap like Littleford, black, probably
illegitimate, aggressive as hell. Everything poor old Andrew
was brought up to despise and fear. Then Andrew gets decency
like religion: social conscience, colour blindness, enthusiasm,
the whole lot. And there is a Littleford on the other side re-
presenting everything Andrew has abandoned, all the greed,
privilege, corruption and the like. He's almost worse than
Andrew's lot used to be. So Andrew pays for everything he
doesn't know he hasn't forgotten, deep down, by attacking,
justifiably, the sort of man he never thought of except as a
servant until he was nearly grown up." We drew up outside the
Newsletter building. He looked sadly and thoughtfully at his
hands on the wheel, and said, "You know what, Stefan? It'll
be a good thing when all my generation in Cayuna is dead. All
of us. Black, white or brown. We tracked too much of the old
dirt in with us. Most of us without knowing it. Worse, pretending that we didn't. This island won't be able to clean house
properly until we're all gone."

The presses had started their running clatter-thud again, in
the basement, and the staff had begun to reassemble at their
desks in the offices upstairs. I waited for Oliver in his room
while he conducted one of the routine progress checks of an
editor on press night.

"Be with you in a minute," he said, coming in and picking
some fresh galleys from his desk. "I'll have to eat and run,
though, if you don't mind."

"Of course not. I'm going on somewhere, anyway."

"Oh?" His brows were knit against the glare from the goose-
neck lamp, and he continued to read as he spoke, "A woman?"

"Hurrah, yes," I said.

"You're now a subject of speculation," he said. "Did you
know that?"

"No. Who speculates?"

"My wife, for one. Jerome Vogier's wife for another. That

172

bitch of a cousin of mine, Dolly Hyde, for a third. You know how Cayuna women like to powder their noses in droves. You can't hear the toilet flushing for gossip, sometimes. Well, the other night up at Eugene Douglas's, I was just about bursting and both bathrooms were locked so I went into the yard behind a blackie mango tree. Just outside the bottom storey bathroom. I could hear every word."

"Now I know where you are," I said. "Where am I?"

He grinned.

"Having your sex life dissected by the ladies I mentioned. They were wondering why you've never taken out any of the women they know more than three or four times. Dolly suggested you might be a queer, incognito. But I think she'd just been reading a book and it had gone to her head. Annette Vogier was more romantic and thought you were having an affair with one of the university women. Sybil was practical and said that if you were, we'd have met her, and opted for a mistress. They were all annoyed at your discretion."

"I thought you knew," I said. "It was you gave me the idea. Bernice is my lover. Bernice Heneky."

"You mean Miss Bernice at Long John's?"

"Yes."

He put the galleys down and squinted through the focused glare of the powerful bulb to where I sat in the shadows.

"Yes," he said slowly, as if aligning a scattered pattern of forgotten facts. "I remember now. But I didn't think. What's she like, Stefan?"

I waited for a second before answering. I have always had an inhibition about using the brief, nearest convenient adjective to describe a woman or a great city: I am always conscious of a sense of loss when I do so: as though the inadequate word has made the experience less.

"I know," I said suddenly. "She's like what Sybil would have been if she hadn't found out she could paint and hadn't acquired all the tricks and graces of our sort of life."

173

"You think those tricks and graces are bad?"

"What d'you think I am? A flat-earther? No. they're necessary. They're what helped turn a dirty little village on the
Seine into Paris. And they're what made Shakespeare claim a
coat of arms. I only meant that Bernice has—— Oh, hell,
Oliver, I don't know what she has. Simple definition in our
age is almost always phoney. We know too much. Like you
know about Andrew. Just let's say she's good. And not that
dreary, good within bad, ultimate sanctification stuff novelists
make money out of, either. It's simply that her passions take to
charity and goodness the way some men's muscles take to
games. That's all. She'd be uncomfortable doing anything
else."

"My God," he said enviously. "You've caught a rare fish,
haven't you!" and, looking at me uncertainly, "You're in love
with her?"

"No," I told him. "I know that for sure. I'm much too calculating for that. I can see too clearly to the day when it would
be important that she couldn't understand why a certain sort
of joke was so funny, or when she'd stop pretending to like the
pictures I hung. But I need her."

"Sex," he said then, in a tone of quiet, almost astonished
fury. "I wonder they've never advanced sex as a proof of God.
Only thought could have created anything as impossible as
that."

"That's not very original, is it?"

"It wasn't meant to be. But then a drowning man calling for
help isn't very original either. Ready?"

We ate in the parlour of a Chinese grocery, about a block
from the office, and popular with the *Newsletter* staff because
of its superlative chicken patties. I wasn't hungry, though I
knew I ought to be: it had been one of those days occupied by
a succession of unusual, closely detailed problems, when even
the thought of food is a bore, until it makes its lack felt and you
find you can't swallow it. I left half my patty on the plate and

drank two beers quickly. We returned to the office down an empty lane.

"I won't come up," I began to say on the pavement by my car, "I'll see you at the week-end——" and it was then that Joan Culpepper leaned from the window above us and called: "Noll, you little brute! Where have you been? I've been waiting hours."

"Oh, Christ!" Oliver said gently. "That's all I needed to make my night."

"I heard that," she warned cheerfully, leaning further from the window, so that she was nearly balanced on her forearms.

"Get back inside," Oliver called up to her anxiously. "I'll be right up." We watched her consider this and then withdraw her torso; an emptily ringing laugh came to us through the open windows as she moved away inside. Oliver made a scribbling motion with his hand, as though trying to put a phrase in the air between us that would comprehend the situation: her sadness and futility, his mixture of tender annoyance and responsibility, the core we have to leave unexplained, finally, at the centre of every human mistake. "Now I'm for it," he said, resignedly. "She's in one of her jocular moods. She'll want company and I'll have to get rid of her, and then she'll get abusive. The hell of it is that a few years ago, when I had nights like that, I was glad to have her to hold onto. It makes me feel a bit of a shit now."

I followed him up the stairs to the office; he and the reporters exchanged impotent, expressive shrugs and grimaces, and he led the way into his room.

She was sprawled on the end of her spine in his big swivel chair, her feet jammed flat against the filing cabinet, wearing the bottle-green skirt and white, pertly severe blouse in which Air Cayuna dresses a receptionist. The skirt was primly tugged over the knees of her raised legs, but the starch in her blouse was tired, and I thought that she must have begun her junket straight after leaving work, without going home to bathe and change. The hard white radiance of the lamp shone full on her face, and I wondered if she had turned it like that, for when we had left, it had been focused on to the desk. She looked as solitary, alert and defiant as a wild animal caught in your headlights on a country road.

"Hi, girl!" Oliver said, in the same loving and conspiratorial tone I had heard him use at Andrew's party; without any of the careful *bonhomie* with which we tend to approach the drunk.

"Hi, boy," she said loudly. "I've come to collect you."

"For what?"

"Listen to him," she appealed to me. "He knows what for, the little bastard. I want to drink down the moon tonight and I need company."

"I can't tonight," he said, sitting on the edge of the desk, looking down at her. "And you know it. It's press night." He glanced back at me. "You remember Stefan? You met him at Andrew's."

She rose with foolish, elaborate care and took my hand, shaking it with the warmth of those who are feeling nothing.

"Of course I remember," she said, and peered at me as though she had forgotten the shape of a human face. "But, Ollie! He's sweet. . . . You're sweet," she explained to me portentously.

"Joan," Oliver said. "Go on home and we'll make it tomorrow night. Promise." He looked at her without much hope.

"You," she said. "I knew you'd have some stinking excuse. You think I'm drunk, don't you? Well, I am. And I'm going to be drunker. And if you don't want my company, Noll dear, you can go and——" She suddenly looked at me with awful archness, and added, "Oh, but this sweet boy would think I'm just a wicked woman if I said what I meant to say. So you have him to thank, Ollie, or I'd have told you what you could do with yourself and your bloody paper and that new leaf you've turned over——" she was gathering her handbag, the trim

176

little cap, and a light tunic from a chair in one corner of the room as she spoke. When she walked it was plain that she was much drunker than she spoke.

"Listen, sweetheart," Oliver said lightly, and gave me a really anxious glance. "Are you driving?"

"Naturally, I'm driving." She veered towards the door, turned, almost lost her balance, and waved a gay, forgiving hand. "Good-bye, Noll, you old traitor." She nodded to me with a parody of regal grace, turned again, fumbled at the door and went out.

"Stefan," Oliver said urgently, "do me a favour and drive her home. I haven't seen her like that for a long time. Generally, she's one of those cold drunks."

"Sure," I told him. "If she'll come with me."

"She will. She only wants company. Come on. Let's catch her up."

She was walking with unnatural precision, slowly, along the pavement, in the direction of the waterfront.

"I've lost a car," she said when we caught her up, accepting our presence without question, and laughing easily. "Can you imagine? I've lost a whole bloody car."

"No, you haven't," Oliver told her firmly. "There it is." He pointed across the street to a little Italian car with a badly dented fender, parked under the light. "Come on, you silly old bitch," he said fondly. "This nice man's going to drive you home. I don't want to have to scrape you off a lamp-post."

"Did you hear what he called me?" she said merrily. "Oh, Ollie! After all these years to be called a bitch by my little Noll." She bent over and gave him a heavy, smacking kiss.

"And it's nothing to what I will call you," he said. I could hear the relief in his voice that he had so easily shifted her intention. He began to manhandle her back to my car. It could have been comic and festive, if one hadn't known that it was another moment in a chain of such moments destined to end, as Oliver had said, with her being indifferently straightened by

177

bored ambulance men at four o'clock one morning, or, perhaps more distasteful, to end in a blurred, sexless sac of facile tears, hazily demanding the attention due to feminine attributes long since destroyed.

"I'll call for you in the morning and bring you down to work," Oliver told her as he helped her into the seat. "Try to remember." He looked at me across the top of the little car with an oblique amusement and apology and said, "It's just past Saviour Spring Corner. Ninety-five. She has the bungalow. There's an entrance to the side. You don't have to use the main gate. D'you think you'll find it all right?"

"Yes. Ninety-five Saviour Spring Road. The bungalow. See you."

"See you. And thanks."

As we drove up through the first, shabby suburbs, I remember, I was recapitulating, with a quietly vibrant pleasure of possession, the lecture I was going to give the next day on medieval bestiaries. It was my own creation: a piece of deliberate, subliminal mischief slipped into the generic pattern of the first-year course, because of the jolt or annoyance it caused to the timid, fact-constipated, colonial notion of a discipline's growth. But this year, a new reader had been appointed to the history department, one of those innately civilized, lethally contentious products from the French islands, who had realized far more about the moral essence of the bestiaries than I, whose blandly authoritative additions to my ideas had compelled me to rewrite my lecture, and—"Eh? I beg your pardon. What did you say?" I asked because she had spoken, into the air rushing past the car, with her cheek still resting on the ledge of the rolled down window. I risked one glance from the treacherous illumination of the road and the recurrent dazzle of approaching headlights.

"I said, 'What about joining me in a drink some place?'" she repeated with grave emphasis. For that one glancing capture, in the deceptive light, all that I could see was her mature comeliness, accentuated by the crisp yet feminine cut of her deep, open collar. Then she sat up suddenly, gave her head a vigorous shake, tidied her hair with the instinctive legerdemain of her sex and smiled at me, and, like the message of a letter dropped accidentally into water, the true lines of her face were smudged by a promiscuous, obstinate conviviality. I had a moment of tempered irritation at the prospect of tedium, perhaps mild inconvenience, and then I said, "Certainly. Where would you like to stop? Or shall I choose?" Another drink, I thought, will probably make her more manageable, save trouble in the long run.

"You choose," she said, and snuggled loosely and awkwardly against me. "I don't mind where, if you promise to have a drink with me."

"I'll have a lot of drinks with you," I told her in an automatically soothing tone, and tried to ease her weight on my arm, and affably cursed Oliver in my mind for the imposition he had wished on me.

I drove past the two night clubs at Cotton Tree on the way up to Saviour Spring Corner: these were the customary rendezvous for people with whom Joan would have grown up, and I felt it would be unnecessary and tactless to expose her to them. Instead I turned into the Chinese beer-garden just beyond, where the tables were scattered under trees hung with minimal, coloured lights.

She walked down the shallow steps into the garden ahead of me with a sort of disdainful steadiness, and I could recognize the learned resilience of the frequently drunk. "Oh, I'll have a whisky," she said when we sat at a table under the lattice-work fence. I had been before and knew better than to wait for service here on the periphery of the garden; so I went to the hatch, on the other side, from which drinks were served. I thought of having to come back again, ordered four doubles in four glasses and returned to her with them. And it was half-way through my second double that I remembered how little I had eaten that day, and knew suddenly that I was irremediably drunk. For an evanescent second, I seemed to hold on to the need for responsible sobriety, as one sees the vanishing significance of a dream. It was no longer than that, and then Joan's face was no longer closed or unreachable behind drink; it had become the face of a desirable companion, with whom one could exchange profundities, delightful candours, equivocal hints and laughter. I put my hand on hers and she turned her palm into mine and entwined her fingers firmly.

"Another?" I asked.

"Whenever you're ready."

"The same?"

"The same."

We both laughed, with our foreheads almost touching.

While the drinks were being drawn, I went to the telephone on the wall to call Bernice: to tell her that I couldn't come down tonight. But I had forgotten her number and when I tried to find it, names and figures scrambled like hair-thin insects on the page. I could not even remember how to call the exchange. Resting my forehead on the cool, black metal of the call box, I said under my armpit to a fat, contented looking black man at the nearest table, "I'm not sober, but I'm happy," and he smiled back with sublime, all-embracing benevolence and said, "A man must get drunk a few time." It made me want to do something to record this moment of selfless empathy forever, like a song, to be played to assure us of the world of real meaning.

We finished our third drink side by side, my arm around her waist, thighs pressed close.

"Damn braces," I said, "bless relaxes."

"What?"

"William Blake," I giggled. "Good old Billy. Friend of angels. I taught myself English from him."

"Really?"

"No. I knew it before. But I learnt what makes the English

go round and round from him. You see," I began hectoringly, "he assumes all the contradictions of the English character...."

"Shut up," she said, rubbing her cheek against mine. "Come on home."

"I'm hungry," I complained. "You don't care, but I haven't eaten since breakfast."

"I'll cook you something," she said. "Come on home."

And then it was morning: a morning that, with a child's intense hope and numbed foreknowledge of failure, I tried to hold back forever in a grey, foetal suspension from which I would never wake; and I was registering subtle differences of texture, pattern and colour in a ceiling I had never seen before, while the memory of the night lay on the floor of my mind, like the corpse of a visitor I had murdered, forgotten, and discovered beside my bed.

II

"You Jews," Oliver said, a year after, when with that peculiar, peremptory and wheedling power he has, he had opened me like a book in a free library. "You breast-beating, impossible Jews. I don't mean the detribalized, trading post trash who are born out here, but the real Mosaic element like you, Stefan. You have this ancestral capacity for making an enormous moral drama out of the most ordinary material, don't you? Of course, it's the only art you have so I suppose you make the most of it."

In a sense, I suppose, he is right. We have never preserved ourselves in stone or paint, or even important music, only in the impalpable word: our conviction of identity must depend on this "capacity", as he calls it, for believing that our every action is weighed. And I am thinking, particularly, of those like myself who grew up in families where conscious faith had been long abandoned for a humane materialism, where there was no longer even any unease about the lapse from observance.

But if what I felt that morning, as I drifted to wakefulness

181

on the grey, scummy waves of a hangover, can be explained by this cultural residue, racial memory, whatever one cares to call it, there was also something else. I remembered us coming home and laughing uncontrollably because I drove through the wide gap in the hedge, which was the entrance to her bungalow, very slowly, with clownish precautions. And I remembered her making me bacon and egg sandwiches in the kitchen alcove, sitting cater-corner from me at the little table in the neat, functional box of a living-room, with her knee pressed to mine. But what I remembered most clearly, with a taste of shame like that of another furred tongue, was the desolate helplessness of desire in her face as I leaned over to kiss her, the utter, vulnerable loneliness and confusion of which I was taking such a gluttonous advantage; for in that moment, with hot food and black coffee inside me, I had recovered enough to know what I was doing. I took her not from physical exuberance, not from the pardonable impetus of drink, but as a miser might palm an unguarded coin of small value, another piece to be hoarded against his own obsessive insecurity. She offered herself to me in the same way that a trapped animal will bite at your hand, a meaningless gesture out of a bewildering pain. And I had realized this even before the strange protesting arc her body made as I entered, even before the whispered groan of, "No, no. Please," uttered with an exhausted, penitent sadness, as though making a last desperate appeal for another whom she had betrayed.

III

So much of love, we think, depends on the right moment—until, looking back on any established love, we see that there were no "right" and no "wrong" moments, that the beast itself adapted through a number of circumstances of which we and our plans were only a part. Love is like evolution: there are, really, no identifiable missing links, only suggestive fossils and isolated species which exercise us with a need for explanation: the exact moment of change, the unique, transitory birth is something we have to accept like the point in mathematics, because we must.

So when love roused itself and seized me, I don't know. Perhaps it was when, with a frightened cry, she clutched feebly at my arm and twitched under me like an overmatched runner fallen on the track. It could have been when I rolled from her passive breasts and belly, to topple into sleep with my hand resting on her side. Or the decision might have been taken for me when I woke, ashamed, angry with myself, yet quick with an odd, obstinate sense of responsibility—as though, during the night, a message I didn't understand, but recognized was important, had been slipped under my pillow—and through the gum of sleep saw her button a white, flare-skirted house-coat about her naked body and go from the room with long strides, her face remote and thoughtful.

I only know that when I came out, dressed, my face and head still cool from a long douse under the tap, and she half-turned at the table in the box-like living-room, I felt my heart, became literally aware of its contraction; I mean, as we do in a moment of fear, or when an unbearable memory arbitrarily returns. She scanned me steadily, with dry, disappointed eyes.

"Hullo," I said softly, and crossed the bright tiles and put my hand on her shoulder. Without seeming to do it obviously, as she might have shifted from a position grown boring, she moved her shoulder from under my touch.

"Will you have some coffee before you go?" she asked. There was a percolator and a second cup on the table before her.

"Yes, thanks," I said, and sat where I had eaten last night. "That would be welcome." I smiled. "I feel as if an orchestra of tiny men are playing a twelve-tone symphony in my head."

She looked up from pouring, with the same level appraisal I had registered when I came in, then a polite flicker drifted across her closed lips and she bent her head again.

I felt strangely breathless. Or rather, I breathed as one does at high altitudes, with the never quite subdued complaint from the body as it gropes for more oxygen. This was not the usual predatory exhilaration of the duel, but a novel apprehension that stirred its heavy wings in my stomach: a complex longing, from which I was somehow excluded, that some response of interest or amusement might animate the dark, withdrawn creature across the table.

"Joan," I said.

"Yes." Her face was as impersonally bleak as a visor.

"Thank you," I said. "Thank you very much."

Into the soft, distant, black eyes there came a moment's hard distaste; nothing so strong as anger, but a kind of impatient contempt. For a moment only, then the visor closed again and she said, "That's a damn silly thing to say. What are you thanking me for?"

"I'll tell you properly if you'll let me see you again. Will you come out with me tonight?"

"No," she said.

"Tomorrow?"

She shook her head.

"Have you finished your coffee?" she asked.

"Yes."

"Then I'm going to ask you to go. I don't particularly want Oliver to find you here."

"Oh, for God's sake," I said. "Oliver isn't a child. Don't you understand? I want to see you again. Please."

"No," she repeated, with a heatless finality of rejection that brought a sudden prickle to my skin. She pushed her chair back and stood. Looking up at her, with my heart blundering around my chest, I remembered the unpitying candour with which she had described herself that morning on Andrew's beach. "Look," she told me now, "why don't you go on home, Stefan?"

"Not until you explain why I can't see you," I said quietly.

184

The jackal's anguish of chagrin in me had begun to feed on its own tail. I wanted an excuse to say something spiteful and to see her sanctimonious and impenetrable reserve cringe a little.

"There's really no need for this," she said, almost sadly.

"Yes, there is. I didn't behave very well last night, but I don't regret it now. And I'm not apologizing. I do want to see you again. Why won't you let me?"

"Because I don't want to, Stefan. I don't even like you."

"Because of last night?"

"No," she said with tired decision. "Listen to me, Stefan, and then leave me alone, eh? There are three sorts of men I've gone with when I get really drunk. Some are like that poor child, Hippolyte, who are all embarrassed the next morning and don't know what to do. Well, that's all right. I understand that. Most of the others take it, honestly, because it's there and don't care any more than if they'd eaten a free dinner. They're not the prettiest men in the world, but they don't pretend to be. And then there are a few like you, who want everything. You think you're just too damn good to be satisfied with what you got. You've got to prove that it wasn't just a drunken f——"

"Don't use that word," I said.

"Why not? That's what it was. You f——d me drunk and now you'd like to see if you could f—— me sober. It would make you feel much better."

"No," I said slowly. "It isn't like that. It isn't like that at all. But I don't even want to convince you now." I got up and walked past her, to the door opening out on the little gravelled yard where I had parked my car. One corner of my mouth was twitching and the skin of my face felt warm and stiffened. I was squeezed tight round a painful rage and confusion. The morning sunlight was still young enough to be pale gold on the grey gravel and the dark green hedge that separated the little yard from the main garden. I turned at the door; she had gone back to the table and stood with her back to me, her hand

185

resting on the chair, her chin sunk on her chest. Under the tight bodice of the house-coat her long back swelled and subsided quickly but evenly.

I said: "I think I was right about you the first time."

"Yes?" she half-turned, with a weary forbearance, an impervious submission to the laws of hospitality, and venom burst from me like the sweat of a breaking fever.

"Yes," I said with careful relish. "I told Oliver you're an emotional parasite. That was a snap judgement. But it was accurate, because I was relying on my intuition. You really are destructive, Joan. And you don't even know it. You simply absorb strength and attention and time like a tapeworm, because that's the only way you can live." The embroideries to my image seemed to tumble out effortlessly like the stuff from a sewer. "You attach yourself to the emotive guts of people and they get huge appetites that do them no good. It's all going to feed you. One way or another, you get something from everybody. And you don't give a thing back. Not a thing." I stopped suddenly, feeling quite sick, my head swimming, and looked at her impassively listening face with bewilderment, as though while abusing a face in a nightmare, I had awakened to find it real. I plunged out of the doorway, walked the five paces to my car and was driving up the road before I really established any connection between myself and what I was doing.

Her passionless and weary contempt seemed to lodge in the centre of my pride like a stone, irritating me into a fierce energy that lasted all day. I went to my lecture determined to hurt. With sadistic pleasure, I watched the faces of my first year as I dragged their raw minds, still sunburnt with exposure to independent study, across a sandpaper of implications, allusive references for which they could not possibly be prepared, and sheer word play. I knew quite well that they were just at the stage when a lecture that they did not understand, that demanded too much of their schoolroom, apprentice skills could cause only numb dismay: they hadn't learnt yet to use us with the critical and sometimes irreverent economy of the older students. In every missed meaning they saw the spectre of failure in their finals. Afterwards, talking of it to Marcel Galbre, the French West Indian whose additional ideas I had so misused, he challenged a great deal of what I had said; I knew he was right, and in trying to justify some of my more extravagant flights, I nearly quarrelled with him.

That night I descended on Bernice with the hard, anxious gaiety of a buccaneer on shore-leave. I badgered her until she left Cherry in charge of the bar and we went up to the Star Garden, where I danced with a frenetic inspiration that gradually turned into a genuine enjoyment, as any harmonious use of the body must in time. We went back to her room late, and the wide, solid bed creaked and shuddered in a storm of love like an old ship.

"Lord God, Stefan!" she said, half-laughing with the flattered sensuality of a ripe woman, holding me by my shoulders at arm's length above her. "How your daddy have such a son, eh? You can't get enough?" She drew me to the sweating dunes of her breast and bit my neck playfully. "Why you never come to see me last night? I did wait up for you."

"I got drunk," I said into the pillow next to her ear.

"You?" I could feel her smile. "But you never get drunk, Stefan. All the time I know you. Not that you can't drink," she reassured me quickly, as if she had made a careless remark about my manhood. "But you always hold it so good."

"Not last night," I said. Sprawled across her breast, my head buried between the soft crook of her arm and her pungent, stiff hair, I felt exhaustion as though my skeleton had turned to soft lead and was slowly by its own weight, pulling itself out of shape. And with this exhaustion, a horrible restlessness, like claustrophobia: sensation itself had become a box in which I had just enough room to breathe. Like sticks caught in the closed circle of a backwater my thoughts struggled to join the

187

main current and were inexorably swept on a course that brushed against the jagged memories of Joan Culpepper's face and words: against the simple fact of her existence. The great journey into mature love that I had made in this bed, with the peerless woman who now held me, was remote, irretrievable as a historic period of which we are inheritors and which we study to enlighten the present. It had died, like an era finally dying with the passing of its last survivor, when some instinct had pushed me into Joan Culpepper's drunken body. I was living now in a new arrangement of forces, trends and references, and like any new generation I could only grope empirically into a new meaning.

"Bernice," I heard myself saying, "I'm sorry. I shouldn't have done you that."

"Sorry?" Her contented voice rose on a tone of amused surprise. "But a man must get drunk sometimes. I didn't mean you to think I was vexed." She tightened her arms comfortingly and kissed the back of my head. "After all, boy, I don't own you."

IV

When I woke the next morning, in my flat at the university, I lay for a moment immersed in a curious langour of relief. I felt like a man who had known by the sour tickle behind his nose and his aching head that he is hatching a bout of influenza, who has elaborately, for a day, tried to deceive it by a zealous normality, and who can now surrender himself to distress without pretence.

I waited until eight o'clock when Marcel Galbre came down from the flat above mine to collect me for our usual stroll across the grounds to the common room and breakfast.

"Go ahead," I told him, "I'll catch you up. I want to telephone."

How mortifying, yes, our physical symptoms of love. But how reassuring. As if they were birth-marks confirming us in the rightful possession of an immense fortune. I took pleasure in the trembling of my hands as I turned the pages of the directory until I found Culpepper, Joan: at the head of a page, I remember, magnified by the shock of her suddenly concrete image. And I took the same pleasure in the huge thudding of my heart as I listened to the exactly recurring buzz at the other end. When the twentieth or thirtieth signal had echoed, I put the receiver down. Hurrying to catch Marcel's distant figure, I felt almost buoyant, as though I had been reprieved at the moment of execution. For how long did not matter. It was not until I fell into step beside him that the possible meaning of her unanswered telephone opened in my imagination like a full page illustration in some gruesomely pornographic work.

For one long and horrifying second, the morning scene around me seemed to waver like the projection of a snagged film. I stopped abruptly. It was unbelievably cruel that one could feel such a grotesque pain and not conveniently faint or shout wildly. The picture of Joan in a bed with a man's arm flung across her was so real, etched itself into the last cowering fragment of responsive tissue with such brutal precision, that I stopped and gasped out a whining croak. I knew this because Marcel had begun to saunter back to me, his pace increasing anxiously, as he said, "Stefan! Étes vous malade?" "Non, non," I said: I seemed to be seeing him through tears. "Ce n'est qu'une espèce de crampe." Kneading my calf vigorously, I fetched a stricken smile. "Speak English, Marcel," I added chidingly. "You know you'll never learn it properly otherwise. Follow my excellent example."

"Yes." He smiled back, but continued to examine my face with critical uncertainty. "You have gone white as death. You are all right?"

"Quite all right. Come on. I'm hungry."

And, indeed, for a few moments, walking beside him over the newly warmed, green odour of the morning grass, the subsidence of pain was more real than its imagined occasion. But as I sat at breakfast, five minutes later, and forced three or four lumps of food into the protesting receptacle of my stomach, the significance of the occasion returned; and I looked at it as a man might look at the healed stump of a severed hand and realize the consequences.

For the rest of the day, I moved about a world so unreal that it eventually became ludicrous. It is not possible, I told myself with a sort of hysterical detachment, for contingent objects to co-ordinate their activities on separate time scales. I lectured, demonstrated and even discussed, helpfully, a brilliant essay on Arachnidae which Lois Gay had timidly handed in a week before it was due. Habits of competence, acquired patterns of communication and simple momentum carried me unobtrusively through a landscape to which I seemed to have no relation, from which I seemed to suck a thin, unsatisfying air.

I telephoned Joan twice at her home and twice at Air Cayuna without any result. By late afternoon, I had assembled and destroyed so many possibilities of approach, contact and acceptance that there was nothing left to feel with. I was emptied. A short-circuit had taken place on the overloaded wires, and as I sat on the little veranda before my flat in the gelid warmth of a dying sun, I could feel myself giving over, without a fight, to a bludgeoned insensibility.

So much so that when the little Fiat dipped to a stop in the driveway under the ebony tree opposite my flat, it took me several seconds to recognize it. It was only when she got out and began to walk across the few yards of grass that I resentfully came back from my temporary solitude, like a conscript posted into the battle again after inadequate leave.

"How did you know where to find me?" I asked stupidly as I went down the steps to meet her.

"I've been here before," she said, and my imagination went plunging like a maddened horse among the possible male flats she might have visited.

"I telephoned you today," I told her gravely.

"Oh? Yes. . . . I wasn't in." She stepped onto the veranda and turned to me, the scarlet and deep sulphur of the sunset burnishing her face with a lurid, translucent clarity.

"I've come to tell you how sorry I am for what I said the other morning," she told me, and the unvarnished sincerity of her voice was like the sound of a hammer on a coffin. Even hope could no longer pretend that there was a second, unadmitted purpose to her visit.

"That's all right," I said. "There's nothing to be sorry for. I asked for it. Won't you sit down?"

"No thanks. I'm going on duty now." She was wearing a freshly laundered uniform. "But I really had to come and ask you to forgive me. I said a lot of things that weren't true. And I hurt you badly." She smiled with guileless contrition. "Will you take my word for it, that I wish I hadn't said what I did?"

"Yes, of course. Please don't say any more."

"Thank you," she said and in the blank happiness of that moment I could only think how ridiculous for her to thank me for anything. She took my hand. "I must be going or I'll be late for work. I expect we'll be seeing each other soon at Oliver's or Andrew's. Good-bye."

I said, helplessly: "I love you, Joan."

"Yes," she said sombrely, and turned on the top step. "I realized that just a minute ago. I wouldn't have come up if I'd suspected. I'm sorry."

"You just can't leave me like this."

"It's no damn good," she said. "Believe me, Stefan. Try to get out of it. I only wish you hadn't, that's all."

I followed her to the little, dented Fiat. Hope had returned like a sly weed.

"You'll have to see me," I told her. "This place is too small for you not to. When d'you come off duty tonight?"

She opened the door and slid behind the wheel. Then she looked up at me as I hung my face like a beggar's before the window. With her elbow on the ledge, she raised her hand and pinched my cheek. And, like any other beggar, I took only the offering: whatever motive inspired it was an irrelevance I couldn't afford.

"All right," she said. "I'm off at midnight." She paused, as if hoping I would protest that this was too late. "You can call for me at Air Cayuna and I'll follow you. Or we can meet somewhere."

"I'll be there," I told her. "I'll wait outside."

I watched the little car scuttle like a self-important beetle around the edge of the wide campus until it was swallowed by the blandly solvent perspectives of dusk. And I stayed there for a little after the car had disappeared, enveloped in a meek happiness and expectancy that would break, I knew, like a stem of crystal with my first movement. As I went back to the veranda, one part of me seemed to clutch with aggressive deference at my elbow like an old employee pensioned off unfairly.

And later:

"No," she said. "No, Stefan. Not even if I was drunk, and I'm not tonight."

"I don't want you drunk," I said sullenly. "I want you as you are now."

"Go on home. I told you it wasn't a very good idea."

"Why did you bother to come out at all?"

"Do you really want me to tell you?"

"Yes."

"Because I was sorry for you. You looked so wretched when I was about to refuse."

"I don't want your blasted pity."

"All right. Then you'd better go."

"I didn't mean that. Give me what you please. Anything is better than nothing."

"Stefan. Stefan, my dear. Please don't try. I've got nothing to give. You were quite right."

"Except to that little swine, Oliver. You'd sleep with him, wouldn't you? Any time?"

"Yes. If I thought he needed to."

"Why don't you marry him then? Take him away from Sybil?"

"I don't want to. And he doesn't want to. You know that."

"You're enjoying this, aren't you? It must make you feel your power. I think you really are a frigid woman who can't sleep with a man unless she's drunk."

"You can believe that if you want to."

"No," I said. "I don't believe that. I don't know what to believe except that I'm in love with you."

"You mustn't. You really mustn't. And it's not that I don't like to hear you say it. I'm still a woman enough for that. It's just that it doesn't echo any more, Stefan. I spoilt myself for that a long time ago. Oliver is the only person I love in the whole world now, and not in the way you want me to love you."

"You could try. You could climb out of that armour you think you have to wear and try."

"Oh, Stefan. I'm not wearing any armour as you call it. Can't you see anybody as they are, without making them over into something you've invented?"

"Then what *are* you? Tell me and I'll know where to start searching."

"You think," she said with a calmly astonished seriousness, as if I questioned the existence of some blatantly obvious fact, "that if I knew what had happened to me, I'd live like this?"

"No. I guess not. . . . Will you come out with me again?"

"Yes. If you want me to."

"Still sorry for me?"

"No. Not now."

"Then why?"

"Because you talk well; because you're one of the handsomest men in Queenshaven and it makes me feel as if I'd scored off the other women to be seen with you . . . and you

193

won't like this, I'm afraid, but because you remind me of Oliver, or because Oliver likes you so much, or a mixture of the two. I'm not sure about that part of it."

"May I see you tomorrow?"

"No. I have a date."

"With a man?"

"It usually is, isn't it?"

"God," I said. "I hate you. At this moment I really hate your damned smug dead face."

"I've done nothing for you to hate me for. Except that I don't want to sleep with you. And I warned you about that."

"You!" I said tiredly; I had clinkered everything except hope in that volcanic moment of hate. "Why couldn't you have just stayed away? You'd be manageable in a big city. Where I wouldn't keep running into you. All right. When can I see you?"

Even now I am not sure whether I could have gone back to her after that night had I really understood what the next few months were to mean. As no man, if he could really imagine the torment of war, could be persuaded to go, even under penalty of death, so I would have rather lost her than gone open eyed into those months and the pain, humiliation, misery, rancorous jealousy and impatient bitterness that accompanied them. Two things, I think, sustained me through them: unquenchable hope, which was perhaps my name for incorrigible egotism, and the fact that I could not blink the truth about her. I could not discover her promiscuity because it was tacitly admitted. There was no shocked sense of betrayal to use as a way out of love: I knew, all the time, before or after. In the fear that any occasion might accidentally inspire love for someone else, I forgot anger or outrage. At times, I nearly forgot myself.

8

★

I

I remember the shocking clarity that would suddenly invest
things and events during those months. Moments of sensation
so intense that they anaesthetized: a sunset of gaudy blood
stabbing my eyeballs like a careless finger; mornings of cobweb
delicacy through which I would walk, suffocated by hung filaments of light; sinister greens and reds forced by some tremendous pressure into the protesting flesh like thick wedges of
iron; a remark between two passing strangers, startling as
another's voice on the moon; faces cut from humanity by acid,
revealed in a flash of lightning. Each experience winding me
another turn round the peg, until I was stretched like catgut,
to a point where I became mildly speculative about my possible
tensile strength. Even a trivial occasion from those months
will sometimes reconstruct itself with a reality that consumes
the present. And when it does, I almost regret the subdued
responses of security and happiness.

The Easter vacation, that year, began a few days after I met
Joan for the second time; and a party of us spent most days of
it in the mountains behind Queenshaven tracing and classifying
the marine fossils which are printed right to the peak tops.

I threw myself into the search with a sort of frenzy rather
than enthusiasm. Every day we would meet, long before first
light, yawning and bleary under the ebony tree outside my flat;
and in two cars, mine and that belonging to Professor Cole, the

head of department, we would drive into the dark mountains: to leave the cars, at dawn in some village or cutting, and go scrambling through the cinchona, juniper, still sopping leaves of ginger lily, down along the valley sides above the wadded mist. I worked in a semi-lunatic fashion, without the long mid-day rest and frequent halts that the others sensibly insisted on taking. For ten hours a day, I would hunt for exhaustion as I traced converging contours up and down slopes steep as filled sails and across the pitons above. By the end of the second week, I was ribbed like an old dog and burnt to an odd rust. The others warned, grew really concerned, and abandoned me to my own stupidity with the half-amused, half-exasperated indifference of those who have been dutiful and been ignored. One day as I came down through a stand of wild pines, I heard one of the advanced students, I think it was Patrick Henry, say from the path below, "Where's our Mechanical Unit now?" and one of the visiting students who had joined us from Jamaica for the vacation, a Chinese girl with a delightful, seductive stutter, replied, "P-p-rob-ably b-burrowing like a drill, my dear. I think he hopes to find b-buried t-treasure."

About the second week, too, my headaches and nausea re-turned: frequent, savage attacks in which the whole sky seemed to crack open on my skull like a huge plate and sickness chilled my warmly rushing blood and goose-pimpled my sweating flesh.

"Is doctor you want," Bernice said, when for the third time in five nights she was massaging the back of my neck, and then, "But, Stefan! I never see you so thin." She pressed my rib-cage between her firm, heated hands as I lay face down across the bed. "You not eating, eh, man?"

She did not say, but I knew she was worried, also, about the unheralded ebb in my capacity for love making. For the first time in my life the act of sex was pinched off from the imagina-tion. I would go to Bernice from a sense of obligation, from cowardice, from habit, I suppose, possessed by an indistinct but overpowering picture of the other whom I had seen the day before—alone or at Oliver's, more unapproachable as our intimacy deepened and became part of a mosaic of friendship —and in the very moment of union, my mind would gutter into blankness and making love was like reading in the dark.

By the time of that Sunday night when we sat together on her bed playing cards, I was dangerously near admission, the only positive release for the frustrated and rejected in love: a kind of instinctive magic we practise, in the hope that by naming we may exorcise.

How closely the impressions of those months seem to rank themselves. Piled, really, not ranked: like a heap of vigorous bodies struggling indistinguishably over one desired objective, so that a foot, say, thrust from the bottom of the bundled forms belongs to the ducking head near the top, and to find the missing pair to a hand grasped at one side, one would have to go round to the other. Yes. The hours of those months are sealed. I feel that I couldn't get the beat of a second hand between them.

And yet there must have been whole stretches of prosaic occupation during which nothing happened and which separated me from the crisis in which, now, I seem to see everything.

How long, for instance, after I nearly admitted to Bernice that I was no longer able to love her, did the by-election in East-moreland Two, that inspired the public emergence of her father, occur? I can't be sure. Although I even saw the air crash which was the indirect cause of the by-election because it killed "Poncho" Gomez, the representative for that district.

Sitting with Oliver and Sybil one morning on the terrace of the art gallery, above the harbour at the end of Queen Charlotte Street, we all saw the early plane from Venezuela bank and turn beyond the Barricades, drop smoothly in its approach —and then hurtle, with a curious, mad air of intention, nose first into the shallows at the end of the runway.

A percussive thud, as from a distant bass drum, struck

across the mile of bright water, and, immediately, there was a burst of brown-smeared yellow flames wrapping the fuselage and clutching for the tail as it lifted over the slowly burrowing nose. Sybil and Oliver said, separately, "No!" and "Great God!" in chorus, and I was clamped by a second's irrational terror, because Joan was on duty at the airport that morning and all impossible probabilities followed until I put the reception hall in its place, a thousand yards up from the crash. Then Oliver had spun from his chair and was past me, darting like a dragonfly, his shouted, "Come on, Stefan!" already an echo to his heels clattering on the floor of the long gallery. I caught him at the bottom of the stairs and he leaped away from me again, out along the pier under the terrace. "Dolphus! Dolphus!" he was shouting. "Start her up, Dolphus! Get her started, man!" and I realized he meant to cross the harbour by the little motor-boat owned by the old wharfman who ran harbour cruises for the tourists who came to buy pictures at the gallery.

I jumped down into the boat as the engine caught on a smoker's cough and the stern dug into the water. Oliver was holding the windshield beside Dolphus, his face schooled into no expression at all, frowning to where, at this distance, the flames glowed like a ball of yellow St. Elmo's fire.

"Quicker this way than round by road," he flung at me, and for the minutes it took us to cross was silent.

The flames had become flapping, exploratory tongues by the time we were skirting the periphery of unendurable heat: the broken back of the fuselage showed through gaps in the fire and there was a tart yet cloying scent to the air. A group of white-overalled airport crew had waded in to push and tug at a broken wing-tip. An untidy stock car race was still in progress down the runway, trailed by sprinting figures. From the two crash tenders, reversed in up to the hubs of their back wheels, twin jets of chemical dampener were being sprayed into the centre of the fire. It was like watching men feed slim wax tapers slowly into the heart of a gas flame. We coasted to a berth at the small jetty at the corner of the runway.

I had told myself that Joan must have been over half a mile away at the time of the crash, but I should have trusted the fool's wisdom of the lover, his fearful prescience of the accidental. Within a few seconds of our running across the tarmac to the crowd opposite that incandescent coffin, we discovered that she, another receptionist and a young Air Cayuna pilot had been the three on the ground closest to the scene. Idling on the jetty, they had heard a whirring over their heads and seen a fragment of metal do ducks-and-drakes on the water before it vanished into the deep water fringing the mangroves. Joan and the pilot were both wet to the waist from a futile dash into the shallows as far as the heat would allow them.

"This girl!" the pilot said. "I've never seen a woman run so fast." He put an affectionate arm round her waist. "Laddie, she was as near as dammit up to that plane before I could catch her and hold her back."

I remembered him now: from some all-day Cayuna Sunday party, months before: a blithely simian half-Chinese who had called all the men "laddie".

"Lester!" Joan said angrily. "Don't be such a fool. You know I couldn't go any further. The heat was enough to knock you out."

She looked incredulously at the flames hissing against the flat water.

"All the same," Lester said—I recalled his name suddenly: Lester Pow—and tightened his arm in another squeeze, "you were closer than I would have gone. I tell you, laddie, she was close enough to burn her eyebrows off."

In that moment, watching his arm around her waist, I forgot the furious death near to us, looked with ignoble envy at their mutually achieved soaking clothes.

Oliver had left us. I could see him darting from one official to another, pausing long enough with each to talk quickly. He turned away from the last, calling over his shoulder, "Thanks. I'll bring it back as soon as I've finished," and trotted over to one of the cars stopped anyhow behind the crowd, got in and drove off up the runway. I guessed that he was going to cable the American agency he represented.

Joan now began to shiver violently: it could not have been the wet for the air on the tarmac was baking dry as the breath from a kiln. Her head was hung in an attitude like supplication, and she said in a thin, cold voice: "Lester, take me up now, or give me the key and I'll drive. You can come up later if you want."

"No," he said. His face wore the careful, excluding set of one professional mourning another and his mistake or misfortune. "No. I've seen enough. Those damn things. Thank God, it wasn't one of ours." He turned to me. "Can I give you a lift up, laddie?"

"No, thanks," I said, "I'll wait here for Oliver."

They walked away: after a few paces she must have said something for he bent to her and tucked his hand under her elbow and led her, his head wagging with the effort of earnest consolation, to his car. I went back to the jetty and sat on a bollard and tried to feel for the still inaccessible, tortured bodies until Oliver came back.

"Well," I said as unpleasantly as I could, "I hope you managed to make the evening edition. Do you think they'll give you a bonus?"

In those days of bitterness, I found myself trying to make companions in disturbance.

He looked straight at me, and down at his watch.

"Why yes, Stefan," he said. "I think I've made the New York evening editions. Just. And I think I ought to get a bonus. None of the other representatives have got round yet. There was only a *Gazette* junior out to meet the flight. I didn't wish for this, you know. I just have to tell people what happened."

"Sorry," I said. "I don't know what got into me."

"That's O.K.," he said. "I don't feel very chipper myself. Is that fool of a girl all right?"

"Yes," I told him. "And I'm glad you got your scoop. Isn't that what you call it?"

"Man," he said, as though he were sucking a penny, "what sort of jazz have you been reading? I suppose you think I told them to hold the front page. Come on, you blockhead, I have work to do."

II

Like co-owners of a golden goose, the two political parties, People's Radical and Cayuna Democratic approached the district of Eastmoreland Two in the weeks before the by-election: coaxing gurgles, shrill, sweet and opposing calls, hands full of promises like grain. Avidly and shrewdly they watched the fluffing tail feathers of obscure opinion: neither side confident that a miscalculated move would not scare the undecided creature across the yard to deposit its shining creation at rival feet.

It had been a marginal and was now a trend-setting seat. "Poncho" Gomez had carried it for the Cayuna Democrats because he had been personally irresistible: an almost indecently masculine, unprincipled brown man, flamboyant with the joy of his tremendous appetites. In a moment of unforgivable bad strategy, the Radicals, during the election when Andrew Fabricus won Eastmoreland One, had accused "Poncho" of fathering two hundred bastards across the Caribbean. The charge had turned a safe race into a romp. "Poncho" Gomez had accepted the lie with the fullness of gratitude possible only for a representative who can hear the mystical rustle of future ballots in his favour. "Which of you," he had asked, with plaintive salacity, "don't have a few brush colt scatter here an' there? If them say that me have two hundred, it must be so. But, God judge me, I never knew say it was so many times I catch." The sober and responsible peasants had come down from their mountain holdings and voted for him as Homeric Greeks might have voted for Pan.

But now he was dead and the seat was being contested by two plodding cab horses, held up by the traces of party organization. Between Barnet for the Radicals, and Porlock for the Democrats, there was no more difference than the fact that the first belonged to the party formed by men like Eugene Douglas, staffed by men like Andrew Fabricus, supported by men like Oliver Hyde, and that the second was the hired hand of a predator like Thomas Littleford. Two weeks before the polls, not even Oliver could tell me which balance to expect. Not even Andrew who, speaking on Barnet's platform, took on a new and disconcerting persona—a folk assumption which conveyed to me how extraneous I still was to Cayuna.

And into the prescribed ritual attitudes of this tournament now stepped Marcus Heneky: a cuckoo in the nest of hereditary legislators.

I first heard of his attempt to influence the election from Marcel, one morning at breakfast in the common room, as he read the *Gazette* propped open on the coffee pot between us.

"Have you seen this?" he asked.

"What?"

"An anarchist has now entered the election."

"An anarchist! Seriously? I didn't think there were any in Cayuna."

"He appears to be. A man called Heneky. He tried to hold a rival meeting yesterday at Martha's Refuge, when Barnet and your friend Fabricus were speaking. It seems that he told the crowd not to vote at all."

"Let me have a look," I said.

There was hardly more than Marcel had said: a few lines in a box beside the main account, saying that a man called Marcus Heneky had appeared during the meeting, on the other side of the square at Martha's Refuge, and tried to attract the crowd from Barnet by telling them that their votes were valueless, pieces of fraud. He had been furiously stoned and the police had warned him off. There was apparently, the *Gazette* said, a connection between him and the Sons of Sheba as he had been supported by a dozen bearded men with matted locks. But that was all. An obligatory mention of an incidental excitement. I passed the paper back to Marcel, tickled by an amused, almost possessive understanding. It fitted what I now knew of Marcus Heneky, but it was nothing to take seriously.

Two days later, he spoke on the racecourse at Bon Accord, a market town up the eastern coast. This time he waited until Porlock and the Democrat speakers supporting him had finished, and then began his own meeting before the crowd had started to disperse. He had been booed, and some of the younger Democrat enthusiasts had threatened him, but there had been no stones. I thought of his passionate and accomplished voice laying siege to accepted meanings, fecundating buried memories of distress, agitating simplicities of belief, and wondered whether the politicians and the press were not unwise in dismissing him as another of the peripheral eccentrics who attach themselves to every election in Cayuna. And Oliver, when he heard him speak, confirmed me in my reservation.

We had gone down to spend the week-end with Andrew. At least, I had gone because I knew Joan was going to be there and I had not seen her for ten days. But for her presence, I would have lied myself out of the invitation: at times during the miserable fever of unrequited love, even the gentle exactions of friendship seem insupportable, like blankets. One only wants to sweat self-pity and unhappiness alone.

Following Oliver's car through the white gold of a Saturday afternoon, along the grey tape of the coast road between the bright green of the cane and the unpossessable blue of the sea, I could nearly ignore the greasy rations of jealous despair I had consumed in the last ten days. I was prepared to enjoy the hours in which we shared the same roof as one appreciated a feast: as something too rich for envy, too special for reasonable desire.

We ate early that Saturday night; and after dinner we all got into Andrew's cavernous, American station wagon and drove through a moonlight like milk tossing in a bowl to a village called Pryorsville, over in Eastmoreland Two, where Marcus Heneky was to speak.

He had already begun when we arrived. The liquid, brass-coloured flames of the kerosene flares around the packing-case on which he stood, sculptured him into harsh, functional planes, so that his black face like a bas-relief, in another, un-named colour, leaped from the blank wall of night behind. Thirty or forty Sons of Sheba, or men with beards and locks, were ranged in a tight, shoulder brushing semi-circle beyond the flares. The crowd facing them formed a tear-shaped blob between the houses and exuded the goatish smell, acid yet heavy, of those who work land under a tropical sun and sleep close together in shuttered rooms. Dark glints, like the sheen from old furniture in a dimly lit, ornately stocked room, sur-faced occasionally in the haphazard rays of the flares. Andrew and Oliver went ahead to the fringe of the crowd and I fol-lowed with the three women. There was a stir of peering curio-sity into the difficult light as we joined Andrew and Oliver, and then faces were turned again, with deep attention, to Marcus Heneky.

". . . an' look at yourselves," he was saying, not on the strained, platform shout, but with the reverberant and capti-vating power of waves crashing on a shore. "You don't dare look 'pon yourselves! Because there is nothing to see, except what them teach you to see. The Lord say his people, his own black and scattered people, will have no countenance until they take up their own burden again, in their own home. . . . Barnet, the black man, come down, an' Porlock, the brown man, come down, an' they is both one an' the same thing. . . . What do they offer, both? Work an' progress! But I say the work they offer is toil in captivity, an' the progress is the strengthening of Babylon's chains an' walls. . . . Ask them for the money your sweat an' labour have earned, which could return we to Africa. No! Do not ask. Demand!" He crouched in emphasis, surrounded by a caul of harsh light like some sudden conception from the darkness behind. I could feel the hidden, accumulative ripple of a crowd drawn in response: a heave like a ground swell in which no single man is conscious of moving but finds himself going forward to meet the echo of a collective emotion. "Demand it!" Marcus Heneky cried, straightening. "Tell them that the white man's vote is a snare an' a delusion to tempt you from God. Your God. Tell them that we are Africa's captive children, an' that we will be children no more . . . but *men*. Men with *one* God, *one* aim, *one* destiny. . . ."

As we drove back an hour later, Oliver said to Andrew quietly: "We're in trouble. He could cost us the seat."

"Him!" Andrew replied. "How do you figure that, Oliver? Because he can hold a crowd? Cho, man! You know Cayuna people. They love a speech better than anything. . . ."

"No," Oliver said. "You're wrong this time. And when I say we're in trouble, the Democrats are too. That old man can kill enough votes to make a difference to either side. The damn thing is we don't know which of us will lose most. He had a lot of people going back there. Too many. I was watching the faces. The men particularly. He's something new, Andrew. You'll have to do something about him. And quick. If he really gets under way before the polls, a lot of votes are going to stay home."

"You're exaggerating," Andrew said. "What d'you say, Meg?"

"I don't know," Margaret replied. "He's an impressive old devil, but he's telling the people not to do something. It's hard to make that stick when they have something they can use."

"Can't both of you see what he was doing there?" Oliver said, with exasperated urgency. "He was getting at the ones who're not sure of anything yet. Not of themselves, or whatever party they support, or their value in this world. If he captures enough of those, even for a little, if he can make them feel proud about withholding their votes, then he can sink us. I tell you, he's taken me by surprise. I didn't realize he was going to be that calibre."

Sybil said, "I think he's right, Andrew. That back to Africa, racial business fills a real hollow place in more people than you'd imagine. And not only Sheba's Sons. Don't leave him unanswered. Where did he spring from, anyway? I've never heard of him before."

"You'll hear more of him," I said, for the sake of something to say, because sitting beside Joan in the back seat I had taken her hand and after a few seconds, she had withdrawn it gently and unmistakably. "If you think he was impressive tonight, you should see him when he really gets going."

"You've heard him before?" Sybil asked, like a hostess to whom a visitor indicates an overlooked facet of her house or garden.

"Yes," I said, "we're old friends. Well, not friends exactly, but we exchange views from time to time."

"Heneky. . . . Heneky," Oliver said. "Oh, I see. . . ."

"What?" Andrew asked him.

"Nothing. I was just thinking aloud."

The big wagon hummed swiftly along the moon-bleached road between the cane-fields on which the light lay like coverlets of pale muslin. I leaned as far from Joan as I could, and rested for a few minutes in abstract and unfeasible dreams of freedom.

To most people Marcus Heneky's counter-campaign in Eastmoreland Two came and went like the shock waves of a small landslide: an unregarded rumble, a brief shaking of the air and earth in which he was the centre of a bewildered specu- lation, and then the fading, occasional noises as he and the Pure Church of Africa Triumphant subsided beneath the sur- face of news. This was all he meant, at first, to most people; all he would have meant to me, except for my knowing him and for hearing Oliver and Andrew discuss him. But he meant more than that to the tough and wary professional organizers on both sides. Like Oliver, they assessed trouble. As the days followed that Saturday when I heard him at Pryorsville, both sets of party engineers put their noses to the invisible gauge and realized a leak in pressure. It was not so much an injunc- tion, but the imperceptible rumour of it that seemed to be following Marcus Heneky up and down Eastmoreland; a bright excitement all the more attractive because it ministered to some lost, heroic purpose of the imagination. What surprised me, knowing the exuberant context of Cayuna politics, was that he was able to make his declarations in peace—until Oliver told me that every day now two or three trucks full of Sheba's Sons left Queenshaven for Eastmoreland. They were present in tranquil but patent readiness at every meeting.

It was during this time that I decided to break with Bernice.

I tell myself that I decided, but did I, in fact, choose the moment any more than I chose to love Joan Culpepper? Was it not rather that I had come to detest passion in the way that one at a dangerous edge of hunger will recoil from food? For in those days, passion sickened me: not only my own, but the tidy fulfilments of it I saw among my friends, even the huge pulse of it that throbs under the skin of the world and is sensed only by the blood.

So that the evening when I went to Bernice, I seemed to be

driven by an overpowering urge to isolate myself from all the tiresome demands of a vast arrangement in which I was now rendered incapable, as by emasculation. By this, and by some perverse and sudden obsession with honesty. Even duplicity depends on intimate, responsible relationship with another, and I wanted loneliness.

She said: "I see." Very slowly, standing before the cash register and looking back over her shoulder at me. The bar was closed, Cherry had gone and she had been checking the evening's take when I told her, in words that seemed to hide like partridges and take flight after my mind had passed. She pushed the till shut, turned and came to the bar: her face was grained, like some stone, with streaks of grey that faded as she looked at me. Leaning on the counter, she said carefully, as if reporting a message given her for me by a stranger: "So you in love now."

"Yes," I said.

"An' you want finish with me?"

"I don't want to. I have to."

"She say so?"

"She doesn't know. Anyway, she has nothing to do with it. She won't even have anything to do with me."

"But you love her bad?"

"Yes."

"I know." She nodded, an abstract concurrence from her gathered knowledge. "That can turn a man foolish. Like it turn you now." She put her hand on mine. I have never felt such guilt as at the dry chill of her palm. "Thank you, mister," she said softly.

For a second I thought she was being sarcastic, before my apathy and self-preoccupation seemed to dissolve in the warm, sad clarity of her statement.

"What are you thanking me for?" I asked. "Don't say that."

"I must thank you," she said. "No, not for the good times we have. But for keeping up a good face all this time when you not happy. I will remember that, Stefan. I was worth that, eh?"

"Bernice. Don't."

"No. I mean it. . . . I know say that this would have to happen one day." She caught her breath, with a faint, whistling sigh. "I know, but I pretend it could go on. I tell you something, Stefan. Is three men I lose in my life. Two others before you. But neither of them hurt like I hurt now. If I did know how much I was going to feel it, maybe I send you away before this." She looked up then and said in a hard, crabbed voice, such as I had never heard her use before. "Who this woman is, eh? What's she have that hold on to you like that?" But, poor Bernice, even in the ordeal of jealous hurt, she was betrayed by her queenly instinct of solicitude and compassion, was deprived even of the inviduous relief of bitchiness. For she added: "Stefan! Stefan, don't look so. Try an' bear it a little. Is the first time a woman ever trouble you, no? Is the first time you never get one that you want?"

"Yes."

"I did think so." She rubbed the back of my hand tenderly, bent and kissed it, and as if in answer to an anxious query, her cloudy green eyes level with mine, said: "But it don't spoil you, Stefan. It only—it only make you proud. An' that will pass."

"Bernice," I said. "I love you. I couldn't have imagined there was anyone like you in the whole world."

"Cho!" she said, and gave a laugh like a green stick breaking. "Love! Love have teeth like a bulldog. The only thing you can do is wait until it let go . . . or until it starve to death."

She put her elbows on the counter and rested her face between her palms. My betrayal lay like a corpse in the parlour of a house where nobody yet believes in the death.

Marcus Heneky was arrested on the Sunday following. He had held an open-air service on the beach at Bon Accord, and the police had waited until it was over, and the crowd gone, before they came to the house where he was eating, charged

209

him with unlicenced preaching, and taken him away. I read of it the next morning as I dressed.

"Hullo, Doctor Cole," I said a minute later, to the head of my department, on the telephone. "Stefan Mahler here. Can you arrange something for my nine o'clock lecture? I must go to the dentist immediately. I think I've woken with an abscess or something."

I went out and drove down to Oliver's.

"You people play a rough game, don't you?" I said. He and Sybil were at breakfast on the wide, red-tiled, white-porticoed back veranda of their beautiful house which was left to them by a friend hanged for killing his unfaithful lover, three or four years before I came to Cayuna: it is one of the few houses in the island where one can feel design like the stimulus of an intelligent mind. In the backyard, the macaws for which Sybil has such a fancy were rasping from their cages like querulous old women. "Whose idea was it?" I continued. "Yours or Andrew's? It sounds like you. Clever, nasty and legal."

"No," he said calmly. "It wasn't my idea. Nor Andrew's. I think Charlie Macintosh"—he named the secretary of the Radical Party—"and Littleford thought it up between them. D'you believe that?"

"I suppose so," I said.

"Good. Then sit down. Have you had breakfast?"

"No, but I'm not hungry. This is a damned dirty trick, Oliver. You don't approve of this?"

"No. But I'm glad for somebody to do the dirty work for me. If the dirty work is inside the law. And it is. Preaching without a licence carries jail in this island."

"If you applied that," I told him, "you wouldn't have enough prisons to hold the people who do. Why poor old Heneky?"

Sybil was looking at me with astonishment: even a woman of her scope, in Cayuna, could not easily relate this much interest on my part to someone like Marcus Heneky.

Oliver said, in a flat tone that repudiated argument or discussion: "You're not a virgin, Stefan. You know why Heneky is going up before the magistrates this morning." His thin, pale face was set hard. "Or, really, you don't know. You're a foreigner and you don't have any responsibility. But too many people like Charlie and Eugene Douglas have worked too hard to get us where we are for an old fool like that to come and knock things down. If he wants to get into the ring then let him learn the rules. He made a mistake and he's been disqualified. . . ."

"Yes," I said. "Of course. You're quite right. I'm sorry if I intruded." I got up quickly. "Bye-bye, Sybil. Oliver. See you soon."

I left them, trailing my words, as I strode with ludicrous briskness from the veranda and through the house to my car in the driveway. Oliver bounced down the steps as I switched on, ran round the front of the car, leaned in at the window and turned the key to "off".

"You're more trouble than you're worth," he said gently. "But I suppose we have to put up with you. . . . I'm sorry. I'm very sorry. Apologies accepted?"

"What d'you think?" I said. "I was just wondering how I was going to come back without looking a fool."

"It's a dirty business," he said. "He'll get six months for sure. The only thing in our favour is that if we spoke Spanish we'd have shot him. . . . That poor woman. She'll be worried. Is that where you're off to now?"

"Yes," I said. "And to get him a lawyer if he doesn't have one."

"Try Gist," he said. "If he hasn't got on to the case already, he's the one. D'you know him?"

"No."

"You'll find him in the phone book. He's one of those professional Irish consciences, but he's a good lawyer."

"Right. I'll remember."

"Good luck," he said. "But he's going inside. . . ."

"Oliver," I asked, "tell me honestly. How much did you know about this?"

"On my word of honour, nothing until this morning, when I read about it. I'm only certain that Charles Macintosh and Littleford must have demanded that the police take action. Both of them know all about that sort of charge. They're old cell-mates. The colonial office put them both away for sedition during the war."

Oliver was, again, right in his appreciation. I went down to Long John's, that morning, to find Bernice fluttery with shock, uncertain of what she ought to do. Anything as ponderous and ramified as an operation of law was outside her scheme: she was hopelessly limited to the simple exercises of individual necessity.

Together we drove out of town to find Gist: a rosy, attenuated Irishman with a lavish beard, who has served a tour before every Bar in the British Commonwealth, wistfully attending on the hope of another Easter Rebellion.

We got him to Bon Accord just in time for him to challenge, unsuccessfully, the right of the court to commit Marcus Heneky to six months at hard labour for serving God without a licence.

9

★

I

On a day when a great weight of cold air had spilled over from the Great Plains, rolled down across Louisiana and the Gulf, and come between the island and its cosy winter sun, I went into Queenshaven to meet Joan.

A bright sea was running and leaping before the wind as if trying to scramble bodily up the sides of the harbour. In Queen Charlotte Street, the girls were tossing their tails like mares, fretting at the bit of a hidden excitement. Clouds being planed like frail shavings from the polished sky. Everyone stropping his mind on the broad, steely edge of the sudden wind. I had a moment of nostalgia for the colder latitudes, for snow and the ringing air of a frozen day.

At this time, I had begun to wonder, with the inflamed ego of my condition, how it was that nobody had noticed what I was suffering because of Joan. Not the men, I told myself, but surely the women must have scented love on occasions when I had been careless or maudlin. But no. I was accepted as another on that tacitly agreed duty roster of friends who tried, unobtrusively, to save Joan, if not from herself, at least from disappearing for too long into her excesses. It would have been impossibly embarrassing had she returned to us in penitence or with promises of reparation. But the courtesy of a fastidious reserve never seemed to desert her when she was with us and not drinking. And sometimes, like the sound of muffled feminine laughter behind a curtain and the sparkle of eyes through a parting in that curtain, her innate sweetness and vivacity would reveal itself: in an exchange, in a recollection, in a gesture of tenderness, in a surrender to enjoyment so spontaneous and delightful that one felt flattered to be its cause. I am thinking, now, not as a lover or a husband, but as I might have seen her had I met her for the first time in a moment when she had shed the infinite weariness of her debauchery, without the censorship she imposed on herself.

But this day, as I drove down Queen Charlotte Street to the gallery overlooking the harbour, I had begun to ask myself, too, when she would begin to despise me, if she did not already: for in the end, any woman must feel a sort of placid contempt for the man who continues to love her without any reward.

Sybil was in charge of the gallery that day, and as I stepped from the head of the stairs into the room, one of her large tapestries which I had not seen or even heard mentioned, seemed to leap from the opposite wall like a rush of fire. It was a Leda and Swan: of such beautiful and ferocious sexuality that I felt the floor of my stomach drop. On the bank of any Cayuna mountain stream, a handsome, ample black girl sprawled naked, her skin still wet and her round face shattered by the terror and pain of her appalling privilege: the god was penetrating her from behind, his feet like enormous spatulas of golden leather curving implacably on her fat thighs as he forced them apart: the pitiless, thick and lovely snake of his neck and great golden beak pinned her neck to the ground, and one could feel the slow beat of the outstretched wings, thudding like pistons, as they drove his divinity into her womb: she had managed to put one hand under her cheek, to save her face from being jammed against the stones, but the corner of her mouth had been cut, and a tender trickle of blood flowed from that uncomprehending, screaming O: her other hand was flung out and clenched into the loose damp earth. Just beyond

214

the reach of her outflung hand lay a faded print dress, a pair of drab cotton drawers and a pathetically frivolous, pink brassiere: the trappings of her snug humanity as she must have dropped them before going in to bathe.

"Well, what d'you think?" Sybil asked. She had come from the desk in the corner to stand beside me as I stared at her spectacular and audacious assumption. "D'you like it?"

"Like it!" I said. "You nearly had my lunch all over your nice clean floor. Jesus, Sybil, it's magnificent. I've never even thought of Leda like that. It's such a gentle myth where I come from. If the government allows that to leave the country, heads ought to roll."

"Can you imagine the row," she asked, "if they bought that? Besides, where would they hang it? I can't see it at Reception House, myself. No. I guess the Americans will get it." She slipped her hand under my arm and began to lead me to the desk. "What can I do you for? I hope you've come to buy a picture."

"No. I'm meeting Joan here. When she comes over from the Barricades. I thought I'd take her to a show and give her dinner."

"Good. Try and head her off taking too many—without using the snaffle."

"One tries. But it's a job sometimes." I stopped. "Yes," I told her. "I will take a picture if it's not tourist prices. That Glendale there." I pointed to a small landscape, all green, of an old house, weathered by rain, sun, time and the cycles of human aspiration it had sheltered, beside a road that climbed doggedly over a background hill.

"Oh, yes," Sybil agreed. "That's one of the best he's done." She went up to it and lifted the little price tab, and looked back at me. "Five guineas?"

"Yes."

I filled in a cheque at her desk, and took the picture and went out on to the terrace. It was cool but still against the wall of the gallery, out of the wind. The sea ran back and forth across the harbour and the sky seemed to tilt over the Barricades. I sat at the table nearest the wall and stood the picture on the chair opposite. In the strong, crystalline light it was even more harmonious and confident than it had been in the gallery, and the house shrugged itself into the surrounding country like a man into an old, indestructible jacket.

"I'll tell Joan you're out here," Sybil said.

"Thanks. She shouldn't be long. She's off duty at four."

I rested my chin on my hands overlapped on the table and studied my picture further. The water was slapping the piles of the pier below with sudden, uneven blows—and—Sybil was shaking me lightly by the shoulder, with the shyness we feel when forced to intrude on sleep.

"Stefan, dear," she said, "I'm sorry, but I'm closing up now. . . ."

The sky behind her head was brilliant with a soaking crimson, and big oily clouds lay like continents because the wind had dropped.

"What time is it?"

"Gone six. Are you feeling all right? I had to shake you for a long time."

"Yes. I'll just wash the sleep out of my eyes. So she didn't show up, eh?"

"No. She's off somewhere, you can bet. Stupid cow."

"Did she telephone?"

"No. Not a word."

In the little lavatory, I ran the water until it was cool and splashed myself awake. Then I began to prepare for the evening ahead, like someone who knows that he must crawl and shudder his car across a great city in the rush hour. As I was drying my face, Sybil came to the door.

"She's on the phone. Just as I thought. Sounds as if she's at one hell of a party."

"Hullo, Joan." I was half-sitting against the edge of the desk

216

because my legs were dulled and slightly trembling. "What a way to treat an old friend."

"There you are," she said with comic, hateful aggressiveness. "I can't make it tonight, I'm afraid. There's this thing going on, and I seem to be part of it." She gave a laugh like tissue paper fluttering down the wind. "I'm so sorry, Stefan. Another time, eh?" I could hear the erratic punctuation of a real wassail behind her.

"Yes," I said. "Have a good time. You wouldn't like me to call for you?"

"No," she said, after the briefest of pauses. "I'm not sure when I'm leaving. It's a sort of airline do, really, for the new pilots who came back today."

"I'm just about to give that girl up," Sybil said as I cradled the receiver. "Fun is fun and friends are friends, but she's getting too much for me."

"You don't mean that," I told her, and considered, seriously, whether it was worth the effort to speak. "You know you're stuck with her, like the rest of us."

She gave the sigh of unconsciously complacent strength.

"I suppose you're right. Where's she now?"

"Some party for new pilots. She's well away."

"Yes," she said. "Until tomorrow. I've told Oliver this: one morning after one of her big dives she's going to kill herself. Nothing dramatic. Just a modest little suicide, with as many loose ends tidied up as she can, to save people trouble. And you know when she'll do it?"

"No."

"The morning she looks at herself and sees that she's ugly. Not simply a bit battered here and there. But squashed around the edges. She'll do it then because she has got taste. And, boy, has she got pride in that body of hers. Not conceit, you know. But the sort of catholic female pride that I can't have because I know I'll never look like that. I don't think a man could understand what I mean, but it's the sort of pride another woman can share even if she is envious. It does us good to see a woman who can look like that and be like that when she's ready."

"Yes," I said. "I understand what you're getting at."

"Well, the day Joan knows for sure that she has no right to that anymore, because she has really coarsened, then she'll finish it."

Ancient superstitions wriggled on their bellies through the dark places of my mind. I smelled bad luck in her words like the odour from a cave of bats.

"I don't know," I said, to deceive the listening, ravenous spirits. "You only think that because you're an artist and you think integrity of line or form is as important to everybody as it is to you. She'll probably just go on until she runs out of fuel."

"Maybe you're right. . . . What a stupid business, eh?" She took her bag and a bunch of keys from the desk and we walked to the door. "D'you want to come up with me and take your chances on dinner?" she asked as she shut the door.

"Thanks, but I'll say no. I've got a dozen essays on my conscience and I might as well get them off it."

I saw her to her car in the street and waited until she had driven off before going to mine. Slowly, attentively, ridiculously, as if I had a brimming bowl of soup on the seat beside me, I drove up Queen Charlotte Street and across town to the public library. I thought: There's nothing more to be done; I'm used up; falling asleep like that this afternoon was a sign; I'm middle-aged; love has aged me; I'm thirty-three years old but age isn't a matter of years, it's experience; I just want to settle somewhere and find somebody to hug my back.

This and similar nonsense accompanied me all the way to the library on Bolivar Street.

I took the airmail edition of the *Times Educational Supplement* from the rack and read steadily through the university vacancies overseas. When I was finished, I took out my pocket diary and pen and copied the details of the three that seemed possible: one in Canada, I remember, another in Hong Kong, and a third in Baghdad. Going from the library, I remembered my Jewish origin and stopped, and scratched out the entry I had made for Baghdad.

A little soft pulse had started to tic somewhere behind my left eye; I smacked my face sharply but it wouldn't cease. Alternatives for the evening lay ahead, and I had occupied them all and found them unbearably confining before I was clear of the city.

So, finally, I drove across the mountains at the head of the Saviour Spring Road: to a small hotel on the northern slopes where I had once lunched with someone I was seeing off at Port Christopher on the banana boat.

But I couldn't finish half of my meal, and even the bottle of Chianti I had ordered was too much after the second glass.

About ten o'clock, I began the long, dark drive back to the university.

II

It is easy to understand why all other ages but our own have believed in demonic possession, personal devils, and the like. Certainly there is something almost improbable in the thought that the sheer wickedness with which I stopped at Joan's house that night belonged to me alone, was my own creation, so to speak. So much mischief and longing to destroy must, one is tempted to believe, have a source outside ourselves. It is too uncomfortable to feel that we carry that power of hate within us like a quiescent appendix.

And I am still not sure exactly what was my intention as I stopped the car after passing the entrance to her bungalow, reversed and turned across Saviour Spring Road into the small, gravelled yard. Some rabid hope of the body, I suppose, which took command when the politer hope of the mind thought itself dead.

Her Fiat was there, tucked into the corner of the hedge, and drawn up behind it, a larger, very smart coupé. I coasted to a stop beside them, and with a bizarre, reeling sense of lawlessness pushed open the shut, unbolted door to the living-room and stepped in.

She was sitting on the divan, leaning her back on the wall, her feet drawn up and her hands clasping her shins. The glass she held was nearly empty and she wore the drink she had already taken with a rakish, secure slant, like a hussar's cap. Lester Pow, the pilot who had been with her on the day of the crash, was sitting in the easy chair, his legs dangling over the arm, his tie loosened. A bottle of vodka, a bowl of ice-cubes and three bottles of ginger-beer stood on the low coffee-table between them. They both looked at me, as I entered, without any pleasure.

"Mahler," Lester said, not coldly, even a shade uncertainly, as if such a grossly ill-judged appearance must be unavoidable. "How are you, laddie?"

"Hullo, Stefan," Joan said quietly.

"Lester," I said. "Joan. Was it a good party?"

I sat at the dining-table, in one of the straight wooden chairs and looked at them expectantly. There was a huge blank territory in my head, like a child's first freehand map. Anything could fill it, and I simply waited for the first shading.

"Have a drink, Stefan," Joan said. "You'll find a glass in the kitchen."

She and Lester exchanged a glance of vexed, mild scorn, and I think, catching that glance, I finally determined to leave nothing behind but hurt and disorder.

"I was passing," I told them, slowly mixing myself a drink. "And I thought I'd look in. Was it a good party? Did you have lots of fun, Joan?"

"It was a good party," Lester said. "How are you, Stefan?"

"You asked me that before," I said. "D'you really want to know, or are you just filling in the gaps? I'm fine. How are you? You *look* fine, but then you can't always go by that. . . ."

"Stefan!" Joan said.

"In one second," I told Lester confidentially, "she's going to ask me to go. That girl, Lester, spends half her free hours asking me to go. It's like a Pavlovian reaction. As soon as I say a word. Crash! And I'm on my way out."

"Too bad," he said. "Well, it was nice seeing you."

"Steady. I haven't even tasted my drink."

"I wouldn't hurry a man over his drink," he said with deliberate evenness. His good face had become cautious and observant. Joan reached forward and patted his arm, a quick, intimate plea that I was grateful for. It helped me to ignore the sense of shame and disbelief that had, at that second, nearly sent me from the house.

"Very good," I said, sipping my drink. It tasted vile. "This *is* a drink." I crossed my legs. "Nice little cold snap we had today. I hope I didn't interrupt anything. If I did you'll just have to hope I don't want a second drink."

"Stefan." Her voice was sad and openly beseeching now. "Don't do that." She breathed harshly once through her open mouth, and shook her head impatiently, as if to clear a buzzing.

"Don't do what, Joan?"

"Don't do what you're doing to yourself."

"Laddie," Lester said, with a real kindness that made me twitch with avid, abject fury. "Take my tip and leave it off. You're making a fool of yourself and I don't think you're a fool."

"To tell you the truth, Lester, there isn't a bigger fool in all Cayuna than me. Ask her."

"I'm not really interested," he said, speaking to the floor, sitting on the edge of his chair.

"Lester!" I said suddenly, with desolate savagery.

"Yes?"

"I think you'd better go, don't you? And leave Joan to sleep it off."

Joan sprang to her feet, snapping her long legs straight and standing on the same jerky thrust. I had come here to hurt, and looking at the heaviness in her eyes, I knew I had succeeded.

"Why?" she asked. "Why did you do this, Stefan? Don't you have any pride at all?"

"I was mistaken," I told them both, smiling. "I thought I was the biggest fool in Cayuna, but I was wrong. She is. If you can't understand why I'm doing this, Joan, you must be stone deaf, and blind into the bargain."

"D'you know what you look like?"

"I have a pretty good idea."

Lester stood, coming up slowly, with a dejected air of resolve. He took a step towards me, and I stood too. And as he lifted his hand, my fist was flung on to his cheek from a release of power like the breaking of a cable. My body was hurled before a roaring wind and the blank space in my head was shaded, now, with a mingled black redness, the outlandish stain of dishonour. I believe that I was blinded with the brutal joy, for I cannot remember seeing Lester's face, but felt my fists, guided with the terrible accuracy of stones from a sling, crashing on their target with a violence that seemed to return to me like new strength. Then I was standing near the wall by the divan and he was holding the wall with his hands reached above his head, as though he were trying to climb it, and all was taking place with a horrifying, slow precision: his slithering collapse on to the divan and from there to the floor, Joan's hands dragging wildly at my arm and her abandoned sob of entreaty, control coming back to my brain, timidly, like silence after the dropping of a huge bomb. (Months later, he told me that when he lifted his hand it was only to touch my elbow in persuasion.)

I said: "I think I've killed him."

"You're not man enough for that," she said tonelessly and knelt by his head.

I went on one knee and felt for his pulse.

"Get some water and the towel from the kitchen," she said,

and lifted his head into her lap. She looked at me as though she were using me, in passing, as a mirror.

In the kitchen, I rinsed the washing-up bowl, and filled it with water and brought it and the towel to her.

"Hold these," I told her. "I'm going to put him on the divan."

I bent and lifted him under the knees and shoulders. I thought, with the ludicrous irrelevance that bangs like a fool's bladder against our gravest moments: I didn't realize I was so strong. For I seemed to raise his slack body with ease. She dipped the end of the towel and pressed it damp.

Propping my shoulder against the wall, arms folded across my chest, I watched her as she sat on the divan's edge and sponged the removable evidence of my barbarity from his face. All the uncounted millions of invisible threads which we spin from the heart and senses, and through which we are nourished by the world, seemed to be breaking without a sound, to dangle about me useless. A streak of music from the club at Saviour Spring Corner leaped the hedge like a stray cat coming out of the night and disappeared. Remorse had gone beyond simple emotion: it had become a problem of containment that felt almost physical. I stood there holding the knowledge of what I had done and what I was, like a man carrying his spilled bowels in his hands, gathering his strength with finical discretion for the next step. Anything I said could only add an unseemly refuse to the rubble they both had to clear.

Lester came to, with a puzzled grunt, and sat up like a horse fallen on an icy road heaving away from the whip. Joan touched her hands to his arms as though he might break in pieces.

"Lester," she said. "My dear. You're all right?"

"Yes," he answered in a voice that hobbled. "Yes. I'm all right."

He glanced at me, in exactly the way that a man might rest his eyes on a distant tree or dog, because one must look at something. Four cuts opened like thin bloody lips where I had

223

broken the skin against bone, and the flesh under his right eye was beginning to puff. Joan tried to smile at him but he wouldn't meet her eyes. His young, mauled face—on which the dapper alertness of his calling seemed to lie like an unfair weight—was shuttered tightly, like the face of a child being teased by the pack about some shameful family secret. He stood up, and looked about him with a groping intentness, as if finding an exact point of inaccessibility for himself between the helplessly pitying woman on the divan and me.

"Well," he said, "that was a bit of a turn. Wasn't it, laddie?"

"Lester," Joan said, holding him. "Lie down, honey. Lie down for a while."

He shook free. Not rudely, nor even with the tremor of personal repulsion, but carefully, as if something independent and susceptible and precious had been damaged and needed utter solitude to be restored. With an irreducible and heart breaking dignity of assumed cheerfulness—all the more moving because you felt it was experimental, a testing of his own broken resources and responsibility for the decent attitudes of life—he said: "It's all right, Joan. These things will happen. I'd better go now. I don't feel like the old Lester we all know and love."

He took his peaked cap, with its prescribed irregularity of drooping crown, from the table, stuck it on the back of his fat, black curls and walked to the door like a man holding an incontinent baby.

"Lester," Joan said. "Don't go because of him. He's not worth it. You're not fit to drive yet."

He turned at the door: sacrosanct as a squire on the vigil before his knighthood. Until that moment, I don't think I had understood how thoroughly my fists had plundered his body and mind. Pride alone kept him going through the door and into the yard. I was suddenly alarmed, as though I had sent a competitively drunk man from my own house to his car. The same warning bell must have sounded in Joan, for we started for the yard simultaneously, without a comment.

Lester was reversing as we emerged. When he saw us, he accelerated with a grating rasp of tyres that spurted gravel against the wall of the bungalow. The car sprang forward to the gap in the hedge—and stopped, its indicator winking above the back fender.

Joan and I began to run, and he must have heard our feet crunching into the gravel: his car leaped again, as though on a hiccough, and by our arrival at the gap, it had vanished.

Joan stopped in the entrance and turned back to the bungalow, as if alone. But some unreasonable and compelling certainty urged me on down Saviour Spring Road, jogging with uneasy, laboured breaths.

I turned the bend in the road and saw the glowing red eyes of his tail-lights. He had drawn up close to the bank under a big guango tree. One of the Saviour Spring Road's exiguous lamp standards was placed just beside the tree, and as I ran up, I could see him drop his head onto the back of his hands gripping the rim of the steering wheel. He was breathing deeply, with the concentrated thoroughness of a seasick man, when I stopped by the opened window.

"Lester," I said. "Please, Lester. Don't try to drive the way you are. Let me take you home."

"Go away, Mahler. I'm all right. I'm just taking a rest."

His voice was weak, and seemed to snatch at the words as if it had made a number of miscalculated dives.

"God, I'm sorry!" I said foolishly. "I'm so sorry that I don't know how to say it. Lester, for Christ's sake, move over and let me drive you home. . . . If I could only tell you how much I wish this hadn't happened. . . ."

He rolled his forehead on the back of his hands, turning his face to me, and smiled as if confronted with the sort of squalor that is unimportant because of its fortuitous rarity.

"Mahler," he advised, patiently, from the misted periphery of stunned detachment, "why don't you go away, Mahler? You're not doing me any good, and you're such a dreary

225

person. Go away, eh? And do something useful for once."

He sat straight, and touched his fingers to his face like someone attempting his first lesson in Braille. He started the car.

"Lester," I babbled. "You can't tell me anything I don't know. Really. If I could only say.... But don't drive, man. It's dangerous when you're like that. Let me. . . ."

"Oh, go to hell," he said with sad boredom. "You stupid animal."

The bonnet of the car rose on the jolting catch of the engaged clutch, dipped, and he was far down the road, already in the bright nimbus of the clustered lights at the corner. He was driving steadily.

I looked along the road to where he had passed from sight. For ten or fifteen seconds perhaps. Then I turned to the great tree under which he had stopped. I looked at my right hand in the gloomy light with the close, cold interest of a surgeon examining a uniquely malignant cancer. The tough, indented bark smelled clean and comforting in the private, midnight air. With the utter, passionless might of derangement I slammed my fist into the dead centre of the trunk: a terrific and shrewdly contrived blow which turned my knuckles so that the ridges of wood shaved my skin nearly to the wrist as I thrust my full weight after the speed of my fist. I seemed to ricochet from side to side of a bowl of pain lit by the macabre glare of sheet lightning, and then I was huddled above the roots of the tree where they disappeared under the asphalted road, nursing my wet hand, and the echo of my yell was not diffusing itself across the savannah but dying to a whimper inside my head.

I went back up the road, hugging the bank as though on the edge of a precipice. My splitting arm was slung into the other, and I gazed down at the raw, glistening smears on my hand like the triumphant survivor of a vendetta. From some residual instinct of pedantry, I latinized the bones I was sure were broken. The gradual rise into the foothills of the road under

226

my feet canted suddenly, as though I had crossed the fulcrum of a seesaw.

The door of the bungalow was shut, and I went past in the way one passes the gates of a palace, with a sense of familiarity but without any thought of possible entry or invitation. I opened the door of my car, sagged before the wheel—and fumbled in the empty keyhole of the ignition. It was three miles to the university and I knew I would never make it on foot.

"Joan," I said, tapping on the door, "I've left my keys on the table. D'you mind if I get them?"

I heard her move across the tiles behind the door, and waiting for her, I pitched down a spiral of humming darkness. When she opened the door, I was humped against the concrete extension from the jamb.

"Here," she said, and dropped the keys into my palm. "What kept——?" and, sharply, "What's wrong with you?" and, "Good God!" as, stepping aside to expose me to the light, she saw my hand.

"Can I just run it under the tap for a minute?" I said, dreamily. Giddiness and pain were surging up my mind like waves up a beach. There was even a repeated moment, like the seventh wave, which seemed to erode an area untouched by the others.

She gave a small, toothy hiss of revulsion and shepherded me through to the kitchen. I rested my arm on the sink's edge and she turned the tap.

"Let it run," she said, and left me hurriedly.

I watched, passively, the red-muddied drops running from my fingers' ends and held to the ravening pain, which now seemed to have found some hitherto undiscovered centre of sensation, as I would have held the last thread of a frayed rope on a mountain face.

She came back into the kitchen, put a bottle of disinfectant on the draining-board beside me, bit the edge of an old cotton petticoat and began to tear it into strips.

227

"I don't have any bandage," she said. "This will have to do."

She mixed a solution of the disinfectant in the bowl we had used for Lester, and I sank my hand into it. Neither of us said anything: we performed the necessary actions like two mechanics over a repair they have done a thousand times before.

"That ought to do it," she said, knotting two strands over a bulky wrapping. "You'll have to go to hospital as soon as you get back to the university. D'you want me to drive you?"

"No," I said, "I'll manage quite easily. I'll hold the wheel between my thumb and hand and go slowly. Thanks. Good night."

"You'd better have a drink before you go."

"Yes."

I followed her into the drawing-room and sat on the edge of the divan like a man with a boil at the end of his spine. She poured four fingers from the half-filled bottle of vodka.

"You want anything with it?" she asked.

"No thank you."

"Ice?"

"Yes thanks."

I took the glass, and she sat on the wooden arm of the easy chair. Her face was almost amiable with wondering question. "Now how did that happen?" she asked, and pointed briefly to my hand. "You didn't trouble Lester again?" Her voice hardened with hope of denial.

I told her: obediently and flatly, as if repeating a multiplication table.

"What was the idea, Stefan?"

"I don't know."

"Lord," she said. "You're a strange one, aren't you? Go on. Drink your drink and get out of here."

Her face was receding into haziness and growing large again with a startling purity of definition.

"Yes, of course."

228

I swallowed and choked.

She said: "Oh, Stefan, why did you have to do that to such a nice boy? You weren't even drunk. And you made him feel so—so damn little."

"No," I said with moonstruck solemnity. "No. It won't be like that. It doesn't matter, really. For him."

"What?" she said coldly. "Why, you——"

"No, listen, Joan." Even to me, my voice was shrill. "I mean it. But not how it sounds. You see. Suppose a decent man like —like Andrew, for instance was to beat another man to pulp. Then there's probably something behind it. The other fellow would have to ask himself what he'd done to deserve it from somebody like Andrew. But a man like me now. There's nothing to it. It's a sort of dirty accident. Like being robbed by a thug who sticks a gun in your back."

"What are you saying?" she said, and leaned forward to look at me with a new uncertainty.

"I don't know," I told her, and as I said this, I felt the first tears on my cheeks.

I thought: this is ridiculous; I haven't cried in twenty years; not since Paris just after the war began.

I looked into my glass, with my head well down and watched from a great inward distance the tears coming past my lids like rain coming through the eaves of a house. I thought then: There's nothing to be done about this, except she mustn't see.

I felt as if someone trusted without question had betrayed me. It was a completely silent, irrepressible weeping, and I tried to halt it with as much success as if I had tried to carry water in my cupped hands.

With my head still bent, my arms across my knees, in an attitude of reflection, I saw the first bright drop fall on my shoe, and felt the second tickle my jaw before it fell too.

She said: "Here! What's this?" In a strange voice, between fright and briskness.

I made to rise, knowing that concealment was no longer

possible, and she put her hands on my shoulders firmly and pushed me back.

"Stefan?" she said, again in that troubled and tentative voice. "Stefan. No. It's not as bad as all that."

She touched my face, gingerly at first, and then decisively as I pulled my head away.

"No," she said angrily. "No, Stefan. Don't." And rose and held my head into the indescribable, cloth and flesh scented softness of her hip. "Oh, you idiot," she said. "Don't."

Then I felt her sit beside me and her suddenly determined arms closed around my shoulders and head and she pressed my face against her breast. Her blouse had the stale, clinging odour of clothes worn all day in the tropics. She rocked me gently.

"Stop it," she said. "It's all right, man. You don't have to worry. I'll look after you. Oh, Stefan, don't cry. Don't cry like that. It's not fair to cry without a noise."

Rocked like a skiff on the warm swell of that unexpected harbour, I cried myself out.

A few minutes later, I said: "D'you want me to go? I'm not holding you to that. I cheated."

She smiled, the sly and carnivorous smile of a woman who has had her mind made up by her emotions.

"You stay where you are," she said, and played with my bandaged hand held between hers like a large, clumsy white mouse between the paws of a cat. "You're my problem now, I guess." She kissed me with soft, confirming calm, as one would spontaneously reassure a child, and then a longer, half-accusing, half-hungry kiss of excitement. "What happened?" she asked, chuckling softly against my ear. "What happened, eh, Stefan?"

A lucid, loving appreciation of the world's farce and beauty had filled me. Happiness was too sudden, yet, to receive even the image of desire.

"I don't know what happened," I told her. "I don't think I'll ever know anything for sure again."

My hand was hurting so badly that I knew I would have to leave her soon for attention at the university hospital. It was not the radiant, flaming pain of half an hour before, but an increasing pressure, as though the ache had petrified.

I looked at my hand, my faithful hand, abused and unconscious ally, and thought of it and my involuntary tears and the body's deep guile.

The next day I went to her at lunch time, driving slowly along as many back roads as I could with the wheel rim slotted between my thumb and the rigid plaster framework about my hand.

"Just tell me how you did it, Mahler," Doctor Robasingh had begged the night before, in the voice of one who has few surprises left in life. "I can't see how you managed something like this. Three chipped metacarpals, one badly bruised articulation at the hamate, compound fractures of minimus and annularis phalanges, flayed to the bone over a limited area. Tell me so I won't keep awake at nights working it out."

"Oh, all right," I had said. "I tried to knock a tree down, if you must know."

"Thank you," he had replied. "Yes. That would explain it. You notice I don't ask why. Simply *how* is what interests me. . . . And to think that one time I nearly went into psychiatry," he had added, indulgently reflecting on an aberration of youth.

She was waiting for me when I turned into the tiny square of gravelled yard: sitting on the step of the open doorway, dressed in the same shorts and shirt she had worn that Sunday morning at the cove.

She said: "I was just beginning to get frightened."

"Frightened? Why?"

"I had begun to convince myself you weren't going to come back. And I didn't like the idea at all."

"You're not serious," I said. "Really? To tell you the truth, I was feeling pretty scared myself coming over."

"Why, darling?"

"I was wondering if you hadn't changed your mind. If you weren't feeling that you have been the sucker in a con game."

"Oh, I know that," she said. "That's what makes it so nice. Darling, how's your hand?"

"Fine. I got off lighter than I deserved."

We stood on the step in the paternal sun of a Cayuna winter, holding hands experimentally, like adolescents, and smiling at each other as though trying our smiles on for size. Then we went into the drawing-room.

"I've been waiting for you to come," she said, "so that I could have a drink. It doesn't seem to make any difference where that's concerned."

"You didn't expect it to, did you?"

"Yes. Was that silly?"

"Not silly. Just part of the jazz, as Oliver would say."

"I don't want to think I'm going to go on as I used to," she said.

"No, neither do I."

"I've always managed to keep it separate from work and things like that," she said hopefully. "D'you think I can make you into a sort of substitute for work, darling?"

"I don't know. I really don't know. I only know that at the moment, I don't care, but that I will in a few weeks. I don't think I could take another man. Not even a nice boy like Lester."

"No more men," she said quickly. "I can't promise about drinking, but I'm sure about the men. I love you so much, all at once, that I feel foolish. D'you believe that?"

"Yes," I said, holding her close with one arm on my lap in the easy chair. "Not as much as I will, but I believe it enough. How about all those drinks you promised me?"

"Yes," she said happily and jumped up. "God, Stefan, I

really want to get drunk today. I'm not going on duty until tomorrow morning. You don't have to go back, do you? You don't have any lectures?"

"No," I said. "I've scrounged the first unjustified day off I've ever taken. I used this as an excuse." I lifted my plastered hand.

She looked me over from head to foot, her black, deeply glinted eyes polished and caressing. Then she went to the door-way between the living-room and the kitchen and called to the maid. I heard the wordless murmur of an answer from the laundry at the back of the bungalow.

"Bring the rum and some ice and sodas," Joan said, "And you can serve as soon as you're ready."

After lunch, she said, directly but looking at her coffee-cup: "I want you to make love to me."

"Yes," I said. "What about her?" And I nodded towards the kitchen where Evadne, the maid, was washing up what she had already cleared.

"This is my business," Joan said. "I don't question hers and I don't expect her to question mine. I want you to make love to me, Stefan. I've never wanted anything so much in my whole life."

And afterwards:

"I have to tell you something," she said, speaking into the pillow, with her forehead on her crossed forearms. "But you must promise not to get angry. D'you promise?"

"No. I'd never make a promise in the dark. Not even for you."

"All right. Will you promise not to interrupt until I've finished?"

"Yes. That's reasonable."

I was lying on my back, smoking. At any second now, I had decided, I'll float right up from the bed and become one of those sun speckles on the ceiling.

She said, in a strained, uncompromising voice: "D'you know where Lester lives?"

"No. Should I?"

"He shares a big bungalow with three other Air Cayuna pilots. They live and let live, if you understand what I mean."

"Yes," I said easily. "The usual bachelor *ménage*."

"Last night," she said; I could hear the words tumble, like the quick rush of water between two damming rocks. "After you left, I drove down. He wasn't asleep. He was sitting up alone, drinking. I made him go to bed with me. I had to, Stefan. It was the only thing I could do. I just couldn't have left him like that. . . . Well?"

"I promised not to interrupt."

"I've finished."

She put a hand out, questioningly, as an animal might sniff from a thicket, and I stubbed my cigarette in the tray on the bedside table and took her hand, squeezed it and began to laugh. I think, now, that my laughter was the last declension, like the slack burr from a run down alarm clock, of the tense, despairing months I had passed.

"Stefan?" she said fearfully. "You don't mind? You understand why I had to do it? I almost turned back, but I had to go through with it."

I finished laughing and raised myself slightly, fell on her face and saluted it with warm, approving kisses.

"And Oliver says," I told her, "that it's we Jews who trail conscience through life like a matador's cape. Of course, I understand. . . . Now you frighten me a little," I added, gravely. "You're too damned honourable. I don't know if I can live up to that."

She tucked her head into the space between my chin and chest.

"God," she said, "you're a sweet man, Stefan. You know that?"

I dug my chin gently into the tousled top of her head, serenely fuddled with the first wonder of possession.

"I'm not sweet," I told her. "But I'm lucky. They look like the same thing sometimes."

When I was nearly asleep, she raised herself on her elbow and hung above me with a face of wan, dogged frankness.

"Listen to me," she said. "You don't think this will make a difference? Later on, I mean."

She tugged a broad lock of her hair forward, splaying it to show the intrusive filaments of grey.

"No."

"I'm older than you."

"By three or four years. I'll catch up on you." I nestled my face between her hanging breasts and she hugged me to her with a little groan.

"You see," she said, "I didn't believe this could happen to me again. I used to hope it would, but I didn't expect it. No. I suppose I didn't want it, really. And I've been a real slut. You're going to have to put up with knowing a lot of men who've slept with me."

I pulled her down with tender roughness.

"You and me both," I told her. "A couple of old sexual vagrants. A woman I once knew used to call it 'going over the hill'. And no matter if you go over a thousand hills or one, it comes to the same thing in the end: the one body somewhere that it's most comfortable to go to sleep against."

"You really believe that?" she said against my chest.

"Almost."

"Good," she said, stretching like a dog until her joints creaked, and throwing a leg over mine. "I don't know if it means anything but it sounds nice and safe."

And in a few minutes I felt the tickle of her breath across my chest, and the endorsement of her parted lips pressed in sleep against my flesh.

IO

———————— ★ ————————

I

Looking back to the few weeks after she first went to sleep trustingly in the crook of my arm, I could almost resent the inadequacy of the language we use to make life real. If what I feel now is happiness, what then am I to call the condition that invested us for a period brief as a heart-beat, timeless as an epoch? For both of us, I think, those weeks remain a romantic projection like Lyonnesse or Camelot: a territory in which we both woke and which we use now, like some great legend, to refund our sober lives with the memory of an ideal and chivalrous conduct. The world outside ourselves was so irrelevant that we did not even find that it trespassed. The necessities of work and social contact were hardly considered any more than the habits of hygiene or the humdrum domestic obligations. In those days, I remember, we both took a great deal of childish pleasure in that capacity lovers discover for making themselves invisible to others without absence. Totally absorbed in each other, we managed to keep our infatuation as secret as the courtship of two wild animals. And we did this, I think, as much from a sense of protection as from a spirit of innocent mischief. We were both vulnerable, we knew without saying, and we realised, also, that this magnificent climate of exclusive generosity and tenderness could not last. Sooner or later, we would have to share the temperate, irksome seasons of everyday living.

"I'll look after you," her snared instinct had prompted her

to cry that night. But in those weeks it was she who put herself into my hands. And, revelling in the unaccustomed luxury of having to be truly responsible for someone, I suppose that I must have done competently. At least, I was always there; and after a while, with the instinct for practical evaluation which seems never to desert women, she must have convinced herself that getting too drunk, too often, deprived her of enjoying my company. She began to get aggressive and boring about refusing a drink when she was balanced between her desire for it and her desire for me, and I took that as a hopeful sign. And the occasions when we disappeared without trace to some private world of mutual discovery grew more and more frequent.

"How long have you been having an affair with her, Stefan?" Sybil asked me one day, with a dry, admonitory concern. I was in her studio, modelling a Spanish Conquest priest for a textbook she had been commissioned to illustrate.

"An affair with whom?"

"With Joan, man."

She put her long brush down and came over to where I stood holding the broomstick that would become a crucifix in her picture. My scarred hand was just able now to bend without gripping.

"How did you guess?" I asked, regretfully, but with a certain smugness.

"Me!" she said. "You forget I grew up in a yard, no, boy? Seven to a room. I must be getting fat and lazy or I'd have seen it before. I began to get the idea last night when she telephoned to ask if you were here."

"In point of fact I was on my way to her when she telephoned. She told me she'd called you."

"I'm not worried about that," she said, still with that hint of challenging and disillusioned grimness in her tone. "I'm asking how long you've been going to bed with her."

"About four weeks. No. Five."

"Look, Stefan," she said with sudden, friendly appeal.

237

"Take it easy with that girl. A man like you could cause a woman a hard time when he leaves her. And I don't think Joan has enough left to take that sort of beating."

"You're a sentimental old gossip," I said sternly, and laughed: the concept of my being able to do without Joan seemed as unreal as Oliver without Sybil.

"What's so funny?"

Her face was lowering with a quick anger.

"You," I told her. "If you only knew. I'm so tangled in this business that I'm even willing to contemplate Mrs. Culpepper as a future mother-in-law." I made a face of only half-assumed distaste. "And that's not only love speaking, Sybil. That's sheer bloody heroism. I went there to tea the other day and she told me that she'd been to a reception the night before. . . . 'The nicest gathering I've attended in years, Doctor Mahler,' she said. 'There wasn't a dark face except for the servants.' She's fascinating in a gruesome sort of way. Like those people in Europe who harp on about how good life was before 1914."

"My!" Sybil said, grinning with relief. "You're a cute customer. Why you didn't tell us?"

"I haven't told you now. Remember that. You're bound to tell Oliver, I suppose. But no one else. Agreed?"

"Sure. You really serious about it?"

"Don't I look it?"

Her handsome, discerning eyes examined my face closely for a few seconds.

"Yes," she said. "You look it. I wonder how I didn't see it before." She smiled again, teasingly. "Close your eyes! Quick!"

I did so.

"All right," she said, stepping behind me. "The dress I have on: it have pleats or not?"

"For goodness' sake, Sybil. D'you expect me to notice that?"

"You!" she said, going back to the easel with a derisive flick of her pleated skirt. "When I first knew you, Stefan Mahler,

238

you'd have noticed what a woman was wearing if she passed you going a hundred miles an hour, on a dark night, in a closed car." And after she had dabbed and touched and stroked at the canvas for a minute, she asked: "Is there a connection between all this and your hand? I have a feeling there is, but I can't quite figure it."

"Women are bad enough," I told her, "at making these *non sequitur* hops into what they think is the truth. But women who happen to be artists are ten times worse. They feel they have a licence to practise. No. I told you how it happened. I lashed out in a bad dream and hit the wall. Go on with your work and leave me to wallow in my own warm muddy thoughts of love."

"But tell me something, man," she said a few minutes later, in the coyly prurient, scandal-hunting voice of women. "How you could hit the wall and that bed of yours at the flat is right in the middle of the room?"

"I'm a sleep-walker too," I said. "I'm the only man in the world who can sleep, walk, dream and fight all at the same time."

And with the playful and sympathetic tensions of this exchange, Joan and I became public property, in a sense. As any prospective marriage must in a society too small for the privileges of anonymity. At times I nearly wished for London, and a basement flat and the indifferent, muffling millions among whom the individual life can make its long explosion without a sound or displacement. We were fostered now by a truly biological process, like symbiosis, in which Cayuna, or that stratum of it which we inhabited, began to digest us painlessly, sincerely offering itself for digestion in return: an interested and hospitable suburbia began to encroach on Lyonesse. The day I opened the *Gazette* and read the announced engagement that Mrs. Culpepper had slipped into the social column, I felt as though I had been towed into dry dock for some utilitarian conversion: from now on I was a cargo carrier on general charter. . . .

It was from the substance of these traditional, devouring platitudes—which we all promise ourselves we'll escape—that I found myself identified once more with Marcus Heneky and his violent, faithful, wrongheaded witness to the inspiration of an impossible dream.

II

Bernice told me when he was to be released from prison. For we did not sever all relationship after I had abandoned her. I had intended to, feeling that my presence, casually drinking in Long John's, would be an imposition, almost an impertinence after my whining and inept desertion. But then her father was arrested, and I had gone to her without conscious consideration, as I might have closed ranks with an estranged relative in distress. During the months that followed, even when jealousy, frustration and panic caused me to blunder through the days like a drunken savage lost in a doll's house, I always kept an implicit appointment: to drive her across to Eastmoreland District Prison, once a week, on a visit. I being no kin was, of course, refused permission to see him. And sometimes at night, or on a Sunday morning, I would sit in my old corner near the cash register and we would talk with the unguarded intimacy, the almost luxurious surrender to self-confession, of those who have loved and have drifted into a stilled and melancholy support of each other.

"The damn old fool," she said one day as we came back through the orange-grey dusk from Eastmoreland. "What him have to go an' get himself in prison for?" She began to weep. Like everything else she ever did, it was a straightforward, unabashed expression of the moment: strong, angry tears that came noisily. I gave her my handkerchief.

"It wasn't his fault," I said. "He got into a fight with professionals, Bernice. He just didn't realize how many places he'd left open for them to cut him down."

"Him should have known better." She sounded like a mother whose son has fallen out of a tree. "An' it making him so hard. Whenever I see him, now, I feel as if I would be 'fraid to touch him. Today I ask him, 'Papa, what you goin' to do when you come out?' An' him look at me sorrowful as if him know me but can't stop, an' say, 'Is try I try to do it peaceful, child. But them want war. All right. From now on this island will dance to my drum.' Now what him mean by that, Stefan?"

"He probably means that the government can't frighten him," I said. "Good. A country needs people like your old man, Bernice. People who shock everybody with their outrageous ideas. You know what the herring fishers in my country used to do when I was a little boy?"

"No?"

"They used to put a dogfish into the hold with the herrings. To keep them swimming up and down, so that they'd be in good condition when they arrived in port. Somebody like your father is a sort of dogfish in this island. But of course the big herrings don't like it. That's why he is in jail."

"You can talk," she said. "But is me have to pick him up when they knock him down."

On the afternoon of the day that he was released, I went down to Long John's. She was making change for a customer at the cash register and looking at her back as I waited, I thought, she has suddenly begun to show her age. Perhaps it was an observation from a cunning conscience anxious to justify my actions. But indeed seen from behind that afternoon Bernice had begun to accept time's contempt: her hair was grizzling, and the backs of her arms, along the triceps, had the first sag in what I remembered as firm fat, and I realized she had taken to wearing a girdle. Then she turned, and her swift, lifting smile of welcome covered the years like a mask.

"Soon come," she said, and went up the counter to her customer: a short, very fat, yellow man, owner of a small taxi-service, and one of her regulars.

"Thank you, me love," he said. "Tell me something, Miss Bernice. That Reverend Heneky? You know of him? I just realize that you have the same name."

"Yes. He's my father."

"True! Lord, I sorry. I didn't know or I wouldn't ask. It's just that I see he was release today."

"That's all right, Mister Roberts," she said drily. "I don't shame of him."

She came back to where I sat. We exchanged the same mocking, pulled down smiles as she came.

"Hello, mister," she said, and held up a beer glass, with her eyebrows lifted in question. I said, "Hullo, Bernice," and nodded.

"I don't see you to congratulate you," she said as she poured the beer for me. "I read the announcement in Sunday's *Gazette*."

"Yes," I said.

She put the filled glass before me and covered my hand for a second as she used to do.

"I glad for you, Stefan," she said. "I really glad. When I first read it, although I know say it was settled long time, I feel bad for a little. Woman foolish, you know. I never really believe it, until I see it in print. But now I glad. Like you was me son."

"You know just what to say, don't you?" I said. "You deserved better than me."

"Cho!" she said. "Don't talk foolishness. After all, I wasn't any baby. I know how life stay. It have a stick for every back, an' you must only hope that you can dodge a few blows."

"How has your father taken his blows?" I asked. "I want to go up and see him this afternoon."

Her broad face tightened with worry, and she shook her head slowly.

"Stefan," she said, almost stealthily, as if trying to creep up on her statement and make it innocuous. "Stefan, I wouldn't go up there if I was you. I did go to see him today an' I don't think him will make you welcome. Him change, you know."

"But, Bernice, I ought to go. How can I not? He knows that I didn't like what they did to him. I even tried to do something about it by getting him that lawyer . . . Gist."

"I know, Stefan. An' him know that too. But . . . but . . . I don't know say I should tell you this. . . ."

Her milky green eyes had darkened with trouble and she looked at me with a gaze that faltered and looked down again as she tapped her clasped hands on the counter.

"Tell me what?" I asked.

"Yes, you better know. I don't like things not open. Him did ask me today whether you an' me ever . . . ever go together. . . ."

"Yes. What did you say?"

"I tell him yes, of course. Why not? Then him say that if I want to be Babylon's whore that is my business, but that him is finished with Babylon for ever. Him say the only reason you find Mister Gist is to please me."

She spread her hands in a brief gesture that seemed to offer me any of life's unreason, pain, sadness and stubborn love from which to take my pick and mix to my own recipe.

"I see," I said slowly. "He's a serious man, eh, Bernice?"

"Him is now," she said. "Before them send him to prison, he couldn't help like people. Even people him mind tell him not to like. But now it seem all that liking was shut out of the prison an' get lost while him was inside."

"He hasn't sent you away, though?"

"No." She gave a dry, gentle laugh of understanding. "I think him really need me now. Him pretend that it's me have to come to him, but I know that him want me to. Just to see me an' use me to talk off the confusion in his head."

"Yes," I said. "I can believe that. But I'll have to see him all the same, Bernice. To keep the record straight. If he doesn't want it, that's his choice. But it must come from him."

"Stefan, man. Don't bother. He can be a hard old man,

243

when him want, an' he will only hurt. An' I know you take these things. You not like me."

"Me," I said. "I'm as tough as old boots. I just want him to know that I feel he was badly treated. You'd better give me another beer if he's going to be difficult."

That afternoon when I drew up outside the yard on the edge of the savannah, got out and went over to the gate, I was stopped before I could put my hand on the latch.

"Hi, mister. You have business here?" the Son of Sheba who had stopped me said. His voice sounded like a razor stropped easily on a leather strap. He lounged against one post and rested his great *coco-macca* stick against the other, not overtly but as if it grew out of the post and he merely held the end. Another of Sheba's Sons leaned on the gate inside and looked at a point past me from under his brows: an alerted, heatless stare in which I was not looked at but taken in as part of the scene.

"Yes," I said. "I've come to see the Reverend Heneky. You may have seen me here before he was arrested. I know him."

"Oh," the man outside said, speaking to the post opposite. "You know him. No. I never see you before. You from de police?"

"No," I said. "I'm a teacher. D'you think you might let me in? I know where to find him."

"An' him," the other man said, but not to me, "will know where to find you when him want."

They both smiled at the air before them.

"Perhaps you could tell him I'm here," I said. I had determined now that I would stand before the gate until dark or until I made them both so uneasy that they would have to act. "If you tell him that Stefan Mahler is outside, he might give you a message for me."

"T'addeus?" the gate-keeper said.

"Yes, Ivor?" the man inside answered.

244

"You ever hear dat Reveren' have any message for de white people dem?"

"No, Ivor. Unless say it's de message dat de Lion of Judah give to de Italian man when dem try an' conquer Zion."

"How dat message sound to you, mister?" the Son of Sheba outside asked me, looking at me with a calculating, gourmet's pleasure, as though tasting me seasoned with his insolence.

"No," I said flatly. "That's not the message I mean. May I go in, please?"

"Dis here is African territory," he said, quite quietly and seriously. "It belong to de Emperor of Abyssinia an' we hol' it for him. White people don't have no call in here. You say de Reveren' Heneky want see you. How I know say dat is true?"

"I never said he wanted to see me," I told him. "I want to see him. We've known each other for a long time, and I haven't seen him since he was arrested."

"Your people arrest him," the man inside, Thaddeus, said. The words seemed to suppurate rather than be formed, so complete was the hatred and dismissal from which they came. "Is your people add dat crime to de oders you commit against we."

"May I come in?"

"I don't t'ink so," Ivor said. "Reveren' put we here as guard against Babylon's intruders an' is guard I goin' keep. Go 'way, white man. Nobody want you here."

"So I can't come in?"

"No. You don't have passport."

I threw back my head on a deep breath.

"Mister Heneky!" I bawled. "Mi-i-st-e-er Hen-e-e-ky!"

I could hear my voice wavering back across the savannah from the hills.

"Here! What you t'ink you doing?"

The stick had been lowered and he looked at me uncertainly, with an interest between alarm and an attempt to conceal it.

"Mister Heneky!" I shouted again, and then to them,

245

normally, "I'll call for him until he comes, or until my voice gives out. And then I'll just stand here and wait for him. He'll have to go out some time."

"All right," he said. "If is so bad you want fe' see him, you better see him. T'addeus, tek him up to de house."

I followed Thaddeus across the yard of sour, greyish earth. There were more brethren from the African societies than I had ever seen at one time before, even on the occasion when I stayed to a service. They were bunched in groups, talking; a number were seated on the front pews of the church, listening to one of Sheba's Sons; and there was a large semi-circle on the brittle grass of the savannah, beyond the gully, in the sun, being addressed by another Son of Sheba who stood in the shade of a guava tree. The little veranda was crowded, some sitting on the boards of the flooring and the rest on the rails. A silence that seemed to visibly thicken the air, attended our progress across the yard; silence and a slow, alert turning of heads, like an experiment in photosynthesis, and an elaborate, impenetrable shuttering of bearded and unbearded faces in which only the hard glimmering of watchful eyes revealed that something was observed and assessed. By this time, I had been long enough in Cayuna to particularize black faces and I felt that many of these were new.

"Stop here!" Thaddeus said at the foot of the steps and went up them quickly, through the crowd on the veranda and into the house.

I waited in the yard and tried to meet the faces turned to me from the veranda. It wasn't possible: an instant before I could make contact with my eyes on any face, it withdrew into some rapt, inward-seeming disinterest, a careful unmenacing separation from what it looked at.

I said: "Good day."

There was a long silence during which my words seemed to be passed through them like a tray of contents they all recognized and examined cursorily.

246

"Good day," one of them said as Marcus Heneky stepped onto the veranda.

Physically, he had always appeared to me to combine the aspects of the noble and heraldic animals: the heavy, stone square of lion's head, the sloping, packed shoulders of the bull, and a body and legs spare and curiously feline despite his age. Now, as he stepped lightly to the top of the steps, these characteristics had only been accentuated by his months in prison. He had always been a lean man and the diet and the bitter heat of his reflections seemed to have worked on him the significant exaggeration we get in art when the unrequired natural details are discarded. His hair which before going in had been grey as uncleaned silver was now white; but the long chin still seemed to be mounted on a gun-carriage and the black deep eyes had the same ready, unfrightened lustre. He looked at me steadily, in silence, and the warm polish of his eyes misted coldly, as though my visit was already relegated to obscurity.

"How are you, Mister Heneky?" I said. "I came to pay my respects. I'm very glad to see you about again. . . . How d'you do, Mister Howard?" I added. "I don't know if you remember me." For the small, neat figure of Mass' Howard, the man from whose house at Gran' Dum I had taken Marcus Heneky months before, had suddenly and nattily bounced from inside the house to stand at Marcus Heneky's elbow with that air of bullying devotion. He still looked as though his clothes were sewn tightly up the back like a model's in an advertisement.

"Your respects?" Marcus Heneky said, and I remembered the bright, testing cruelty of his voice the first time we met. "But look here, boy, your friends in government already pay respects. Six months of it, like an animal in a cage, because I recall my people to their God."

"Not me," I told him. "I didn't agree with that. And not my friends, either."

"Them wasn't sorry, though," he said, and waited for me to deny that. I said nothing. "But no matter, boy. It give me time

247

to think, an' it was punishment for my weakness that I didn't submit more of my life an' heart to God's command. I know better now. I finish with Babylon an' all its servants an' citizens. No man can ride two horses. Except him perform in a circus." White grins spread momentarily among the bearded dark faces. "An' this life is no circus, you understand." He paused and a brief, almost reluctant chuckle escaped him, and I wondered what incorrigible satiric spirit had made its secret comment on his last words. Then his face tautened like a mask of leather drying and shrinking. "So don't come back here, boy. This is we place. Black man's place. An' we want keep it free from the taint your people bring with them. Leave we now, an' go back to your friends an' your country, an' don't try come into ours. I make myself clear?"

"Yes," I said. "Good-bye, Mister Heneky."

I turned, hoping that the burning in my cheeks was not too patent as a flush, and began to walk back down to the gate.

When I had gone about twenty yards, I heard him say, "Hi, Samaritan!" as he had said it that day I went to see him in the hospital: teasing without malice, the wry sharing of an iron ration with an enemy during a lull. I turned and saw him coming across the yard after me. He walked deliberately and heavily, but without the stumping shuffle of the aged: it was, rather, like watching the padding slow swagger of an old tom-cat unhurriedly coursing its own bailiwick. He came up and put his hand on my shoulder.

"You understand it must be so?" he said. "You understand that the destiny of my people an' yours come to this? History dig a gulf between us, boy, an' it don't fill in yet. Not yet." Like the glint of a bright accoutrement seen for the merest registration of the retina in a wall of forest, a flicker of what might have been kindness, regret, liking or perhaps pity passed across his face. "I don't thank you for bringing that white man lawyer to me," he said. "I know say why you do it, but you didn't have to. Him is the only man of your people I need in

248

this country of wickedness. None of the rest of you is good for we. Now go on, boy."

I walked quickly to the gate, followed by the same slow, poised turn of heads that yet took note of movement, of my position in space.

At the gate, held open for me by Ivor, I turned. Marcus Heneky stood where I had left him, feet apart, hands pushed down into his pockets, looking at me, but of course at that distance I could not read his passionless, still face. The various brethren had begun to close in on him, the Sons of Sheba in their para-military shorts and shirts standing nearest. There were some big, coarse-veined and muscular men among those around him, their beards adding a powerful masculine emphasis to their bunched force; but at that distance it was they who looked faded and almost slight beside the lean, compact old man.

III

A few weeks before, I suppose, I would have seized on this with the morbid hunger the unhappy have for anything that will increase their distress. But happiness has its own serene egotism. What had happened between Marcus Heneky and myself seemed to me regrettable, even unnecessary, and for a little, I enjoyed the emollient satisfaction of having been unjustly wounded, but I could not make it more. The jealous hand of new love plucked at my attention firmly and led it off to its own interests.

So it was that when the police sent for me, anything but Marcus Heneky and his passion occurred to me as the cause of the summons.

I was lecturing that day. It must have been a first year anatomy group for I seem to remember the skeleton of Cayuna's scavenger, *Vulturus vulturidae*. And I must have just made one of those pedantic jokes, which like dim, inextinguishable

249

torches have been passed through the centuries from the first lecturers in the grove at Academe.

I remember because I was still modestly grinning my acknowledgement of polite student laughter when Claudie, the laboratory servant, touched my arm and said, "Police outside, want see you, Doctor."

In that moment, my first idiotic thought was that Joan had been in an accident and had called for me, maimed, semi-conscious, perhaps dying. Perfect love may cast out fear; but with our roughly contrived human facsimile of it we begin to nourish fear like some ugly, greedy changeling left on the door-step of the heart. With a dry mouth and a brain stuck like a badly changed gear, I hurried through my office to the veranda.

"I beg your pardon, Doctor Mahler," the police constable said. "Superintendent Barraclough down at Central presents his compliments and wonders if you would find it convenient to call on him later on today. Entirely at your convenience, sir."

He was a tall, high-brown man, just over the hump of youth-ful gawkiness, and he had the steely and immaculate beauty that sometimes comes to the uniformed young who are serious and intelligent about their calling. From his shimmering boots and faultless, dark blue puttees to the death's head crash helmet, he was as crisp as a nun: his body rose like a stem from the sheath of a crimson cummerbund exactly bisected by a black, silver-buckled belt: under the poinsettia beyond the veranda, was parked the red, 500 c.c. police motor-cycle.

I said: "Thank you, officer," with a relief that would have surprised him, then, "Superintendent Barraclough? I don't know him. Any idea what's wrong?"

"I'm afraid I can't say why he would like to have a word with you, Doctor Mahler. But I'm sure there's nothing wrong. He said entirely at your convenience."

He was taking in every nuance of my reaction; not suspi-ciously, but as a matter of routine that might save future work. He was very young, almost desexualized by starch and pride, and I thought: he won't be an ordinary dispatch rider long.

"Yes," I said. "Well, I have to teach after lunch. Will you tell the Superintendent that I'll report to him at five o'clock, if that's all right?"

He grinned appreciatively at my choice of the meek verb: he was not only very bright, but subtle. Nothing would stop him going as far up the force as he cared to go.

"Five o'clock, Doctor. I'll tell Super. Good day, sir."

He pulled out of the space before the laboratory on a fast, unshowy semi-circle which might have been followed by a compass and pencil, and I went back to my class.

A tawdry, vague anxiety began to nag at me as I showered that afternoon. A significant and malleable part of my life had been spent justifying myself to police, at times even proving my existence: too much of it for me ever to feel sanguine about any interest they might take in me. Somewhere along the path that had brought me from the Rhine to Cayuna, my confidence in the organized forces of protection and order had suffered a permanent dislocation. Before leaving, that afternoon, to drive into Queenshaven, I unlocked my cabin trunk and took out my passport. The stranger's face stared glumly at me: the universal passport countenance of a moronic criminal backed into a corner, sullenly trying to placate his pursuers. That was properly stamped; so was the expiry date; so was the Cayuna residence visa. I put it into my pocket and left.

At the Central Police Station on Constitution Avenue, the junior superintendent on duty in the office was Soames, a man I had happened to meet, through coincidences of invitation, three or four times and find drearier on each occasion. He was remarkable for his affectation, even in a colony where so many of the English expatriates become carriers of an agreed myth: of an England resting in the haze of some golden Edwardian latitude, where the country houses stretch from Land's End to John o' Groats and every pub nestles to a hawthorn bank overlooking green fields.

"Hullo, Soames," I said. "I think Superintendent Barra-clough wants me."

"Ah, yes, Mahlah," he said, getting up from his desk. "He asked me to usher you in. Been breaking the law, old man? Can't have that, you know. Sets a bad example. Eh? Ha-ha!"

The *sahib* accent, depressing as the tie of a minor public school, hung uneasily from his adenoidal native Midlands.

"I think I'm clean," I said. "But we'd better go and find out."

"Quite right, old man. This way. . . . And how's that charming little lady you've got yourself engaged to?"

"She must have grown since you last saw her," I said. "She tips the scales at ten stone now. But she's still charming."

"Eh? Oh. Yes. Ha-ha! Well, here, we are, old man. The question chamber. Bright lights. Rubber truncheons and all that, what? And, 'When did you last see your father?' "

He tapped at the door half-way along the grey-walled, red-linoleumed corridor down which he had led me.

"Come in," a voice called, and Soames opened the door.

"Doctor Mahler, sir," he said.

"Thank you, Soames," Barraclough said and rose from be-hind the grey metal desk and came round it to me. Another senior superintendent sat in an old-fashioned Windsor chair beside the desk.

"Good afternoon, Doctor Mahler," Barraclough said, shak-ing my hand. "I'm sorry to have to drag you away from the university. It was very good of you to give up your time so promptly. We thought perhaps you might be able to help us."

"Glad to, if I can," I said as he showed me to another Windsor chair in front of the desk. Among the metal furniture, maps and statistical charts of the office, it looked incongruously leisured.

"That'll be all, thank you, Soames," Barraclough said.

"Right you are, sir," Soames said, and left us, closing the door.

"Now," Barraclough said. "May I introduce you to my

colleague, Superintendent Cowell. Brian, this is Doctor Mahler, from the university. A zoologist, I believe, Doctor Mahler?"

"Yes," I said, and shook Cowell's hand. He was a big, very dark Cayunan, layered like a bear in hard, healthy fat. He pressed my hand with only the firmness required by good manners, but I could feel strength in his grip as one feels the thrumming of high voltage beneath an insulated wire. Two blobs of cold, dark aspic jelly surveyed me without a sign of interest or even thought, and a small, bud-like mouth pursed in an automatic smile.

Barraclough went back to his swivel chair and leaned across the desk to proffer me his opened cigarette case.

"No thanks," I said. "I just put one out."

"Brian?"

"No thanks, Jock," said Cowell, without taking his eyes from my face.

"I know how busy you must be, Doctor Mahler," Barraclough said, lighting a cigarette for himself. "So, I'll make it as short as I can. D'you think you could tell us anything about Marcus Heneky? Anything at all?"

He fanned the match out and held the stick while he looked at me, waiting for my reply. He had a face that could have hung unremarked in a butcher's window, and in it the cigarette looked absurd and feminine: nothing but a huge, black pipe, I felt, could possibly match those scarlet, heavy features and the angry red moustache.

"Marcus Heneky!" I said. "What could I tell you? You know more about him than I do, surely?"

"Yes," he said amiably. "But we felt that someone like yourself who knows him ... socially, so to speak ... might give us something extra."

Cowell said, in the thin, soft voice of some big men: "You've known him for over a year, Doctor Mahler. You've visited him several times."

"Yes, I can see you must have had his place watched, but I don't understand what I'm supposed to know about him. He runs a church, and he believes that all people of African origin should return to Africa, and you arrested him for preaching without a licence. Anybody who reads the *Gazette* could tell you that."

"Let me put it this way then, Doctor Mahler," Barraclough said, with friendly insistence, as though we were mutually conning a problem and offering suggestions for each other to criticize. "Have you, when you've visited him during the past year, noticed anything or overheard anything at that so-called church of his that might be termed 'political'? Anything that really doesn't have much to do with religion?"

"I don't see how one can separate the two," I said. "Not if you're serious about the religion."

"True," he said with a smile like a row of small yellow tombstones. "Joshua, for instance. Or Mohammed. Or the Cromwellian Puritans. I agree with you."

I suddenly realized that the brutally caricatured imperialist's face was no signature of the imagination behind it.

"You haven't really answered the question, Doctor Mahler," Cowell said.

"Oh, I'll answer it," I told him. "I wasn't trying to dodge. No, I've never noticed anything political. I was as surprised as anybody else when he opened fire on the regulars in the Eastmoreland election."

"Yes," he said, in a tone that might have meant anything I chose to read.

"I'm going to ask you to think back and think hard, Doctor Mahler," Barraclough said, settling forward, elbows on the desk. "Remember: anything, even if it seems completely unimportant or casual to you, may be just what Mister Cowell here or myself are looking for. You know: a chance remark that seemed slightly puzzling or odd at the time; anybody hanging around who looked suspicious or untrustworthy to you. Any activity going on in the house or the yard which you could hear but didn't see. That sort of thing."

"No," I said firmly. "I go there because I like the old man, in a way. We talk and I leave. He gives me a cup of tea sometimes. Or a rum and coco-nut water. Although he doesn't really approve of alcohol."

I had decided I would say nothing of being turned away from Marcus Heneky's yard.

Barraclough said: "He wouldn't approve of his daughter's occupation, then? You know she keeps a bar?"

"Yes. A very good bar. No, he doesn't altogether approve, but he forgives it. He tries to be a fanatic but humanity keeps breaking in."

"It often does, doesn't it?" Barraclough said warmly, almost happily, as if asking me to share with him the hope of this redeeming factor. "Now, the daughter. Miss Heneky. Has she ever mentioned anything? Not deliberately, you understand? Nor even knowing what she had said. Nor, if you'll allow me to confuse things, even knowing that she'd observed anything that had prompted her remark." He looked down at his desk with a discomfort and embarrassment in which, strangely enough, I believed. "I understand you and she have had a close association for some time."

"We were lovers," I said, in a flat, empty voice. For I had noticed, as he spoke, what had inexplicably escaped me up to then: the buff file on the blotter before him. I knew, with absolute certainty, that it pertained to me, and felt as though I had woken to discover the first blemish of leprosy or syphilis on my body. No matter how complete or quick my cure, from now on I would be that much weaker by the first, unchecked development of the disease.

"Then you don't see her anymore?" Cowell asked.

"No. . . . Is that my *dossier*?" I added to Barraclough.

"Your *dossier*? Good heavens, no, Doctor Mahler. We don't have a *dossier* on you. You're not under any sort of suspicion."

The scarlet, meaty face had become almost alarmingly flushed with the sincerity of his denial. "It's simply some information we gathered when we were investigating Heneky. There's hardly anything here that you wouldn't have to tell your insurance company."

He opened the file quickly, his small, brilliant blue eyes sliding from mine after a glance of pleading and apologetic ruthlessness. "Yes," he said. "Absolutely nothing here to take exception to, Doctor Mahler. It's all information you've given yourself at one time or another. We just collected it for our convenience. . . ." He continued, using the text as if refreshing his memory. "Stefan Mahler . . . born Brunau-am-Rhein, 1925. . . . Refugee in Paris, Bordeaux, Lisbon, 1939. . . . London, 1940. . . . Yes. . . ." He looked up. "You had a remarkable war record, Doctor Mahler. After your internment. I never got to it, I'm afraid. I found myself well and truly stuck out here."

In some curious manner, he managed to nearly convince me that his envious admiration was simple and genuine, like his embarrassment.

"Remarkable?" I said. "As a medical orderly? TABT injections and FFI inspections are hardly remarkable, Superintendent. Even if I did become a corporal."

"You wouldn't call two medals for gallantry in two months remarkable?" he asked; the little, intense chips of his eyes were still now, equivocally searching. "I would. One of them is a *very* good medal. It was a bit more than TABT injections, wasn't it?"

"Oh, I see," I said suddenly, after a moment of uncomfortable protest. "You're either trying to flatter me or embarrass me. The latter, I suppose. You couldn't have imagined that I'd enjoy all this talk about my war record and medals. You hope I'll get rattled and blurt something."

"You're quite right," he said simply, with open admission of surprise, and we both laughed. "How did you know that?"

256

"You haven't read far enough," I teased him cheerfully. The atmosphere seemed to have become fresher, with a positive pleasantness, as after rain. "Further on it ought to say that they transferred me to intelligence after the war. I must have remembered some of the tricks."

"Oh, well," he said, with the congratulatory but superior smile of a fencing master scored on by a clever amateur, and closed the file as he swivelled his chair sideways to stretch his legs. "But seriously, Mahler. Can't you tell me anything that might help us?"

"I really can't, Superintendent. I don't even know what you're looking for."

"We're after treason, Doctor Mahler," Cowell said, with a sort of clicking harshness. "Treason and violence. It's being plotted up there and we want to step on it before it goes any further."

"Treason!" I said. "You're not serious. Old Heneky is a strange man, all right, and he has some uncomfortable ideas, but he isn't plotting treason. He's a man of God before he's anything else. He wants to do violence to people's souls, if they have any; but that isn't treason."

"Have you ever heard of a man called 'Tiger' Johnson?" Barraclough asked.

"No."

"You've heard of the Jungle?"

"Yes. A picturesque name for an atrocious slum. I've heard of it."

"Johnson is the king of it," Barraclough said, and grimaced as though asking me to forgive the cliché. "He's also one of the finest criminals this island has produced in a long time. Anything you can think of from murder to receiving. But what we really want him for is ganja. That's where his money comes from. Not from the small peddling, but large scale exportation. You ought to know, too, that he's a black racialist. He wouldn't allow race to stand between him and money, but he's pretty

257

serious about it. The Sons of Sheba and the other racialist societies pay him a sort of loose homage, you might say. And he buys the ganja they grow. . . ."

"What does all this have to do with Heneky?" I asked. "Everybody knows that most of Sheba's Sons and the rest of them smoke ganja, the way you and I smoke tobacco. But Heneky doesn't. He doesn't even like it, although he can't stop it. He's no ganja smuggler."

"But he has taken up with Johnson," Barraclough said. "They're seeing too much of each other. And a lot of Johnson's special boys, both in and out of the Sheba movement, have begun to gather too regularly up at Heneky's church since his release."

I remembered the number of new faces I had noticed in the yard on the afternoon I last went to see Marcus Heneky.

"Well," I said, "if this Johnson, whom I've never heard of, is an African racialist, and Heneky gives real words to that idea, isn't that your connection?"

"Doctor Mahler," Cowell said suddenly, and the soft, short of breath voice was impressive with its seriousness. "You don't know this country. You don't know what a man like Johnson or your friend, Heneky, can cause when they're ready. They don't want progress and order and what a man has to work for and build up. They want violence. Where they can rise. Particularly Johnson. Whatever he gets into, you can be sure it's bad. African racialist! Who could be more African than me? It's because I'm an African that I want to stop a man like Johnson, and a man like Heneky. I have something to lose when men like that lead a lot of my race into crime and disorder. They could make hell in this island, and when they were finished men like you and Jock Barraclough here would look at me and my colour and wonder what right I had to wear these." He lightly slapped the three silver stars on the epaulette of his bush jacket. "*I* would know I have the right, but you would question it. Not openly. Not even in your minds. But you couldn't help asking

258

it, even for a second. I know where I stand and I'm proud to stand there. My people built this island and your people helped. Now my people rule this island and if your people want to share it still, you're welcome. But I don't like to sit here and see a man who looks like me turn what we have done into a disgrace. That's why I want to know what you've heard up at Heneky's place, Doctor Mahler. It's not only you and your colour he's against. It's me. And people like me. And I will settle him gladly for all of us if I get the evidence to act. You sure you don't have anything to tell us?"

"No," I said. "And I'll be honest with you. If I did . . . if I even suspected something that might help you. . . . I couldn't tell you. I'm not an informer."

"Yes," Cowell said, in the voice a man might use to confirm a statistic transmitted to him from a colleague. "Thank you, Doctor Mahler." He rose. "Good night. Good night, Jock."

He had reached the door, opened it and closed it on his retreating back before one properly realized the noiseless, ursine glide.

"Good night, Brian," Barraclough said to the closed door, but looking at me. "You heard," he said to me. "You think I want to see Heneky in jail, don't you? You think I'm just a second-rate English copper who wants to make himself important finding treason in a little colony. Well, you're right. I'm pretty sure that I'll have to arrest him sooner or later. But not for my sake alone, Mahler. For everybody's. So that I can go on working with a chap like Cowell without even thinking that he has a black face and used to be an ambitious country constable when I first came to Cayuna. D'you know where his ambitions had to end in those days? Sub-inspector in Records, if he was lucky. I thought it was only natural, then. Nowadays I wonder how I could have been such a damn fool as to deprive myself of equality with a man like that. And I wonder that he has the generosity to allow me to stay on in his country after the way we treated him."

"You're much too imaginative to be a policeman," I said uneasily. "You'll come to grief, Barraclough. All the same, you're wrong about Marcus. He'll cause trouble. But good trouble in his peculiar fashion. You don't really see what he's getting at. If I was black, he'd have something to say to me. Even now."

"Oh, I know what you mean," he said. "Othello."

"What?"

"Othello." The massive, nearly animal face, florid as a freshly cut steak, was oddly shy, like that of a man admitting a risible vice. "It's an idea I've thought of occasionally. Did you ever imagine you were a Walter Scott knight, Mahler? Or Robinson Crusoe? Or, later on, one of the real men, like a great general or a politician? Figures like that from stories or life?"

"Yes. Of course. Plus a few like the Maccabees that you wouldn't have heard of."

"Now, take the case here," he said. "You're black, and as a child you'll imagine yourself being all those people. Part of a story or real history. But then you grow up and if you're sensitive at all you find that you can't. You're not part of it. Stories and history that are part of a big pattern don't belong to you. You joined the pattern as a slave. Very late in the day. Although you're now part of it and can't ever escape. You don't have any legends or history that's your own to build on. Except Othello. The only black face that everybody accepts that has any dignity. I think it's a hell of a fix to be in. It's why you get somebody like Heneky. Even 'Tiger' Johnson, although he'd be a crook anywhere he was born. I mean, they're both trying to find a state where they can be Robinson Crusoe instead of always being Man Friday."

"Yes," I said. "That's almost exactly what Marcus Heneky believes, even if he puts it differently. When did you start to think like that?"

"God knows," he said, rising. "I just woke up one morning and looked at what I have to put up with in the mirror and thought of it."

260

I rose and we went to the door together.

"Tell me," I said, quickly, as a sudden realization of circumstances formed in my mind. "You don't think that Bernice —Miss Heneky has anything to do with whatever might or might not be going on? You're not going to trouble her?"

"She's all right," he said. "We're sure of that. We questioned her this afternoon, very discreetly, at her place. You'll find that out when you go to tell her we questioned you. But she doesn't know anything. It was you we were depending on. If we only had an idea what Heneky and Johnson are cooking between them, we could move in on them when we were ready. As it is, now is too soon and later might be too damned late."

"D'you believe that I know nothing? That I hadn't even thought of anything until you called me?"

"Yes," he said. We were standing on the top step of the flight leading down to Constitution Avenue: a flaunting sunset of red and green and umber cloud distended the sky over the sea. "I believe you, Mahler. So does Cowell, or he'd have stuck into you harder. Good night."

"Good night," I said going down the steps to my car parked a little way up, in the gutter beside the pavement.

Until I started to steer along the empty street and felt limp, I did not realize how rigidly I had held guard during the interview.

I I

★

I have asked myself since if Barraclough and Cowell did not conceive these two interrogations—of Bernice and myself—with the primary objective of a double bluff: a purposeful tipping of their hand so that Marcus Heneky and 'Tiger' Johnson would be tempted into an unplanned change of movements.

"Tell your father," I said to Bernice, that same evening, a few minutes after leaving Barraclough, "that the police have been on to me. I'm not quite sure what they think he's doing, but they're out to get him again. So if he has any schemes that they could jump on him for, tell him to be careful."

"Stefan," she said, in a real anguish of impotence. "What am I to do with that old man, eh? Preaching without a licence is one thing, but ganja is another. What him think him doing?"

"Is that what they told you they're after?" I asked.

"Yes." Her face became still and prepared. "What them tell you, Stefan?"

"They talked about treason," I said. "Treason, for God's sake. They mentioned ganja, but by the way, if you get what I mean. Chiefly because of this fellow, 'Tiger' Johnson."

"That's another thing," she said furiously. "What him want to go an' mix up with a real bad man like Johnson for? It's not only today I hear about Johnson. Them should have lock him up long time. Him just don't go up there to hear papa preach. I know that. Lord, what am I to do, Stefan?"

"Tell him what has happened and advise him to keep himself out of trouble. If he's able to do that. What else can you do?"

So it might have been our concern for him, and the warning that he was being watched, that prompted Marcus Heneky to change the hiding place for the small arms he was collecting, from the tangled, almost overlapping shacks of 'Tiger' Johnson's Jungle to the uninhabited bush of the rocky hills overlooking the savannah.

All this is only speculation. For all Johnson would say later at his trial was, "We would have brought war to dis country. Big war. But bad luck hol' on to we. Bad luck an' dat dam' fool."

The fool he referred to was Mass' Howard, who as a lettered man was sent to Cuba to arrange for more of the various small arms which were gradually being smuggled into Cayuna in exchange for 'Tiger' Johnson's bulk supplies of ganja.

In a moment of loneliness or a need for the comfort of fresh inspiration, Mass' Howard wrote a long letter to Marcus Heneky in which he made a reference to "the triumph of our arms which come to you in God's cloak of darkness". It was a short step between the interception and the re-forwarding of this letter to the time when the police caught one of Sheba's Sons on his way up to the hills beyond the savannah with the stock of a Sten gun in his shirt. In the raids that followed, 'Tiger' Johnson was captured in a refuse pit in the Jungle, supervising the burial of three hundred rounds of .32 revolver ammunition and a kerosene tin of explosives. Marcus Heneky and fifteen of Sheba's Sons escaped across the gully and savannah into the hills while Ivor, the gateman, and two others held the police off until the fence on either side of them was broken down and they were beaten senseless.

And then, during the next few hours, while the excitement of the news was still a *frisson*, the whole affair ceased to be an abortive upheaval from a visionary fringe of our society. It became murder.

Following Marcus Heneky into the razor backs and vertical

dry gulleys of the bushy hills, Superintendent Cowell discovered an arms' cache under a huge rock dug out, rolled away, and then settled back. The earth had been freshly scooped from under it and it was obvious that arms had been removed. Cowell split his party into groups and they began to throw the search up the accessible contours. Just before nightfall as Cowell was about to pull back his men, he heard two stammered cackles of Sten gun fire from the first low peak a mile away. When he reached the area from which the sound had come, he and his assembling men pulled the bush nearly flat over a square of about a hundred yards before they found the three men of the fourth group shot dead at very close range. In accordance with the regulations, they had full magazines to their rifles but no charges in the breech.

II

At his trial, 'Tiger' Johnson also said: "It was me teach Reveren' to t'ink war. Before me, him only t'ink words. Is me send de message to him in prison say, 'When you come out, you an' me will give de white man an' de brown man an answer dem will listen to. Wid you to preach war an' me to mek it, we can win dis country back to Africa.' An' we would have wait our time until Reveren' message spread fuel ready for we to light."

I believe, though, that if it had come to the sort of war they had planned, it would have been Marcus Heneky who would have made it and taught 'Tiger' Johnson how to make it.

Certainly in the weeks that followed on the murder of the three policemen, he taught a number of experts what it means to hunt a man who will not be caught. Had there been one hundred and fifty instead of fifteen men for him to lead in that wild dash across the savannah and into the hills, he probably would have tried to bring war to Cayuna. In the hope, perhaps, of becoming the active symbol of a belief to which more and more of Cayuna's people would subscribe. As it was, with only fifteen men to sustain his ecstatic conception, he concentrated his unyielding energies on the simple assertion of liberty.

For the first week or ten days, while the island still winced and throbbed from the strange sense of amputation that the sort of murders he had committed must inspire, we all wished fervently for his capture. These murders and the extent to which he and Johnson had already prepared for violence had penetrated too suddenly the placid surface of Cayuna's imagination. Those of Sheba's Sons to whom no share in the plot could be ascribed, who had been kept ignorant of it for security or because of their suspected pacifism, had to walk cautiously about the city; and many of them shaved their beards and heads.

Then as the first fortnight passed and he kept finding hole after hole for himself and his followers in the professional cordon being built around them in the Blue Range, some forgotten demon of anarchy and wager seemed to recognize the appeal of his doomed struggle. The half battalion of the West Indian Regiment in Cayuna and the police were patiently and precisely pushing him east across the high, forested spine of the island; but each time that they sealed him into a shrinking box—cube, really, because of reconnaissance aircraft—he would lead an insolently original or audacious break out down some impossibly difficult ridge or up through the last ten minutes of a closing gap across a peak.

There were no more deaths: they were unable to get near enough to him for an exchange of fire. This, I think, and his age in society where years command almost instinctive respect, brought the search out of the realm of cruel spectacle into which a man-hunt devolves and made it almost a contest of immitigable destiny. Imperceptibly, he was being hammered by ancient inspirations into a dimension that could contain the shades of the pristine adventure: memories, I suppose, of an abandoned, wild self-sufficiency in which fear, conquest, defeat and courage are not categories of feeling dependent on artificial considerations of society, but all one in an humble, keen exhilaration of risked life. He was at once abhorrent and thrilling. I don't pretend to know exactly what my feelings were about him as he moved his inscrutable, tragic life to a close across the mountains of the island. I only know that the morning I passed a wall along one of the back streets of the city and saw, scrawled in thick, unpractised strokes of chalk, the words "M.H. SOUL IS MARCHING ON", I seemed to understand what had promoted them, without being able to explain this shared comprehension, and although I knew I couldn't approve of the purpose he had attempted.

To feed themselves, he and his band had to raid the small holdings that fringed the three thousand-foot contour under the forested heights. They came down at night, at places far from the tentatively cast but inexorable patrols, and carried off yams, cocos, bread-fruit and sweet potatoes; occasionally a chicken or a tethered goat. And at each place from which he had to steal, Marcus Heneky left a note, in the careful handwriting that he must have acquired when he kept the ledger at his little bakery: *One God, one Aim, One Destiny*, he always wrote. *This is to certify that the Pure Church of Africa Triumphant, Zion's light in Babylon darkness, borrow food from her children. Present for repayment in the day of our victory, Marcus Heneky (Healer of the Wound).*

The austere promise of these receipts began to add to the peculiar stature he was achieving as he was worked steadily towards the lower St. Joseph Mountains. They seemed to epitomize the incorruptible obstinacy of an ideal as meaningful in essence as it was mistaken for the time and place. They seemed to confirm the integrity of his blind and impermissible challenge. And in the midst of the fear, shock, outrage and deep anger that he had aroused, one could often hear the note of a reluctant admiration, a secret respect, and sometimes even the warmth of moved pity.

All this, of course, was then. When his constancy of endeavour to remain free, his astonishing skill in doing so, and his fidelity to his bizarre revelation stirred unconsidered sympathies or disturbed accepted presumptions. Now, he is almost forgotten, is a part of that shadowy compromise the mind makes with those it cannot explain with real justice. As I had agreed with myself to leave him alone until Oliver's quest for a journalist's truth revived the troubling reverberations of his eloquent face this afternoon. . . . The half-starved, bearded face that stared, without astonishment or protest, only with a sort of indomitable question, at the hard, glazed sky over Caymanas Marsh. . . .

III

That Saturday morning when Marcus Heneky finally ran out of space, Oliver woke me at about six o'clock. It was the Saturday before term ended and I had been correcting papers until four o'clock: the tickets for Joan and myself, to England on my end of tour leave, were already locked in the cabin trunk, between the centre pages of my passport.

I was pulled from sleep, by the electric buzzer, like an exhausted but still pugnacious trout fighting from the shallows.

"Step on it, Stefan," he called through the slats in my jalousied front door. "I'm in one hell of a hurry, man. I wish you had a telephone."

"What?" I said, opening the door. My attention was still shambling across the floor behind me.

"They've cornered him," Oliver said. "Down by the shore on the far side of Caymanas Marsh. He's dug in and it's going to be the devil to get him out. D'you want to come over with me? I'll give you a press pass."

"What?" I said again. I was as awake as a plucked guitar string. "What d'you mean Caymanas Marsh? He was reported from upper St. Joseph night before last. How did he get to the coast?"

"He must have gone through the cane fields in the dark. I

267

don't know yet. Central Police just phoned me. I don't even know the place where he's been trapped, but it sounds as if it's going to be next to impossible to get at him and his people without loss of life."

"Can't they wait until they're so hungry they have to come out? They can't get out of the marsh if they're against the sea."

"They raided a shop in a place called Gran' Dum. D'you know it? Up in the mountains?"

"Yes."

"They raided the shop there and loaded up. But instead of taking off into the high ground again they turned south. They'd have got away with it, but one of the fishermen from Caymanas Village heard them talking early this morning, when he was off-shore. I don't think they could have realized how sound travels over water. Are you coming?"

"No, thanks," I said. "It was good of you to ask, but I haven't any part to play there. I could only watch. And I don't particularly want to see him hunted down."

"Yes. I know what you mean. I almost wish this place had a frontier so he could have a fighting chance. . . . I really came to tell you because I knew you'd want to know; because of Bernice. She might need a shoulder or something. It'll be general news any minute. See you, Stefan."

"Yes," I said. "And thanks for thinking of everything."

He was already crossing the strip of lawn to his car. I watched him as he tried to get more from it along the drive than it had to give, and went back to the bedroom and turned my portable radio full on. While I was in the shower cubicle, the special report started to come through.

I listened carefully, but what they had to say hardly added to what Oliver had told me: the rushed encirclement of the area by police and troops, the fact that Eliot, the young Minister of the Interior, had gone down, the appeal to Marcus Heneky to surrender and his refusal were all what I had expected. The only factor that I didn't know, or hadn't guessed, was the place where he had come to bay: Loud Shore, a segment of the great swamp I had seen about two years before. Remembering it, I knew that if he was determined, Marcus Heneky could make his arrest hideously expensive. As soon as I had dressed, I went out and drove through the gradually quickening streets to Bernice.

During those weeks, she had changed. No. Not changed. But it was as if even her huge, calm vitality was choking to death in a dust column of sorrow and care. Helplessness, of course, added its own penalties to what she had to bear. I remember the two deep lines that appeared, while I seemed to have looked away, between her eyes; and I sometimes try not to recall the trembling that would take her hands, while pouring a drink for a customer, or at the till, as though, in those moments, she saw what had happened through a sudden lift of mist.

"I've always heard," she said one night very late: a report on her father had just come through from a village in the hills north of Serena and we were waiting to hear the follow up, if any. "I've always heard that it's the children who cause parents grief. But that old man pay back for all the grief parents feel, eh, Stefan?" And then, with a wickedly painful, cautious steadiness. "You think they will hang him when they catch him? I know say they must catch him."

"I wouldn't answer that now," I told her. "I wouldn't even discuss it until a jury brings a verdict."

This morning I rapped on the side door in the lane until she came down. Oliver had woken me so early that this section of the city was still unopened. The air was bright as though with the visible sparkle of an invisible dew.

"Yes. I hear it on the radio," she said when she opened the door. "I knew say you would come down as soon as you hear, Stefan. Thank you."

She led me up the stairs to the room I had not entered—for how many months? And I sat on the edge of the bed with my back to her while she finished dressing.

I said: "D'you want me to take you out of town somewhere? Anywhere. Until it's over. It won't be pleasant just waiting and trying not to look grateful when the customers who know the connection don't discuss it. You just say what you want to do."

"No," she said. Her voice was calm, almost serene. "Thank you. You're the best man I ever meet. But I going to wait until they bring him in. Maybe they will allow me to see him for a little."

"Bernice," I said. "They're not going to bring him in that quickly. It's going to be a long, ugly business."

"How you mean? Them surround him now. Him must give up. Even him."

"You know him. Besides that place he's got himself into. Long Shore. It won't be easy getting him out. It's all rock and tide on the sea face. It's so bad there we've never been able to collect specimens. And there's swamp before it, and mangroves. One man could kill twenty before they take him. Let alone fifteen."

"More deaths into this?" she asked quietly. She came round from the dressing-table and stood before me, her solid, dependable body held as if expecting a sack across the shoulders.

"I think so," I said. "It looks so, Bernice. Unless he allows them to take him. If I told you differently it wouldn't be any kindness in the long run."

"Jesus Christ!" she said suddenly, on a kind of held explosion, and sat beside me. "I did think it was all over. More dead men. And for what? Him can't see it finish now? How many him want see killed before he feel that his work done?"

She put her elbows on her plump knees and rested her big, greying head on her fists. I patted her shoulder. There didn't seem anything useful that I could say.

She remained like that, staring at the floor until, perhaps fifteen minutes later, the radio announced that an attempt had been made to move in on the fugitives at Long Shore and that a policeman had been shot in the stomach. During the carefully modulated excitement from the little box, she was quite still. When it was finished, she rose, with an even, matter of fact decisiveness.

"Is me should be down there," she said. "I can talk him out. I should have think of it before. But it's so long since I even try to think straight. I must go down there, Stefan. You will take me?"

"You can't go down there," I protested. "You don't know what men are like when they've been hunted like those poor devils for nearly six weeks. They'd kill you. You can't talk him out, Bernice. Not even you."

"I can talk him out, Stefan," she said, with that undeviating serenity, the calm of immutable decision, not even trying to convince. "At least, I must try. Suppose another man get shot like that one? Or him get shot? And I know say that maybe I could have prevent it. How you think I going to feel?"

She was slipping on her shoes, and now she went to the mirror and began to make up her face. Like a woman going to a job.

I said: "Bernice! Be sensible, woman. They'll have closed that area to everybody. You wouldn't get within two miles of it. Besides they won't allow you to try. Suppose you got shot, maybe killed? By mistake even. That wouldn't look too good in the press for the people running things. This business has caused enough confusion already. The whole island feels like a pan ready to boil. That's why they want him out of there with as little fuss as they can. An arrest, not a bloody battle."

"Stefan," she said, turning from the mirror. "I'm not a fool. I know that I can't just walk in there an' say I come to take over. Take me up to Central Station. Let me talk to who ever up there in charge, an' beg him to send me out there. How much more foolishness an' death you think I want to hear on the radio an' know is somebody call Heneky cause it?"

"You don't realize what might happen. Even if they do allow you to risk it."

271

"You going to take me up to Central? Or I must walk up?"

She stood there, waiting steadily on my reply, suddenly and astonishingly isolate in a tremendous pride, beautiful and durable as a rock made flesh.

"Yes," I said. "I'll take you up, but it won't do any good. I don't think they'll consider it."

"You will come with me as far as down there?" she asked, and I think in that moment I realized that whoever was on duty at Central would have no more chance against that steadfast and unstoppable conviction than I. She would be passed on as I was passing her on. "I would like you to come with me, Stefan. You think they will let you?"

"If you say so," I told her, "they'll let me."

Eliot, the young, bony Minister of the Interior, said: "It's not a decision I like to make. But if she really feels she can influence him. . . ." He looked dubiously at Barraclough, Cowell, the deputy-commissioner of police, and the major in command of the military support. Bernice stood beside him, looking at him with the implacable, commonsensical appeal that had defeated me in her room.

I stood with Oliver and the others from the press, a little way apart, straining like them to follow the discussion.

Before us, the swamp reflected from an opaque surface like dulled, grey-green metal. Mangroves or long, virulently green saw grass bordered the swamp on three sides. On the fourth side, a quarter of a mile away by the shore, there was a small, sloping patch of grey earth, dotted with scrubby bush, and an enormous rock. Heaped in front of this rock was a long, straggling cairn of small stones, its ends curving back to touch the massive face. Winding across the eastern corner of the swamp was firmer ground, like a causeway, of rancid grey earth in the middle, with a wider skirtings of squelching mud and grass. It led to the shelf of dry land on which Marcus Heneky and his men had built their wall. The police and the soldiers had tried to get across by wading under the shelter of the path, but it was impossible to climb from the glutinous, mephitic mud on to the dry land opposite without exposing themselves defence-lessly. There were more men trying to find a way through the mangroves on the far sides, to take up positions from which they might command some line of fire. All that could be seen of the shore was the burst of spray that seemed to hover con-tinuously beyond the rock at Marcus Heneky's back, and which held a pale spectrum. Barraclough, Cowell and the major were coated with drying grey mud, like dead flesh, right up to their arm-pits, and under the solid, noiseless pounding of the sun, Barraclough's face had assumed a colour like a brass mask in a bed of coals. Behind us, cars and wagons were parked among the dildo and skeletal, flat-topped trees. When we had first arrived, in a police car, at a wrenching seventy miles an hour over the rutted dirt road, it had seemed to me that every policeman and soldier in Cayuna must have been brought down to close the chase.

"Let me have one more go at him, Minister," the major said. "If I can get a dozen men through those mangroves over there," he pointed to the eastern border that did not outflank Heneky's position far enough, "and you keep them busy from half-way along the path, Barraclough, we might rush them."

"If you try that," Cowell said, "you'll lose three or four men doing it, and even then you won't reach them. They'll get you as you come through the mud. I'd say they have at least eight Stens or Thomsons among them, not counting pistols."

"The military wanted to use a mortar," Oliver whispered to me. "But Barraclough and Cowell dug their heels in. And Roger," he nodded to Eliot. "I wonder how old Heneky found this place?"

"The Sons of Sheba had a camp not far away. Between here and the village." I whispered back, "One of them must have known about it."

"Mister Eliot," Bernice said, politely, as I was whispering,

273

"why you don't allow me to try, eh? He won't hurt me. I promise you that. An' him won't allow them to hurt me, either. Just let me try."

"Are you sure, Miss Heneky?" Eliot asked. He looked at her hopefully, as if trying to convince himself from her placid determination. I could almost read on his long, knobbly face the tensions between his need for an arrest without more deaths, and a trial, and his anxiety for what might happen to Bernice on her way to that wall of stones, or behind it.

"Sure," she said. "Just use that loud speaker you have an' tell him it's me coming across. Lord, Mister Eliot. Do it, eh. Enough death an' wounding happen because of him. I know say I can calm him down enough so that him will see another death is useless now."

"All right," Eliot said, almost briskly. "I don't have to tell you what we all feel about your offer, Miss Heneky. I don't think I could put it into words now. Mister Barraclough, would you tell Heneky that his daughter wants to come across?"

Barraclough left the group and walked past us quickly to the nearest car. As he did so, Harper, the photographer from the *Newsletter* and the *Gazette* photographer plunged forward. "No, no," Bernice said. I had never seen her so awkward and discomfited. "What you want pictures for? Cho, man!"

"Please, Miss Heneky," Harper was saying when Barraclough's unnaturally clarified voice smashed its way from the car loud speaker across the swamp. "Heneky!" the monstrous, dehumanized tones called. "Heneky! We are giving you another chance. Leave your guns and come out with your hands on your heads. Listen to us, man. You're caught. Be sensible." In the pause, as air seemed to return with a sigh, the steady, white glare was smeared with the flashes from the cameras. Bernice turned away with the fretful pleasure of the truly modest who know they have received deserved flattery and attention. "All right, Heneky!" the paralysing voice continued. "Listen! Your daughter is here! Your daughter! Bernice! She wants to see you! Will you let her do that? Will you let her do that?"

"We waited in an endless drifting pause. During it, I left the others and went up to her and took her hand. With a pang of impotent protectiveness, I felt that she was sweating cold. And on that realization of her fear, a long, disembodied, "Ye-e-s. Tell her, ye-e-s. She alo-o-ne," floundered across the swamp, so faintly that it seemed to crawl from it and drop on the baked earth at our feet.

She was gone while I still felt the damp, cool twining of her fingers. We watched the deliberate, sailor's roll of her heavy stride take her up the harder ground in the centre of the path. Against the primaeval, stagnant landscape, she was almost ludicrously anachronistic in her vogue-imitated, urban clothes and high-heeled shoes, holding the very good handbag I gave her, exactly as if she was trudging reflectively past the shop windows on Queen Charlotte Street. Towards the end of the path her figure seemed to grow dumpy, as though by a sudden settling of forces she had become the personification of a dogged, industrious resolve. Then she was walking across the stretch of open land, up to the low half-circle of roughly piled stones.

At the Central Police Station in Queenshaven later that day, Albert, the sublimely idiotic Son of Sheba whom I had once seen at the hospital with Marcus Heneky, made his deposition on what happened.

"Reveren' tell us," he said, " 'Is me daughter dat. She don't belong to we. But let her come, because she is my blood.' So she come an' she stand outside de stones an' she say, 'Papa, come. Enough deat' happen because of our name. Don't be the cause of any more.' An' Reveren' say, 'Is destiny bring me here, child. Destiny you cannot understand. An' I must stand wid my people until de end.' An' de daughter say, 'Stand wid dem, Papa. But don't bring dem into deat'. Some of dem wid you will live if you come out now. God an' destiny never tell you to lead men to dis sort of deat', papa. You know dat. Is blood fill your head now.' An' is so dem talk. An' little by little, Reveren' go near her. An' den him hol' her hand an' she stroke him head an' say, 'Papa, is time you come now. Tell dem to come wid you. I know it hard. But you can't allow dem to stop here an' get kill like animals. Come out an' tell people why you do what you do.' An' Reveren' shake him head an' t'ink. An' den him turn to we an' say, 'You see where we stand? Babylon oppressors surround us. But de fight don't done. Let we go out an' face dem wid scorn an' speak de truth of what we do for Africa's children.' An' I t'ink all of we glad to hear dat. Because is a long time we run an' hide an' we tired. All of we glad except Ralston, an' is tired an' sufferin' turn his brain to madness. . . ."

We saw Bernice turn away from the wall, and then a figure follow her—even at that distance I could recognize Marcus Heneky. Another figure followed, scrambling over the long pile of stones. And another. They didn't put their hands on top of their heads, but the hands were empty.

"My God!" Oliver said beside me. "Don't tell me she has really done it. Stefan! That's a woman and a bit, you know!"

Comment and exclamations were being snatched away on excitement like a wind, as over two hundred of us ringing the swamp's edge watched her trudging stride lead Marcus Heneky and his followers down the path.

The last figure half-vaulted, half-heaved over the long cairn and began to splash past the file which was keeping to the firmer ground in the middle of the way. He came, compactly bounding, with an odd gambolling prance, nearly up to his knees in the gluey mud, coursing for Marcus Heneky like a large, hairy puppy. And Heneky had pitched to his knees before we really saw the dark sliver of the machete in the man's hand and he was on to Bernice as I yelled with a power that seemed to rip a layer from the inside of my throat, "Bernice! Look out! Bernice!"

The man turned with a flickering swiftness as the sweep of his cut flung Bernice off the path, face down in the mud. He was up to his waist when one of the policemen shot him. The ripely bursting repercussion seemed to shatter the tranced second that had passed between Marcus Heneky's abrupt, knee-bent slump and the savage force that had hurled Bernice, leaving a dark jet across the air, into the slime: movement, comprehension, incredulity, all came rushing back into us like air into so many vacua.

I realized afterwards that it had taken place so quickly that even Cowell had only partly fumbled his revolver from the flapped police holster: I saw that, as meaning returned, with the still vividness of a flash photograph.

I looked at Marcus Heneky once as they laid him on the dry ground. He had become unbelievably thin during the six weeks of his driven pilgrimage. For some reason, it had never occurred to me that he would be unable to shave: the curling, silver mat of his lower face was a strangely gentle frame for the harshly emphasized bones of the nose, brow and cheeks. He looked as if he had died in the middle of some absorbing conversation and was holding himself still as though to surprise an echo meant only for the living.

Bernice's head had been nearly severed and her drained face, now that it was no longer quickened by her prodigal sensitivity to the moment's complex adventure, had a graven calm quite other than the usual indifferent faces of the dead. It had the unflinching assertiveness of a death mask rather than a lifeless face.

The man who had killed them both, Ralston, Albert's companion that day in the hospital, stood under guard as his broken arm was given a temporary bandage. He was muttering and smiling frequent congratulations to himself and glancing at the bodies.

"Is two traitors my sword search out today," he said, largely, to us all, and grinned again and nodded in agreement. "The sword of Zion find two traitors to strike down. 'I have pursued mine enemies, and overtaken them. . . . I have wounded them that they were not able to rise.'"

He laughed and shook his head as though relieving himself of an excess of delight. His pitifully starved, vaguely responding face was not even fierce. The other brethren being named and handcuffed looked across at him sadly.

"I'm glad this whole world is just an accident," I said to Oliver. "If I thought it was created, I don't think I could stand it."

"I second that," he said gravely, as if I had said something profound.

IV

By two o'clock that day when I was driven back into Queenshaven, the *Gazette* reporter had already telephoned the story through. The newsboys were shouting, and the bundles of the special bulletin under their arms were selling well.

I had arranged the night before to meet Joan at one o'clock in the Shell Bar at the Palm Bank. She was waiting for me in one of the booths, "like a serpent sweetly simmering in its own venom", as Oliver once said of a woman we had watched waiting for her date.

"Well, hullo," she said in a pointy sort of way. "Aren't there any telephones where you were? At least three sets of people have asked me to join them. I expect they were afraid I was starting on a solitary binge."

"I'm sorry," I said. "I was held up. I should have phoned."

"Oh, dear," she said, "I've started nagging already, and we're not even married. Forgive me, darling." She gave my cheek a discreet, apologetic peck as I slid on to the shell-pink leather beside her. "Have you heard about Heneky? You must have." She smoothed open the crumpled bulletin she had

278

bought and looked at the pictures of Marcus and Bernice. "Poor old man," she said unaffectedly. "What made him do it? And that poor woman. What a horrible thing, eh? After what she did. I used to drink at Long John's sometimes. Long ago. But the men didn't like it, so I stopped. I haven't been there for nearly three years. You men will miss her." She examined Bernice's picture more closely. It wasn't one that the *Gazette* photographer had taken. They wouldn't have had time to get it back for the bulletin. It was one I had taken, well over a year before, one Sunday morning when she was thinking with her head down and I had said, "Bernice", suddenly. She had looked up, smiling, and I had caught her: it had turned out so well that I had enlarged it in the laboratory darkroom. I guessed that Cherry must have lent it to the *Gazette*, taking it from the bureau where Bernice had put her copy in a frame. "She has got such a sweet face," Joan said. "To think of someone like that going in such a way."

The waiter came across and I ordered a beer for Joan and a double whisky for myself.

"That's new, isn't it?" she said as he left. "You hardly ever have spirits before night. You're a real sundownah Limey."

She laughed and patted my cheek.

"I need it," I said. "I've had two already. On my way here. With Oliver. But I ditched him. . . . I was out at Caymanas today. That's why I'm late."

"Stefan! You should have said. Instead of letting me go on. I'm sorry. It must have been rotten. Did you go out with Noll?"

"No," I said, "I went out with her." I rested my finger-tips on Bernice's picture. "At least, we were both taken out by the police. In a way, I'm almost responsible for her going out. It was something I said that started her thinking of it, and I took her up to Central Police this morning."

"But," she said in a puzzled, slightly wary voice, "but I don't quite understand, darling. Why you? I mean how do you fit in like that?" Her questioning gaze suddenly became shrewd

279

and she stopped talking, then, "Oh. I didn't realize you knew her that well."

"I knew her better than that, Joan," I told her as the waiter came back with our drinks. "I knew her much better than that."

Her sooty eyes continued their steady and methodical assessment of whatever was showing on my face. She reached down and took my hand resting on the seat between us and held it tightly. Then she lifted it and pressed the back of it snugly against her blouse, just under her heart.

"Listen," she said softly. "You can tell me now over a few drinks. Or let's go home and you can tell me there. Or you needn't tell me at all if you don't want to. But I think you ought to tell me. You're not very good at trying to live with things all by yourself, are you, darling?"

"No," I said. "I don't suppose I am, really. I was going to tell you, but I was just wondering how to start. It's hard to find a beginning sometimes."

About the Author

John Hearne writes of himself: "I was born in Montreal about thirty years ago, but grew up in Jamaica, where both sides of my family have been settled since the early part of the eighteenth century.

"For the most part we have been planners, soldiers, civil servants and churchmen; but writing probably came into the family a generation or so before the French Revolution when two journalist brothers who had played too close to the encyclopaedist fringe were forced to choose between prison or exile, and decided that the British West Indies offered more freedom if less scope.

"The Hearnes were originally an Irish family but since about 1750 the main stream has received generous tributary strains of Scottish, African, English, French, Jewish, Spanish and American Indian blood."